Wildflowers in Winter

Naomi Wark

Naomi Wark

ISBN-13: 978-1734432916
Library of Congress Control Number: 2019921035
Dragonfly Press
Camano Island WA

Wildflowers in Winter is a work of fiction. The events are imaginary; the characters are fictitious and are not intended to represent actual living persons.

I'm now an old woman ... and nature is cruel;
'Tis jest to make old age look like a fool,
The body, it crumbles, grace and vigor depart,
There is now a stone where I once had a heart.
But inside this old carcass a young girl still dwells,
And now and again my battered heart swells,
I remember the joys, I remember the pain,
And I'm loving and living life over again.
I think of the years ... all too few, gone too fast,
And accept the stark fact that nothing can last.

Anonymous. Excerpt from "An Old Lady's Poem"
retrieved from http://www.poemhunter.com

Acknowledgements

The process of writing is solitary, but the inspiration for this book came from many individuals. *Wildflowers in Winter*, my debut novel, would not be possible without the journals left behind by a beloved family member whose early life inspired the flashbacks for this story. I owe my success in bringing my dream of honoring a woman who wanted her story told, to the Skagit Valley Writer's League and especially, my critique group, the Sno-Isle Writers, who inspired me with their talent, encouraged me with honest critique, and continually helped me improve my craft. Thanks to my daughters, Rebecca and Erica, who proofread the manuscript along with numerous others, and my biggest thanks to my husband, Dale, who supported a project that spanned many years and throughout that time always believed in me.

Prologue

Wildflowers in Winter is a work of fiction. Edna Pearson represents many aging individuals who live to a ripe old age, but are cursed by failing bodies and minds. Edna, like others, has outlived her spouse and her children. Suffering from progressive Alzheimer's, she fears spending the last years of her life alone and isolated. Although Edna's story is fiction, the Alzheimer's flashbacks portrayed in this novel are inspired by excerpts from diaries left behind upon the death of one much-loved old woman.

(If we ask Our Father, He will grant our prayers, if He determines the right to grant. The grants will be the ones God sees fit to grant."
E.M.P. diary August 1921

Chapter 1

The telephone's shrill ring jolted Edna awake. Fighting drowsiness, she blinked a few times, before she fixed her focus on the red, lighted display of the alarm clock. Five-thirty. Her heartbeat quickened. Early morning calls always mean bad news. Restrained by the nightgown twisted around her legs and hips, she trembled and groped for the dial phone on the nightstand. She paused, closed her eyes, and took in a few breaths before lifting the receiver, stretching out the tightly coiled black plastic cord and bringing the phone to her ear.

Choked back sobs from across the line made it difficult for Edna to recognize Alicia's voice. "Grandma, Daddy's dead."

Edna paused as she struggled to absorb the news. Without her hearing aids, the words came muffled, garbled, barely audible above her pounding heartbeat.

"Alicia, speak up, you're not making sense."

"Daddy's dead."

This time, Alicia's words landed like a blow. Edna's mind reeled as she fought to comprehend. She must have misunderstood. Her son couldn't be dead. She'd seen him only yesterday. He was fine. "Larry? Larry's dead? I don't understand."

"Yes, he's gone."

Pain gripped her chest, now damp with perspiration. She flung back the bed covers that ensnared her and pulled herself to a seated position. She flipped on the small brass reading lamp on the nightstand. "What happened?"

"He suffered a stroke last night and never regained consciousness."

A dam of emotion released in a torrent of sobs. Edna had worried about his health and nagged him to quit smoking, but he wasn't supposed to die. Not like this, so suddenly, so young, only sixty-four. "What am I going to do without him?"

"I don't know. It's going to be difficult for all of us, especially, Mom. Dad took care of everything. I'll call you later to let you know the details when we've made the arrangements."

Edna straightened on the bed, shivering from the cold. "When can I see him?"

"I'll let you know when he's been taken to the funeral home. It's going to take a while to harvest his organs."

"What are you talking about? What do you mean, harvest his organs?" Resentment rose, like the taste of bitter coffee in her throat.

"Dad was an organ donor. We've been told his kidneys, eyes, and tissue are still viable for donation."

Edna shook her head. "There must be some mistake. He would have told me he was an organ donor."

"Well, I guess he didn't tell you everything."

Dazed, Edna returned the phone to its cradle. It didn't sound like Larry to want to be dissected upon his death. Surely Kora-Lee, or more likely, her daughters, had put him up to it. "It's not right." She pounded her fist into the pillow.

Too early to call anyone, Edna motioned for her only consolation. Missy, her black terrier, pounced on the bed and nestled into the crook of her arm. Salty droplets fell on the dog's long, matted fur. She cried out her frustration, burying her head into Missy's fur. "Why, God? Why didn't you take me instead?" It wasn't fair. Parents aren't supposed to outlive their children. For a few moments, she let her shock dissipate through her tears. A surge of loneliness gripped her like a rogue wave at the thought of losing her last child.

Though forty years had passed since her daughter, Bernice died, memories raced through her mind like a flash flood. Then she had Jacob and Larry for emotional support. Now, with her husband and son both gone, the hollowness in her heart echoed her grief. Drawing on all her physical and emotional strength, Edna climbed from her bed and plodded downstairs to the living room. She pulled the drapes open, hoping the sunlight would overcome the darkness filling her. Instead, the opened curtains revealed a still darkened, gray sky, skirted with low ragged edges, suiting the somber mood. Edna shuffled to the sofa and gathered her favorite cover around her. She buried her nose in the quilt which had warmed her babies and herself throughout the passing years. With closed eyes, she inhaled the mix of sweet and bittersweet memories. Each memory unique, like the multi-colored, tulip shapes she had carefully crafted and sewn into the quilt. Fingering one corner of the worn cotton spread, she spied the small rips where Larry had used the quilt for teething. Remembering the warm memories of the past helped keep the early morning chill at bay. Numb, she sobbed in the silent empty house until, drained of tears and emotion, she drifted off to sleep.

The brazen rays streaming through the exposed living room window reawakened Edna. For a single heartbeat, she welcomed the new day, but a dull pain pulsed in her clouded head. She closed her eyes to quell the pain. Blurry memories of anger and tears swirled in her mind. Maybe it had been a bad dream. As her eyes focused on her surroundings, she realized she wasn't in her bedroom. Wads of tissue littered the gold shag carpet. Reality resurfaced, reviving her grief. She trudged to the kitchen, poured water into a cup, and turned on the microwave. Opening her small metal canister, she pulled out a tea bag, inhaling the spicy blend which she favored and Larry always bought for her for special occasions. Its smell alone always helped awaken her. Normally favoring a breakfast of bacon, mush, and maybe toast with homemade jam, her stomach rebelled at the thought of food. Instead, she stirred a single teaspoon of sugar into her tea and sipped. Clutching the cup, her hands warmed, and the scent of the sweet apple and spicy cinnamon blend soothed her aching heart.

Missy barked at the ringing phone and she scurried to answer it. Without sobs, Alicia's voice came clear and harsh. "The arrangements are set, Grandma. There will be a viewing on Thursday evening. The cremation will take place early Friday before the funeral service later in the afternoon."

"Cremation?" Edna stiffened, her heart beat with increasing speed to keep pace with her swelling anger. "Larry didn't want to be cremated. We talked about funeral plots next to Bernice and Jacob. He wanted to be buried next to his sister and his father. How can I visit him and leave flowers?" Not wishing to start a fight, Edna held the phone receiver at arm's length, too stunned to face any more shocking news. She stewed unable to move for a few beats before she pulled the receiver back in time to hear Alicia.

"Mom prefers to have him cremated. It's less expensive than a standard burial."

Edna snapped, "How can you talk about money? Doesn't anyone care what Larry wanted, or what I want? I have money if you need money."

"Daddy would have wanted to go along with Mom's wishes. They'll eventually be placed side by side in a wall at the cemetery for cremated remains. You'll still be able to visit and place flowers."

Edna fumed but fought back her anger. After all her son had done for that woman, marrying her when she was with child, and accepting her five-year-old daughter as his own. How could Kora-Lee have such disregard for what Larry wanted?

"I'll let you know the time. We're still waiting for the final details from the funeral home."

Without saying goodbye, Edna disconnected the call. She sank into the overstuffed brown recliner she no longer had the strength to tilt back. Though she expected Alicia to side with her mother, as always, she resented her for defending Kora-Lee's decision. It was hard enough to accept Larry was gone, now hearing he would be cremated and permanently resting alongside Kora-Lee, instead of Jacob and Bernice was more than she could take. She never felt so alone, so irrelevant in her entire life.

With Larry gone, Edna no longer had anyone who loved her and would look after her in her remaining years. She didn't think of Kora-Lee and her girls as family. They weren't blood. Kora-Lee's daughters called her Grandma, but Edna knew they only did it to pacify their father. Besides, they didn't treat her like family. They often spoke in hushed whispers about her when she visited. Edna wondered what would happen now to the already strained relationship with her daughter-in-law and granddaughters. Would she continue to see Kora-Lee or her daughters? She fumbled in her handbag for her handkerchief and dried her eyes and wiped her nose. Her gloom overshadowed the bright sun poking through the window announcing a new day, a day Edna wasn't sure she could face. Her body and mind were numb and her will to go on as dead as the body of her last child now lying in a morgue.

She reached for the phone and dialed her dearest friend, Barbara, her only friendly contact for caring, comfort, and consolation.

Chapter 2

David frowned at the intrusion of the persistent ringing as the family sat gathered for their dinner on Wednesday evening. He set rules for phone use and refused to let a phone call disrupt the family meal. He glared across the table with raised eyebrows at fifteen-year-old Rachel and twelve-year-old Emily, guessing either was the recipient of the call.

David's wife, Jean, got up and glanced at the phone number displayed. "It's from a 509-area code. Do you know anyone in eastern Washington?"

David shrugged. "No one I've spoken to in years. Maybe an old high school or college buddy."

"You might want to get it." Jean grabbed the receiver and hit the speaker button on the phone, against her husband's protest.

"Hello."

"Hi, I'm trying to get ahold of David Bryant. My name is Alicia."

From the dining table, David shook his head, unable to recall the name. The unfamiliar voice continued, relaying a clue. "I'm Larry Pearson's daughter."

Stunned, David's mind wandered back to the father he had seen only twice since he was five and his brother three, and their parents divorced. He grimaced as he remembered the lanky soldier who smoked constantly and was barely home for his sons. A vague memory of his stepsister, Alicia, whom he met only once when he was eleven, popped into his mind. It was the last time he'd seen his father.

"Hold on a moment please." Jean put the call on hold and held the phone out to her spouse. "You should take it."

"Why? We haven't spoken in thirty years."

"It must be important for her to call you."

David's stomach tightened, in spite of his lack of concern over the stranger who was his birth father. All eyes were on him as he pushed his chair back and grabbed the phone from Jean. "Alicia? This is David. What's up?"

"I'm so glad I located you. It took some work finding you in Washington. Last I knew you were in California, but I guess it's been a while."

David held his tongue and resisted stating the obvious. Her sniffles through her breaking voice across the line stifled his wisecracks. A lot of time had passed since they were children.

"I've been trying all day to track you down. I thought you and Nathan should know your father's dead."

"Larry's dead?" David swallowed. He didn't know what to say to her. He barely knew her. Hell, he barely knew his father. "I'm sorry. I hope he didn't suffer much."

"No. He suffered a stroke Monday night, and he passed away early this morning while in a coma. He never knew what happened."

"How are you and your family doing?" The words spilled out like a well-rehearsed routine, formal and out of proper etiquette. What else was there to say? He wasn't sure why he should be concerned. David paced back and forth in the kitchen, uncomfortably aware his family watched and listened between bites of potato salad and baby back ribs. To avoid their looks, he walked into the living room and plopped onto the sofa with his back to the dining room.

Alicia struggled between sobs. "We're all in shock. Mom isn't sure how she'll handle things alone. Dad always handled the bills and all the house repairs, as well as being the income earner."

David shifted on the sofa, struggling to hang on to each word while he tried to push aside the thought his dinner was getting cold. He remembered Larry's oldest daughter, Lorraine, about five years older than he whom he'd met while she was in high school.

"On top of that, Grandma's driving Mom and me crazy with her constant sobbing and complaining over the arrangements."

David straightened; his interest heightened at the reference to his paternal grandmother. "Grandma Edna's still around? How's she doing? I haven't heard from her since high school. She got mad when Nathan and I moved to California. She accused Mom of doing it out of spite."

"That sounds like her. She's having a tough time right now. Dad's always been there to help her. I don't know how she'll get by."

"It's good she has you and Lorraine, and your mom."

"Lorraine's in Minnesota now, so she's not around to help out with Grandma and Mom and Grandma have never gotten along. I guess that leaves me, and frankly, the old woman isn't getting any younger. She's getting senile and she's a little difficult to deal with. We haven't exactly been close lately."

Alicia's comment sounded cold, under the circumstances. "Well, I guess being difficult is to be expected at her age. How old is she now?"

"Ninety-two."

David grinned. The one positive thing he could say about his family was a tendency toward longevity. Both his maternal grandparents, midway into their eighties, were still alive, also.

Alicia continued. "The funeral will be Friday, with a viewing Thursday evening. We're still working out the exact times. I'll call you with the final times and addresses tomorrow. I assume you and your brother will want to come."

David mulled over all he had heard in the past few minutes. His mind reeled with fragmented thoughts. It didn't make sense to disrupt his whole life to rush off to a funeral for a man with whom he had no relationship, even though it was his father. He didn't need another interruption in his already hectic schedule of overtime, putting in a yard, and coaching Emily's soccer team. David stifled a groan and glanced toward the dining room, his family still watching him. He didn't know how he should respond to the recent news but tried to control the situation. "Nathan's in the army. He's stationed at Fort Bragg, North Carolina, but last time I spoke with him he was leaving for the mid-east, something fairly top-secret. I doubt he'll be able to get away." For a moment, David wished he had such a simple, guaranteed excuse.

"No wonder I couldn't track him down. Is he married?"

"Nah, he's single. Career military." Wanting to stay focused on the reason for the phone call, David changed the subject. "So, the service is on Friday, the day after tomorrow?" He paused and decided to give himself an excuse for not attending. "I'm scheduled for a flight on Friday. Let me call you after I've seen what I can do about work."

"A business trip?"

"No. I work for Boeing, testing their new airplanes. Most flights are there and back the same day, but they're unpredictable."

"That's fine. I'll give you my number so you can call if you have any other questions. Otherwise, I'll phone when I know anything for certain. Will you let Nathan know?"

"Sure." David returned to the kitchen and grabbed a pen. Though he had no intention of returning her call, he jotted down the phone number. "Got it."

"You know, it's too bad." Alicia paused before she continued. "He used to talk about you and Nathan a lot. I think he would have liked to see you both again before he died. We were planning a sixty-fifth birthday party for Dad and talked about having you and your brother come." Her voice trailed off. "I guess you never know when it's your time. We should all have tried harder to get together."

David noticed the sun beginning to set through his large living room windows. He shook his head. He didn't buy the line that Larry had ever talked about him or Nathan. Besides, why should he be concerned with any guilt Larry might have had, which he doubted anyway. God knows David wasn't about to feel guilty for not keeping in touch with a man who hadn't been a father figure in his life for nearly forty years. With a sigh, he released his bitterness. There was no point in taking it out on Alicia. She had nothing to do with Larry's decision to ignore his sons, though he suspected Alicia's mother, Kora-Lee, had plenty to do with it.

With the aroma of mesquite still in the air, Dale glanced toward the dining room. "Whatever. Keep me posted. My dinner's getting cold." He flinched and immediately regretted his last remark. "Thanks for calling." David hung up the phone and blew out a deep breath. He collapsed onto his chair at the table. His family all turned their attention to him. He didn't know what to say first. "Well, I guess my birth father passed away this morning."

"Are you sad?" Rachel exchanged glances with her sister. "You never talk about your dad. What was he like?"

David looked down at his cold ribs. He hesitated, knowing he should have shared more about his father and his stepsisters with his children long before it came to this. "No. I've never had much of a relationship with Larry, so I don't feel any loss. He was gone a lot. I was young and he was in the army the whole time Mom and he were married. I haven't considered him my dad for a long time." David thought about his relationship with his step-dad, who raised him. "You know I'm not

Naomi Wark

particularly close to Ray, either. He could be mean, but I consider him my dad, not Larry."

David tried to remember what he could about his father. There wasn't a lot. He remembered the constant fighting and long absences. How could he respect a man who left his wife with two small sons and married another woman and her ready-made family? No. There was no way David was going to drop everything to go to the funeral for some stranger, father or not. He had no desire to take part in a memorial for a man for whom he had no respect. How could he make small talk with two sisters he didn't know, or his father's wife who he later learned was the primary reason for his parents' divorce?

"How come you never saw your dad or your sisters?" Rachel twirled her curly hair around her finger avoiding her mother's disapproving look.

"When Mom and Larry split, she brought us back to the states from Korea where Larry was stationed. Mom married Ray, and we moved closer to her folks in California. Larry married a Chinese woman, Kora-Lee, who already had a daughter, Lorraine, and was pregnant with my other stepsister, Alicia. After that, Larry pretty much ignored Nathan and me. He was never a part of our lives. He had a new family, and from what I gathered early on, Kora-Lee would just as soon Nathan and I never existed. It's been easier to let it be at that. The way I always looked at it, if he didn't care to see me, why put myself out to see him?"

"You have two stepsisters, cool." Emily looked at her mother and motioned to be excused.

"Can I please finish my dinner, since everyone else seems to be done?" David shook his head and went to the microwave to zap his plate with a few rays. Carrying her plate to the sink, Jean stopped to rub David's shoulders. "How's your grandmother doing? I heard you say she's still around. This must be very hard on her. Larry was her only child, wasn't he?"

Emily wiped the counter then hung the dishtowel on the hook and joined the conversation. "She's got to be getting old, huh, Dad?"

It wasn't fair to his family to take his jumbled emotions out on them. He smiled in answer to Emily's broad grin clad with recently acquired braces. "Grandma's ninety-two. I guess she's doing fine. Alicia says she's crying a lot. I guess that's to be expected, under the circumstances. Her only other child, Bernice, died before I was born. My granddad died close to twenty years ago."

Rachel, who took after her mother with her persistence, excused herself from the table and went to the sink. "I'd like to meet her. I think it would be cool to have another grandmother. Don't you, Emily?"

Half-heartedly, David responded. "Maybe someday." He opened the microwave, carried his plate back to the table, and sat down. He gnawed at a rib, taking a few bites before he spoke. "I never told you girls, but I lived with my grandma and granddad for several months when Nathan and I were five, shortly after Mom divorced Larry. I guess having two energetic troublemakers was more than Mom could handle alone." David smiled. "Nathan and I had a great time with them. She was big on vegetables and made us clean our plates before we were excused from the table. But after dinner, she always had homemade desserts. She loved baking." David took a few more bites before he sensed Jean watching him. Seeing her smile, he knew the look and realized his mistake. He had subconsciously given her a reason to encourage him to go to the funeral.

She kissed him. "If you don't care about saying goodbye to your dad, at least think about going to the funeral for your grandmother's sake. The girls are right. It would be good for them to know their great-grandma. After all, who knows how she's really doing and how much longer you'll have the opportunity to get reacquainted with her."

David cringed. He hated falling into the guilt trap, unconvinced he owed anyone anything. His appetite diminished after his conversation, David excused himself and dumped his plate in the sink. He snatched the phone before one of his daughters could dash off with it for their nightly phone marathon. "I'm going to call Nathan." Once again, he retreated to the sofa and dialed his brother to share the news.

Nathan answered after the third ring. "Hey, brother, what's up? It's got to be important for you to be calling."

"Funny. You know I'm not much for talking on the phone. Besides, when was the last time you called me? Anyway, I got a call from Larry's youngest daughter, Alicia. Larry apparently died from a stroke this morning."

"A stroke, huh? I had him pegged as a sure-fire cancer or emphysema victim. He smoked like an eighteen-wheeler burning oil the last time I saw him."

David shifted in his chair. "I remember. You saw him a while ago, didn't you? When was that? Early eighties?"

"Yeah. Right after I graduated from West Point. I guess it's still been twenty years though. I had this crazy idea I should visit him again since I was heading out to active duty and likely to see some heavy action. You never know, especially with all the stuff that's going on over there in the desert. It was a stupid idea though, seeing him again."

David couldn't remember the specifics about the visit. "Why? What happened?"

"Nothing, really, I got the feeling it didn't matter to him if he saw me or not. I'm not sure if he just didn't give a damn or if he was uncomfortable seeing me again after so long. His wife, I can't remember her name, anyway she made it very clear she wasn't pleased to see me." Nathan paused for an instant. "So, are you going to the funeral?"

"I don't know. You know Jean. She thinks it's the right thing to do, especially for Grandma's sake."

"Grandma Edith's still around? How's she doing?"

"Fine, I guess so. She's ninety-two. Alicia says she's senile but who knows. Did you see her when you stopped to see Larry?"

"Nah, I asked Larry how she was doing. She was out of the country somewhere. Asia, I think." Nathan took a moment before continuing. "Do you remember when we lived with the grand folks the summer after Mom and Larry divorced?"

Some of the depressing thoughts of the last hour seemed to fade as he thought back to his childhood. "How old were we? Five? That was probably the best summer we ever had. Remember how Granddad always took us to the creek and we'd go fishing? Funny thing is we never caught on that we were never going to catch anything in that tiny old creek." The memory of the long-ago summer lightened the discomfort roiling in the pit of David's stomach.

"Didn't Granddad pass away sometime back?"

David's smile faded. He recalled hearing about his grandfather Jacob's last trip to Madigan Army Hospital in Tacoma. "It's been a while. Shortly after you left. Right after I moved back to Washington, following those few tough years in Los Angeles after college."

"Well, I won't be able to make the funeral. These classified missions don't make for an easy out. I figure I'll be here in the God-forsaken desert for at least another year. I'll make it back to Washington someday. Tell Grandma 'hi' from me and let me know what happens."

Sending his best wishes, David clicked the phone off and returned to the kitchen. With a sense of defeat, he reluctantly replaced the phone on its base. He turned to Jean. "Okay, we'll go to the funeral. I'll call Alicia tomorrow. It's the right thing to do under the circumstances, and it will be nice to see Grandma again after so many years."

Chapter 3

Barbara came by in the late morning with cookies and a macaroni casserole, offering her comfort and a sounding board upon which Edna could project her anger and sadness. Edna first met Barbara at the church she attended after two young men in suits rang her doorbell one day. An unselfish woman who took joy in caring for others, Edna could always count on Barbara for support, or as a last-minute chauffeur. She asked for no recognition or compensation for her deeds, believing her reward lay in the afterlife. As the day wore on, grief cloaked Edna like low-lying clouds on a rainy day. Though Edna had outlived most of the teachers with whom she had taught for over forty years, many garden club associates, and both her children, she welcomed the visits from the congregation and from her neighbors, Fred and Marge, who stopped in to offer their condolences. Barbara greeted them with coffee and tea, accompanied by her home-baked cookies.

By dinner time, the house fell quiet and empty. Barbara set the table and brought out her heated casserole and rolls. "What time is Alicia coming to take you to the viewing at the funeral home tomorrow?"

"Around five-thirty." Smelling sweet yeast adrift in the air, Edna's mouth watered. Barbara was heating some rolls. Edna realized she hadn't eaten all day. Barbara took a seat next to Edna. "Will you need any help getting ready?"

Edna patted Barbara's hand. "No. I'll be fine." Edna snatched a roll and devoured it in no time, then gobbled down the heated tuna and cheese macaroni. Embarrassed by her poor manners, Edna's cheeks flushed as she smiled at her friend. "I didn't realize how hungry I was."

Barbara cleared the table and washed the dishes. "Are you sure you're okay? Let me know if you need anything. I'll see you on Friday at the funeral." Barbara hugged her friend and departed.

Alone in the house, Edna reflected upon how quickly Larry's sixty-four years had passed. She warmed, remembering the love that surged from her as she gazed into her newborn son's deep intense blue eyes. Edna shut off the lights downstairs and trudged up the stairs to her room, which unexpectedly seemed lonelier and quieter than the night before. She tossed and turned in bed. There would be no peace or sleep tonight. Instead, long ago memories flashed like old silent movies through her mind, tiring her. Still, sleep evaded her.

After a fitful night, Edna woke Thursday to a sharp pain squeezing her chest, her breaths came short and shallow. She mused over the irony of having a heart attack on the day of Larry's viewing. Panicked, she struggled to sit, but lightheadedness forced her back on her pillow. She rubbed her fingers together to stop the tingling and to distract any thoughts that perhaps she was dying. Edna tried to imagine her granddaughters and their mother planning her memorial. She wondered if Lorraine would trouble herself with her already too-busy schedule to assist with the arrangements and pay her respects. She doubted they would expend much energy on a suitable service in the event of her demise. The reflection both amused and saddened her. After a few minutes, the pain subsided and her breathing returned to normal. It was only stress.

Feeling stronger, she marched to the bathroom to prepare for the day. Nonetheless, she reminded herself to talk further with Barbara about her affairs. She certainly couldn't count on Kora-Lee or her granddaughters to carry out her last wishes, especially now, knowing they were disregarding what she and Larry had discussed for his arrangements.

Alicia arrived the next morning as promised. She rang the bell several times before Edna could get to the door. "Are you ready to go?"

Edna frowned at the hint of impatience and grabbed her purse from the dining room table. She followed Alicia to the car, opening her door and climbing onto the well-worn, black vinyl seat which had absorbed the intense heat of the day and smelled of old cigarettes. Edna shifted uncomfortably, both from the hot sticky vinyl and the oppressive tension between them. "Where's Lorraine?"

"She was at the viewing earlier. She had some last-minute arrangements to make with the funeral director. I called David though, and he might be there."

"David? You spoke with David?" Edna straightened, turning her gaze to Alicia.

"Yeah, it sounds like he and his wife are planning on coming to the funeral. I'm not sure if they will make it in time for the viewing though."

Edna's anger lessened and with it the tightness in her body. She couldn't remember the last time she had seen either of her grandsons. "What about Nathan? Is he coming, too?"

Alicia shook her head and shared what little she knew about Nathan's situation. Edna wiped the corner of her eye with her finger. "It would be nice to see him, too, sometime."

"Well, I wouldn't count on it. It's not like they've gone out of their way to keep in touch all these years." Alicia looked across the seat, her dark eyes awaiting a response.

Edna bit her lip. The resentment she'd buried for so many years returned with a fury. Her pulse raced. She knew Kora-Lee had never allowed Larry to keep in touch with his sons. She didn't blame the boys. They were so young, not even school-age when their parents divorced. Edna swallowed her words. She would not get into it. Not today. Today her mind was on her loss. But today God had answered a long-sought-after prayer. After so many years, she was going to see David again.

Chapter 4

Overcoming the urge to call off the trip, David put the luggage and funeral attire in the car ready to hit the road.

"I wish we could go." Emily wrinkled her brows. "I really wanted to meet Great-Grandma."

"I know." David offered a weak smile. "Another time. She's going to be overwhelmed enough getting over Larry and with seeing me again. I need time to find out how she's doing. Besides, you don't want to miss your soccer game this weekend."

After hugs and reminders, they climbed in the car. David turned the key in the ignition and they were on their way, for better or worse, headed for eastern Washington.

"Are you doing all right?" Jean rested her hand on her spouse's leg. "You're unusually quiet."

David shrugged. No point thinking too much about a relationship that never existed with his father. Now, it never would. "I'm only doing this out of obligation. Don't go trying to make this into some big happy family reunion, okay?"

Though Jean verbally agreed, David knew her mind was spinning a fairy tale ending on the whole awkward circumstances.

"Did you grab the address to the funeral home?" Jean peered over the seat to check for the usual forgotten items, which always was the case with family trips.

"I have it in the GPS." Tired, from waking at six o'clock to work a half-day before the five-hour drive across the state, David didn't feel like talking. He focused on the tedious drive ahead.

The parking lot at the funeral home was nearly empty when they arrived during the last hour of the viewing. A solitary older model, blue Ford Taurus with splotches of primer on the rear driver's side stood parked in front of the chapel, along with a few hearses lining the side of the building.

"I guess this is it?" David took a last gulp of coffee from the now-empty thermos then stepped out on stiff legs.

Jean took his hand as they headed toward the entrance to the funeral parlor. Inside the lobby, David was taken aback at the sight of a woman taller than he'd expected, dark eyes, and shoulder-length auburn hair, not black as he remembered, but then the color could be from a bottle.

"Alicia?"

The woman rushed toward David; her arms open for an embrace. Caught off guard, he half-heartedly put his arms around his stepsister, patting her back.

Jean approached offering a hug. "I'm Jean, David's wife. It's too bad we have to meet under these circumstances."

Eyes smeared with black mascara; Alicia dabbed at the tears with a well-used tissue. "I never got the chance to say goodbye. It happened so fast he never regained consciousness." Alicia sniffled as she reached for a fresh tissue from one of several boxes scattered on tables around the lobby. "Come on, I'll take you to the viewing room. Grandma's still inside." Alicia led them down the hall.

Their steps echoed on the gleaming gray and crimson marble-tiled hall. David clutched Jean's hand, a subconscious display of affection, or maybe an indication of much needed emotional support. Alicia stopped at a small, dark, wood-paneled room. A single casket sat atop a wheeled cart, visible near the front. David noticed the stooped posture and slight frame of the solitary visitor. "Is that Edna?"

Alicia exhaled as if exhausted or exasperated. "Yeah, we got here around six. She refuses to leave until closing."

Alicia's rough words bothered David. Not overly emotional, he could easily imagine the difficulty of saying goodbye to a deceased child. His shoulder and neck muscles clenched both from the long drive and the uneasy situation. He tried to relax with deep cleansing breaths, thankful Alicia's mother, Kora-Lee wasn't present in the small grieving room. "Your mother and sister aren't here?"

"No. Mom and Lorraine came by earlier. I told them I'd stay with Grandma until she's ready to leave."

Impulsively, David patted Alicia on the shoulder, his best attempt at consolation. He tipped his head in the direction of the casket and headed toward it with Jean by his side. They approached Edna with short slow steps. David hadn't been to many funerals, with all his relatives living to a ripe old age. He had never viewed an open casket and was unsure how he would feel. Stopping a few steps short from where Edna stood, David watched her as she stood hunched over the simple, blue satin-covered casket. She plucked a yellow rose from one of the few arrangements sent in memoriam. Placing the rose in Larry's hand, she bent over and with uncontrolled sobs, she kissed him.

Alicia came over to David. She shook her head. "That's disgusting, kissing a dead person like that. She's still upset about Larry being cremated, but she knows Mom can't afford a fancy all-out funeral like she wanted to have for him."

The comment seemed inappropriate. David turned to Alicia. "I didn't know he was being cremated. How does that work, since the funeral's tomorrow?"

Alicia explained after closing the funeral home for the night, the body would go to the crematorium, and by the early afternoon ceremony, Larry's remains would be in the receptacle she and her mother and sister preselected. Alicia paused to dab her eyes. David couldn't help feeling perhaps her sorrow was over-dramatized, though he had nothing upon which to measure her grief.

Alicia fumbled in her purse. Her keys jingled as she pulled them out and looked imploringly at David. "I'm tired and I've had a long day and need to get home to my daughter. Would you mind taking your grandmother home when you're through here? Also, I need to be here early tomorrow before the guests arrive. Do you think you could bring Grandma to the funeral tomorrow?"

"Sure, it's not a problem." David shrugged. "As long as you think she's okay with it."

"I'm sure she'll be fine. I think we need to take a break from each other for a while." Alicia paused before managing a feeble indication of concern. "Of course, I'll still be here for her, but I think it's best if I support my mother right now. You understand?" Giving David a pat on the back, she smiled. "Thanks for coming."

Convinced his eyes would give away his feeling of disbelief, David leaned in and offered his best attempt at a sincere hug to avoid eye contact. After Alicia walked away, David shook his head and contemplated the position in which he now found himself. He guessed the obvious resentment between Grandma and Kora-Lee was Alicia's real motivation for inviting him to the funeral. He now understood his role. Intermediary.

David glanced at Jean. "I'm going to check on Grandma." He approached the casket, wiping his clammy hands on his jeans. Reaching Edna's side, he hugged her. "Hi, Grandma, I'm here."

Edna turned and looked up. Her moist eyes widened. A Cheshire cat grin spread across her face. Her wiry trembling arms reached out as if in praise. "David? Is that you?"

Shocked by the deep-set wrinkles of time and the folds of her turkey neck, David hesitated before welcoming her embrace. "Yes, it's me. I'm sorry Nathan can't be here. He said to say hello to you." David noticed his grandmother's appearance. She looked far from groomed. Perhaps the food-stained dress and untidy hair pinned back haphazardly were only signs of her advancing age. Maybe burying her last child was more grief than she could take. Possibly she no longer cared about her appearance. David tried to push his shallow thoughts from his mind.

Edna continued to cling to David. "I couldn't believe it when Alicia told me she called you. After all these years, thank God you are here."

"It's nice to see you too. It's been a long time."

"I don't know what I'm going to do without Larry. No one else cares about me. What's going to happen to me?" His grandmother's grief matched the tears that began to flow.

David pulled back, troubled by the remark. "You'll be okay Grandma, I'm sure you have lots of people who care about you. You have Kora-Lee, and your granddaughters, and I'm sure you have friends." Already questioning Alicia and her family's commitment to Edna, he justified the white lie about their concern as the right thing to do under the circumstances.

Grandma's eyes narrowed. She glanced around, as though she were checking for spies. "No. Those people don't care about me. They've just been pretending all these years because of Larry. Besides they're not family."

Stunned, David studied the frail woman. Her resentment was obvious, yet David was certain she hadn't overheard Alicia's earlier comment. He spoke with a gentle concerned tone. "Of course, they're family. Why would you say that?"

Edna shot a glance back. "No. They're not blood. You and Nathan are my only real family now."

Jean slipped in to join the exchange. She shook her head and raised her index finger to her lips. She narrowed her gaze toward her husband. He knew the leave-well-enough-alone look. He swallowed his unspoken comments. Jean took Edna's hand. "Hi. I'm Jean, David's wife. We care about you and we'll be here for you."

The worried drawn lines of Edna's face relaxed. She smiled at the granddaughter-in-law she was meeting for the first time.

With Grandma calm, David wavered before he glimpsed the casket. His stomach churned and gurgled, perhaps from the sight of the still and stone-faced corpse, but possibly only in response to the lack of any substantial food during the long and hectic day. He stared at the gaunt man in a medium, gray, pinstripe suit. His thin face showed deep-set lines around the lips, obvious smoker's pucker. His wrinkled and mottled skin looked older than his sixty-four years. David drew back slightly, not sure what he was expecting, but the deceased who lay in front of him was unfamiliar and aged beyond David's imagining. Somehow, he expected to feel his skin crawl and smell the scent of ammonia or some whiff of death hanging in the air. Instead, Larry looked at peace, as if he were simply asleep and a faint lavender scent floated on the air, likely from the arrangements of white and purple flowers gracing the white pedestals around the room. Aware his grandmother stood watching him, David swallowed, rolled his tongue, and wet his lips to stir some saliva to his parched mouth. "Larry looks nice, doesn't he?"

"Yes, I bought that suit for him. You should have seen what Kora-Lee wanted to bury him in."

David smiled and patted her arm. "You did a good job."

Jean put her arm around David. "Are you okay?"

"Sure." David lowered his voice. "It's like I'm looking at a stranger. I'm more concerned about Grandma." Glancing at this once important person from his past, now near-stranger, at his arm, a hint of weirdness made his head spin. In the past few minutes he had been reacquainted with Alicia and already had an uncomfortable gnawing feeling in the pit of his stomach. He'd seen his grandmother for the first time in over thirty years, and before him lay the body of a man whom, if he passed on the street, he might not have recognized as his own father. David looked back toward the door. Alicia was gone. Relieved, David blew out his breath and turned to Jean. "Thank God I don't have to say anything else to Alicia tonight, because frankly, I would find it difficult to be civil to her after her last comment. Are you ready to go?"

David took one last glance at his father's body. He contemplated saying some inspirational verse or verbally sharing some deep, personal, father-son memory pulled from the recesses of his mind, but sentimental memories and words eluded him. From the corner of his eye, he noticed his grandmother looking on. He reached for her arm. "Are you okay?"

She scanned the room. Her voice came halting and fearful. "I don't see Alicia."

"She asked if we could take you home. It will be a good chance to get reacquainted. Is that okay?"

Her moist, red eyes, sunk deep in their sockets, instantly brightened. She nodded, supporting herself on David's arm.

"Ready?"

With a slight smile, Edna turned and stepped unsteadily to the door.

"Thank you." David shook hands with the funeral home attendant who stood waiting by the door, most likely anxious to have them leave so he could lock the business for the evening. David looked at his watch. "I'm sorry. I didn't realize it was so late."

"It's quite all right, Sir." The dark-suited man held the glass door open.

Jean hurried ahead and swung open the wide front door of their Mustang convertible. "This isn't the best car for you, Grandma. It's a little difficult to get in and out of."

David assisted her into the bucket seat, supporting most of her weight as he lowered her onto the black leather.

"It's just fine, Dear. It's so nice of you to take me home." Grandma held on an extra moment to David's arm before he was allowed to release it and close the door.

22

With Grandma situated and buckled in, Jean went around the driver's side and climbed into the back seat.

David looked across the front seat. "I don't know the way to your house, so you're going to have to show me." He reached across and patted her hand, as much to gain her attention as to express his concern. "Are you still living in that rambler in Kennewick?"

Not hearing, or oblivious to the conversation, Grandma sat grinning and humming to herself.

David looked at her. She appeared lost in her own world. Perhaps her hearing was weak. He raised his voice slightly. "Grandma, do you still live in Kennewick?"

She startled and looked at him. "Oh, my Lord, no, Dear. I sold that place. I moved to West Richland two years ago."

"Okay. Why don't you give me your address and I can find it from there?" David looked in the rear-view mirror and caught a glimpse of Jean's broad smile and her attempt to stifle her amusement.

"That's okay. I'll show you the way."

David tensed; he had a feeling things wouldn't be that simple. He pulled the car around to the exit and waited for Edna to direct him. He flipped on the GPS on the dash and noticed the car was facing north, so he made a left turn out of the lot. "I guess we turn right and head west?"

Edna's eyes darted around. "I'll tell you when to get on the bypass. It's a little way down the road."

David turned his attention to driving in the unfamiliar city, which always made him uncomfortable. The long day was wearing on him and his patience was growing thin.

Grandma shifted in her seat. "It's so nice having you both here."

Leaning forward, Jean put her hand on Edna's shoulder. "I'm glad we're here too, after all these years. I'm sorry I never got the chance to meet Larry."

With Grandma's attention elsewhere, David was forced to keep her focused on directing him to her home.

Edna looked around, seemingly confused. "Turn left at the next light."

David obeyed, continuing a few blocks. His hands gripped the wheel a little tighter. "Where to now, Grandma?" His voice came harsher and sharper than he intended.

Grandma's eyes widened and her face tensed. "No, wait, this isn't right, I don't know where we are. Did you pass Columbia Drive yet?"

David sensed Jean's calm-down-and-breathe gaze burning through the back of his car seat and took a breath of frustration. He pulled the car off the road and into a parking lot. "How about you give me your address. We have a gadget which will lead us right there."

Edna furrowed her brow, obviously upset with him., but she gave him the address. "3971 Morningside Avenue."

Removing the GPS from the window mount, David handed it over the seat to Jean. A twinge of pain stabbed at his temples. A head-ache was one thing he didn't need on top of everything else.

Edna straightened. "Oh, wait, there's the turn. Turn right at the Market Place store. I know where we are now."

The tension in David's shoulders and neck muscles eased as Grandma directed him into the drive for the townhouse units where she lived.

"It's the last unit on the left. That's my white Buick parked there."

David raised his eyebrows. He hadn't considered the possibility she was still driving. He noticed the well-dented metal shed that lay dead ahead a few feet, speculating how the dents got there as he pulled alongside her car. "So, this is your house. It looks nice."

"It's a lovely home. Would you like to see it?"

David checked the clock on the dash. "It's late, and we've had a long day, between work and the long drive over. How about we see it tomorrow?" He assisted his grandmother from the car. "Alicia needs to be at the funeral home early tomorrow. If it's okay, we'll be by a little before noon to pick you up to take you to the service. Is that going to allow us enough time to get there by twelve-thirty?"

"Of course, but why don't you stay here tonight?"

"I'm sorry, we've already reserved and paid for a hotel."

At the front door of the townhouse, Grandma fumbled with her key. "I wish you would stay. It would be so nice to have my grandson stay with me."

"I'm sorry, Grandma, maybe another time. Are you going to be all right alone tonight?"

"I'll be fine. Thank you, Dear." Edna hugged David goodbye.

Saddened by his grandmother's drawn, aged face, David returned the hug, then watched as she shuffled inside and closed the door.

Chapter 5

On their way to his grandmother's house the next morning, David mulled over Alicia's request. "Don't you think it's odd I'm picking up Grandma, not Alicia or Lorraine? You know I don't mind, but I'm a near stranger to her next to her granddaughters who've known her their whole lives."

"I don't know." Jean looked at David. "Maybe they don't feel they have the time to share in her grief when they're so overwhelmed themselves."

"Maybe." David shrugged, unconvinced. "But Alicia sounded like Grandma was a bother to her and her family, and based on Grandma's comment, she doesn't exactly consider them family, either." He pulled the car into the driveway, hopped out and strode to the door. After the first knock, his grandma stepped out like a newborn fawn on gangly legs. She clutched a tan, old-fashioned, vinyl purse to her chest as she steadied herself. "Hi, Grandma. It looks like you're ready to go." David's heart ached as he scanned the fragile woman, who had recently lost her last child. She had outlived her only sister, her spouse, and now both of her children. The thought of losing all his loved ones made his gut churn. He tried to imagine the emptiness she must be feeling.

In spite of the warm day, Grandma wore a heavy brown tweed coat, showing many years of wear. Her brown slip-on shoes were beyond well-worn. Her hair, strewn atop her head, was a beautician's nightmare of long fine white hair pinned in place with loosely held bobby pins.

Jean leaned over to David. "She can't go to her son's funeral looking like this."

David looked at his watch. "I don't know what we can do about it now." Regret gripped him. "I wish we had come earlier. Maybe we could have helped her clean up a bit." He shook his head. He doubted Grandma was aware of her appearance or would have accepted help anyway. He remembered her strong-will, and even with her advanced age, he had a feeling she maintained this trait. He reminisced on the once young, prim and proper, always tidy, school teacher, who never would have allowed herself to look so unkempt.

He noticed her eyes were less red than the previous night, he guessed she had slept fairly well. Still, he imagined the deep-set wrinkles were etched by a lifetime of tears and sadness as well as good times. "Do you need any help?"

Her eyes shined and she flashed a brief smile. "I'm just fine, David. You look so handsome in that navy-blue suit."

David reached out, took her free arm, and lowered her into the car. With the GPS loaded with the funeral home address, David backed the car out of the drive.

Grandma gazed out the window as David drove. "Do you know where we're going?"

"I'm ready today. I have the address this time."

"I see. I wasn't too sure about that. No one has told me anything about where we're going today."

David turned to see her. "We're going to Mueller's Funeral Home, the same place we were last night."

"Oh yes, I almost forgot. The funeral home. Are we going to visit Bernice?"

Taken aback at the mention of his long-deceased aunt, David glanced in the rearview mirror at Jean. He raised his brows with a slight shake of his head and eyes narrowed with concern. "No, Grandma, we're going to Larry's funeral."

"Larry? Yes, that's right, they told me he died too." Her voice drifted off. "Today's his funeral you know? Is he going to be buried next to Bernice?"

Uncertain of the disposition of the urn, an uneasy and unexpected burning sensation speared his eyes. David tried to blink it away. "I don't know where they made plans to bury him. Maybe next to Bernice."

"Oh, I wondered about that. Those people never told me."

Saddened by his grandmother's confusion and obvious resentment toward Alicia and her family, David wondered what to expect when they got there. Arriving only a few minutes behind schedule, David scoured the sparsely filled lot for a close parking space. He offered Edna an arm to exit the car. Once inside, he searched the lobby for Alicia's familiar face or even Kora-Lee's. Though he wasn't sure he would even recognize her, he imagined he could make an educated guess.

Only moments later an attendant in his crisp black suit and tie approached them. "Are you Larry's son?"

"Yes, I'm David." Extending his hand to the man he introduced Edna and Jean. "I don't see the rest of Larry's family." David noticed a nervous reluctance from the emotionless, dark-haired, middle-aged man as he straightened his horn-rimmed glasses before directing them down the hall.

"Your room is this way."

David grabbed his grandmother's arm and followed the attendant. He stopped and opened a door revealing a small sitting room facing the chapel which David assumed was where the memorial would be held. "What's this?" David glanced around the room filled with several dozen sturdy wooden chairs with deep red corduroy cushions, all in neat rows and all empty. A wall of large windows looked into the chapel area, slowly filling with people. A modest selection of recently added colorful bouquets joined the previous night's assortment of white and purple flowers adorning the stairs and circling the podium. "Where are the rest of the family members?"

The attendant shifted his weight. "This is the private grieving room the widow and the Pearson family selected for your comfort. They will be entering the main chapel shortly, where they'll be seated with the other guests."

David shook his head in disbelief, suppressing his first thought. Knowing he was putting an innocent man on the spot, he prodded the attendant nonetheless. "Is there a reason we're not all seated together?"

"Mrs. Pearson thought you would be more comfortable grieving in private, separate from the immediate family." Light reflected off the beads of perspiration on his forehead and the attendant mopped his forehead with a white handkerchief from his pocket.

David held his tongue but allowed his mind free reign. *Yeah, right! This was done for our sake.* He asked the attendant to explain to Kora-Lee and her daughters his concern. "I think we should all be seated together. We're all Larry's family, especially Larry's mother." David patted Edna's arm.

The attendant hustled out to relay the message. It didn't matter, David knew what the response would be the moment the attendant departed. A slight pang of remorse stabbed at his conscience for putting the attendant in the position to try to reason with a group of people who obviously couldn't be reasoned with.

Returning, the attendant motioned David over. "I'm sorry, Mr. Bryant, Mrs. Pearson prefers the existing arrangements. Please, if there's anything else I can do, let me know."

It wasn't the attendant's fault. There was no point in pursuing the awkward situation further. David extended his hand and thanked him for his help.

David returned his attention to his grandmother who stood looking out to the gathering crowd. She looked fragile and frightened.

"I'm feeling faint." She turned and reached for David's hand. "I don't think I can make it." Her knees buckled.

David caught her under the arms as she sank to the floor. Jean was already heading for the door as he called for help. "See if you can get a glass of water, and maybe a wet cloth."

With quick assistance from the attendant, David dabbed at Edna's forehead while Jean bent over her with the water. "Are you doing okay?" David awkwardly helped her to a seated position. "Let's get your coat off, it's too warm in here to be wearing a coat." Removing the coat, David notice food stains sprinkled across the front of her cream-colored floral dress. A run ran up the side of one mismatched knee-high nylon, which showed underneath the torn hem of her dress. Her appearance made him wonder how adequately her needs were being met by her supposed loving and caring son and his family.

After a few minutes, Edna's color returned. She looked around with wide eyes as if she were seeing the room for the first time. "Where is everyone else?"

David could almost fathom Kora-Lee seating him away from the crowd like a waiter might seat a bum in a swanky restaurant. But the idea of Larry's own mother being asked to sit apart from the other mourners, especially Kora-Lee and her daughters, pissed him off. He motioned for Jean, who steadied a chair while David eased Grandma in place. "We have a separate room so you can grieve in private. I thought it would be less stress for you than sitting with the rest of the guests."

Grandma didn't question further and appeared to be satisfied with the answer, but David boiled at the inane dealings of the whole thing, briefly wishing he hadn't come and put himself through this. Then he looked at his grandmother who sat weeping and abandoned by Larry's wife and his daughters. He leaned toward Jean. "I wonder what would have happened to Grandma if we hadn't come. Don't these people have a conscience?"

His father was dead, he should feel some emotion, yet how could he? He had only seen him twice since he was five years old. He didn't feel like he had lost anyone special to him, because he hadn't. Funny, Grandma considered family the bloodline, regardless of whether there was any emotional contact involved. Whereas, David considered family the people who were there for you, emotionally and physically, whether blood or not. His grandmother had apparently tried to forge a relationship with Kora-Lee and her granddaughters, but from the looks of the sorry arrangements here, it was obvious the only relationship forged was forced by his father's marriage to Kora-Lee. Now, with Larry gone, their blatant disregard toward her was clear. Any family relationship that may have been carved by the passage of time seemed severely splintered now. Grandma's last child had died. It was the cruelest and most difficult event for a parent to face. Her closest relatives geographically, and by association, did not appear capable of showing compassion. He hadn't cried since he was a small child, and no tears would fall today. Not for his dad. The only grief revealed would be for the tragedy faced by the old woman next to him. Overcome by the circumstances, he patted his grandmother's cold hand. "Do you need a Kleenex?" He found a tissue box from a small end table and handed it to her.

David turned to Jean. "It's not right. I know Larry was her son, but with my limited exposure to how his family is treating Grandma and us, it's hard to imagine him as a caring man." The thought of how this other family could be so dysfunctional boggled his mind. Larry certainly hadn't been a role model to Nathan or David. He never gave their mother or his sons a second thought, or even child support, once he returned to the states after his time in the military.

The minister entered the chapel from the side vestibule, interrupting David's thoughts. Impeccably dressed in the appropriate garb for the occasion, black suit and tie, pressed white shirt and shiny patent leather shoes, he strode to the center of the altar. In the front row, David noticed

Alicia seated next to a young girl, undoubtedly the daughter she mentioned, Larry's granddaughter, Edna's great-granddaughter. Beside Alicia's daughter sat Kora-Lee and Lorraine. Buried in his thoughts, he hadn't seen them enter and take their seats.

The preacher addressed the small crowd from the podium, his voice carried into their private room from the speakers on the wall. "We are gathered to pay our final respects to Larry Jacob Pearson and we pray for his wife and family who will sorely miss him." The words came loud and clear as he continued with the expected well-rehearsed lines, the norm for the occasion. When he finished, he bowed his head in prayer over a small brass urn, then he invited Alicia to the front.

She strode to the podium with the stature, allure, and attire of a model walking a cat-walk. Prim, proper, and poised, she faced the audience with confidence. Pausing, she brushed back her deep auburn hair from her eyes before starting. She began with some trivial stories of her life with her father and told those gathered how much he would be missed by his wife and daughters. After Alicia finished her part, Lorraine joined her sister on the altar and took the microphone. She shared stories of being Daddy's oldest daughter, and his pride and joy, and all the related hoopla about her wonderful father.

There was no acknowledgment of David, Nathan, or Edna. No sign of respect for Larry's mother left alone without her son, her last child. How could his father have allowed such disrespect toward his own mother? David had already decided he didn't wish to associate himself with this family. He shook his head and squeezed Jean's hand, inwardly grateful for the love and respect of his family.

Throughout the speeches Grandma sobbed openly, gasping into a wrinkled flowered handkerchief. "Larry was all I had, he took care of me, and he was the only one who truly loved me since Bernice and Jacob died. Now he's gone, too. What am I going to do?"

For all the negative thoughts which had passed through David's head in the previous few minutes, Edna's words relayed what David failed to recognize. Larry was her son. He loved her, in his own way, and she loved him. Maybe that was enough. David put his arm around his grandmother but turned to Jean with a low voice. "To hell with Kora-Lee, and I'm not sure what to make of her daughters. They may have been Larry's family, but they have made it clear they don't want to be part of my life and I wonder if they intend to be part of Grandma's life."

Acknowledging, Jean put a hand on David's leg.

Tuning out the continuing drivel from Lorraine, David took a deep breath. He draped his arm around his grandmother's slumped shoulders. "I'm sorry he's gone. You still have Nathan and me. And we love you. We're your family and we'll be here for you." A stitch of resentment pierced him for the position and responsibility in which he now found himself. He didn't need the stress. He was already swamped with six-day workweeks and still finishing the basement and clearing the acreage surrounding his new home.

David looked back at the chapel in time to see his stepsisters return to their places. The minister concluded the ceremony by thanking the congregation for their support of Larry's loved ones and invited everyone to the reception downstairs before he turned and disappeared from view.

"We'll help you through this, we promise." Jean took Grandma's arm and led her out into the hall.

The attendant greeted David by the door with a weak obligatory smile. "Don't forget the reception in the hall downstairs."

David shook his head. He had no intention of being ignored by Larry's family any longer. He looked over at his grandmother. "I think Larry's mother has had enough for one day."

Edna stopped mid-shuffle. "Oh, no, Dear. My friends have all come to the funeral. We need to go to the reception."

Sighing, David conceded. Edna's presence at the reception was appropriate and necessary, though he doubted his ability to be patient or civil toward Alicia and the others after the way they'd been shunned the past hour. Nodding at the attendant, they followed him to a room laid out with long cafeteria-style, tan tables covered with white cotton tablecloths and lined with tan upholstered folding chairs. "Come on, Grandma. Let's find a place to sit, and then I can get you something to eat if you like." David steered her toward a nearby table and helped her get settled. "Would you like something to drink?"

"Are there sandwiches or crackers? I haven't eaten anything today."

Jean scooted a chair closer and sat next to Edna. "I'll sit with Grandma while you get a small plate for you and her."

David headed to the end of the short refreshment line. He looked over the crowd for Edna's supposed family. In a small way, he hoped to at least speak with Lorraine after all these years. A pleasant-looking middle-aged plus woman approached. He refocused his concentration.

"Hi, I'm Barbara. You must be David. Your grandmother was so excited when she called me last night to tell me you had come."

David extended his hand which Barbara accepted. Her warm relaxed smile showed genuine concern.

"I'm so pleased to meet you at last. I've known your grandmother through the garden club and church for over ten years. I will tell you, it means the world to her to have you here. She's shared so many stories about you and your brother."

The comment surprised David. After all these years, his grandmother had still spoken about him and Nathan. "Really?"

Barbara gestured toward the moving line. David swept his arm out, motioning her ahead. He examined the assorted tea-sized sandwiches, egg salad, cucumber and tomato, and either tuna or chicken salad, dressed with olives and pimento. Though his stomach was empty except for a quick continental breakfast at the hotel, nothing looked appetizing. He selected several assorted sandwiches for his grandmother, served a small serving of fruit salad with apples, grapes, and melon, and some macaroni salad which smelled heavily of vinegar. He grabbed a clear plastic cup of non-alcoholic punch. He'd come back and get some much-needed coffee for himself in a few minutes and stop for a burger or sub sandwich on the way home when he was more in the mood for eating.

Barbara glanced over where Edna was seated. "I'm so thankful you are here to help her through this. It's a relief for me. I won't have to worry so much about what will happen to her now." Barbara must have considered herself too forward and presumptuous. She paused and brought her hand to her mouth before continuing. "You will be keeping in touch and watching out for her, won't you?"

David closed his eyes. His mind spun like a whirlwind before he drew a deep breath, realizing the commitment he faced with his answer. "Of course."

Barbara smiled her approval and David followed her to the table to join Jean and Edna. Setting the plate in front of his grandmother, David waited for Barbara to take a seat before introducing her to Jean. He looked forward to chatting with Barbara further.

"Come on, let's offer our condolences to Kora-Lee." Jean grabbed David's arm.

"Why?" He pulled away, disgusted by the whole charade being played by Kora-Lee's grieving family, and their cold-hearted treatment toward their grandmother.

"Because it's the right thing to do." Jean turned to Barbara and Edna. "Excuse us for a few minutes. We'll be right back."

Nudged on, David followed Jean. "Let me get myself some coffee first." He grabbed a Styrofoam cup and poured a cup of steaming java. He could tell from the aroma it was strong and had probably sat around for a while on the hot plate. He splashed it with cream before he unwillingly wove through the crowd to where Kora-Lee stood. As he sipped his too-hot coffee, he watched with interest as Kora-Lee, dressed in all black, accepted condolences from friends while dabbing at her eyes, heavy with mascara.

Jean pushed on, unfazed. "Hello. I'm Jean, David's wife. We're so sorry for your loss."

Kora-Lee turned. Her dark brown eyes widened and her jaw dropped in unsuspecting surprise. She stood motionless for a beat before speaking. Her expression of gratitude weak and emotionless sounded disingenuous. Obviously uncomfortable around them, Kora-Lee shifted her weight and glanced around the room. With her gaze focused elsewhere, she hurriedly excused herself to chat with other mourners. With a jerk of the head, she dismissed them.

Alicia stepped forward with more grace, and certainly more manners than her mother. "We're glad you could make it." She put her hand on a young girl's shoulder and beamed. "This is my daughter, Lacey."

David and Jean took turns shaking hands with the composed dark-haired girl around ten years old. Lacey resembled her mother in many ways, but some of her characteristics appeared to come from her father's side. "We're pleased to meet you, Lacey." David recognized Lorraine standing next to Alicia. Lorraine smiled and extended her hand. "Hi, David. Remember me?"

"Sure. Nice to see you again Lorraine." David studied the two sisters standing side by side. The contrast in height and features was obvious.

Lorraine was several inches shorter than Alicia with a tawnier complexion, and a smaller nose, like her mother's. It was hard to picture them as sisters. However, Jean and her sister looked nothing alike, either, one fair-skinned and the other dark enough to look Italian. "It's been a long time. I'm sorry about your dad. But then, he was my dad too."

Lorraine wore a pasted-on smile and too much flowery perfume. Like her mother, her words lacked much emotion. Not knowing her, David withheld judgment and accepted her words with his own fake smile. Talking with the strangers who were his stepsisters was uncomfortable, and forced, as he expected. "Well, I'm glad I could be here to pay my respects and help Grandma Edna through this. I hate to leave her alone during such a difficult time." David glanced back to where he had left his grandmother. "I'd like to stay and chat, but Grandma could use the company." David pointed in the direction where Edna was seated. "I'm sure she'd appreciate you stopping by when you have a moment, to see how she's doing. She's taking Larry's death hard, as you might expect." He shook his sisters' hands, then he led Jean back toward his grandmother. Nearing the table, David noticed Edna sitting alone and looking around, unconsciously pushing the fruit around with her fork. He hurried back and sat down. "Where's Barbara?"

"She had to get home to her husband. He's quite ill. Wasn't it nice of her to come?"

David patted her shoulder. "Yes, it was. I was hoping to talk to her some more, though."

"She said she would get your phone number from me and call you sometime next week."

A couple friendly faces emerged from the otherwise aloof, if not hostile, crowd. David and Jean introduced themselves to Grandma's neighbors, Fred and Marge.

"Hi, your grandmother told us all about you. We're so pleased she has family who will take an interest in her." Fred glanced at Edna before continuing. "I'm not sure how much you know about her situation."

"Not much. If today's experience is any indication, I can imagine." David looked around the respectable crowd. He guessed they were there primarily to support Kora-Lee and her girls. Grandma sat mostly ignored. David didn't mind being shunned by these people, but neither Larry's spouse nor his loving children appeared to offer Edna a kind word or caring hug.

The hand had been dealt in a game David was still trying to understand. There was nothing left to do but finish out the play. After all, Edna was family, and family always takes care of family. David motioned to Jean then stood to leave. Pulling back his grandmother's chair, he took her arm. "Come on Grandma. Let's take you home."

Chapter 6

Back at Grandma's house, David took her keys, unlocked the door, and held it open for her. Stepping inside, the stench of urine abruptly announced a pet in the home. A pet that most likely did not get out or get its box cleaned. David wrinkled his nose and glanced at Jean. Grandma's small, black, stringy-haired mix of cocker and terrier yapped and trotted to greet them. It looked and smelled sorely in need of a bath. After seeing his grandmother's appearance, David doubted she managed to bathe herself often, let alone the dog.

"Hi, Missy. I'm home. Did you miss me?" Grandma bent down and rubbed the dog's neck fur with a playful pat.

David wrinkled his nose, his nasal passages burning from the overpowering odor of ammonia.

Jean shook her head and looked around. "This place looks terrible." She took a deep breath before she headed toward the living room.

David led Grandma across the stained, gold-green shag carpet to her dirty, shredded, cat scratching post of a sofa, an obvious breeding ground for bacteria. He didn't see the cat, but the odor was tell-tale. The semi-closed dingy blinds allowed little light into the room. Under these circumstances, it was almost more light than David cared for. He thought back to thirty years earlier when he had last seen his grandmother's home. Surely this was the same sofa. It looked at least that old. He would bet it hadn't been cleaned since.

With trepidation, David glanced around at the dust-covered blinds and the cobwebbed ceiling. He went to the windows, hesitating before he drew the blinds the rest of the way open. With the bright sun illuminating the room, David looked closer at the cobwebs and behind the curtains. His eyes widened at the small black specks darkening the corner. His skin tingled and he brushed away imaginary crawly things on his arms. "Good God." He covered his mouth at the sight, examined the black specks, then closed his eyes momentarily in denial. Hundreds of tiny moving arachnids, the size of a pin head, moved about. He looked back at his grandmother seated on the sofa with Jean and wondered how she could live in such horrendous conditions. David gestured with his head for Jean to come.

Jean went to the window leaving Edna still playing with the disheveled dog. "What?" Her eyes followed David's gaze. She drew back, shaking her head. "Tell me that's not what I think it is."

Baffled by the situation, David watched his grandmother fumble with a Chapstick laying amidst magazines, coffee cups, even pink foam curlers wrapped with loose hair, scattered across the dark pressed wood coffee table. He took in the cluttered room. Ragged outdated issues of Better Homes and Garden, Sunset, Flowers and Garden, and other magazines and papers littered the floor. Old baskets of faded, yellow and red reed, possibly hand-made, cluttered the room along with shoeboxes filled with yarn and dozens of half-finished sewing projects, looking like sprouting weeds in an unkempt yard. Beaded Christmas ornaments flowed over odd-sized boxes and trays on the over-sized rock fireplace hearth. The living room furniture was a strange melding. A gold ratty sofa, an oversized brown chair, cheap end tables, and beautiful antique mahogany pieces. He walked over to a curved mahogany dresser along one wall.

Watching him, Edna smiled and pushed off the sofa. "The furniture belonged to my mother and father." She met him at the dresser, which sat to the left of the smoke-stained fireplace. She lifted the ornate wood mantle clock and caressed it. "This clock was a wedding gift for my parents in eighteen-ninety-one. Look, it still runs perfectly."

David looked at the clock, which read eleven forty-two. He listened for the pendulum's steady beat, ticking time, not quite accurately. He noticed lettering across the wood back verifying the date of the gift. "It's a beautiful clock." He tried to recall his last visit to her and envisioned a younger woman in control of a neat, unpretentious, home with everything in its place, a true showcase for her needlepoint and sewing talents.

Grandma beamed and replaced the clock before shuffling back to the sofa. Reluctant to sit on the sofa, David stood next to Jean. "Is this what happens when people get old? They stop caring about their homes?"

Jean wiped the top of the dust-covered mahogany dresser with her hand and looked around. "I don't think so. It's more likely her eyesight is failing and maybe something else more serious. Who knows? It's obvious though, she's not able to properly care for herself, let alone the house. She probably doesn't even realize how dirty it is. I don't understand how Alicia and Grandma's friends can see how she's living and simply ignore the situation."

Edna blew her nose and tossed the tissue on the table. "I could use some water."

"I'll get it." Jean excused herself and headed for the kitchen.

David suspected she welcomed the escape from the spiders, which had always terrified her.

When she returned Edna accepted the glass with eager gulps. With a sideways glance, Jean whispered to David, discreetly updating him on the living situation. "I can't leave this place in this condition and feel good about myself. How could Larry allow her to live like this? Hasn't anyone else noticed how dirty it is? There's a pile from the dog in the corner of the kitchen."

Jean led David into the filthy kitchen, reeking from dog poop and stale air. The light green Formica counters were cluttered with food scraps, some, atop white Styrofoam meat trays. David looked at the gold and brown stain covered, kitchen carpet and held his breath. He didn't have to guess what the stains were from. He noticed the dog dish, alive with flies, rejected even by the dog, filled with dried table scraps from only God knows when.

"How long do you think it will take to make this place presentable?" David looked at his watch. "I know it needs a lot more work than we can do today, but maybe we can at least clean the kitchen and bathrooms and remove the spider's nests."

Jean sighed. "Let's see what we can get done within a couple of hours. I'll call home and let Marie know we'll be a little late, and then I'll get started on the kitchen. See if you can find a vacuum." Jean peered under the sink. She pulled out a well-worn sponge and can of cleanser, shook it, and frowned at the hollow sound. Spying the laundry room, she opened the cupboards and rummaged around. "Maybe there are more supplies in here."

"Grandma's going to wonder where you are."

"Tell her I'm making a cup of tea, and ask if she'd like one, too." Jean returned empty-handed.

David left, stopping to use the bathroom on the way. The brown stained porcelain bowl, and grime-covered sink disturbed him all the more. He scrunched his face at the sight. How could anyone live in a home for only two years and have it fall to such a frightful condition? Against his better judgment, David joined his grandmother on the sofa, Missy plodded over and jumped into her waiting lap. Glaring up with a raised lip, the mangy beast snarled at David.

"Missy is a sweet dog, and she's so protective of me. She always barks to let me know if someone is at the door, or if I don't hear the phone." Edna's tremulous hand stroked her beloved pet. "I used to have a cat, too." She cast her eyes downward. "She was a wonderful companion, but she died a few months ago."

Relieved at least there was only one pet to battle over odors and cleanliness, David resisted the urge to comment, choosing to change the subject to something more productive. "Grandma, where do you keep your vacuum? Jean thought maybe we could spend a few minutes helping you out while we're here."

"Oh, you. Don't start sounding like Barbara. That's not necessary. I can clean when you're gone. Where is Jean? I want to show both of you my home. Larry sold it to me while he was in real estate."

David's mouth fell open. How could a man consider selling a two-story home to his elderly mother? It should have been obvious that by ninety, taking the stairs would begin to present a challenge to most people. Was this man so hell-bent on making a real estate commission that he'd sell a home that was unsuitable for a senior citizen, especially his own mother, to make a buck?

Grandma pushed herself off the sofa and shuffled back down the hall calling for Jean who stepped from the kitchen into the hallway with a cup in hand. David wondered if it held tea or was merely a prop. Grandma led her visitors into the still darkened dining room pointing out her needlepoint hangings of orange oriental poppies, vibrant purple pansies, and roses in shades of red and pink scattered across the once white walls. Jean flicked on the light switch to better see the meticulously crafted artwork. Fine quality detailed works showed the patience and persistence of Grandma's younger years.

"My friend Barbara loves this picture of pink and red roses." Edna pointed to a gold framed needlepoint. "I promised it to her after I'm gone."

She removed the picture from the small nail and turned it over, revealing Barbara's name and a date, scrawled in shaky black letters on the backing. "You make sure she gets this." Edna showed off beautiful moss green, woven, oriental silk hangings of intricate flowers in vibrant hues of orange and red. "Larry brought those back for me from Korea." Her voice lowered before she continued. "When he returned with his new pregnant wife and her young daughter."

David doubted he would ever understand the relationship between his grandmother and Kora-Lee and Larry's stepdaughters.

Edna moved with slow concentrated steps, gripping the stair rail as she climbed the first flight of stairs to the landing. At the small landing, she stopped. Her chest heaved. She bent over a small corner table and tapped a black fluted vase shaped like a tall cylinder. "I grew these and dried them myself."

David glanced over the assorted dried flowers that filled the dusty vases and chipped garage sale pots, now broken and faded by time, suiting the surrounding décor and the resident of the home. He forced a smile. "They're very nice, Grandma."

Upstairs, his grandmother's bedroom was spacious with a full wall of mirrored closet doors, a large white and gold dresser, and surprisingly, a neatly made bed covered with a white and yellow spread. A wood clothes drying rack stood by the window draped with several personal unmentionables. David rolled his eyes as he followed his grandmother into the master bath. The bathroom was equally appalling to the one downstairs with a mirror bearing the spray of many washings and teeth brushings. A blackened sink had not seen cleanser for some time. Edna pushed open the door to the guest-room. David turned to see Jean's wide eyes. The double bed, adorned in a red crushed-velvet bedspread, took up most of the small room. Red glass lamps with dingy yellowed shades sporting gold tassels flanked the bed on small, mismatched, dark wood-grained, nightstands. The gaudy room lacked only plastic beads to complete the look of college dwellings in the late sixties.

"This is my craft room." Edna creaked open the door to the last room. Clutter buried most of the space. Clearly, the keepsake room, bookshelves and file cabinets bulged with fabric, yarn, and patterns. David glanced at the vintage treadle sewing machine and table covered with a visible layer of dust and wondered how many years it had gone unused.

"Well, what do you think?" Grandma's smile relayed her pride.

"It's very nice." David and Jean nodded their heads in unison, then dutifully followed her back down the stairs.

Jean veered off at the bottom of the stairs. "I think I'll duck into the kitchen and get back to the cleaning I started. Holler if she gets suspicious."

David joined his grandmother by a gold metal plant stand at the living room window.

"These are my African violets."

Bending over to examine the plants, David noticed a half dozen of the largest pink and purple African violets he had ever seen, stretching nearly two feet across. "I've never seen African violets as big and healthy as these." He wondered how her plants were maintained so well while her house looked like a tornado had swooshed through it.

"I've taken a dozen clippings from this one plant. My garden club is always telling me they've never seen anything like them." Edna's eyes sparkled as her fingers stroked the deep green velvety leaves. "I have a green thumb if I do say so myself. I'm a master gardener, you know."

Though her home was beyond dirty, Edna's stance and confident tone conveyed her pride in her abode and her many talents. David glanced at the sofa cushion. A few brushes with his hand failed to dislodge the dog hair coating the gold velour. A large pillow wedge and blankets sat piled at the end of the sofa.

"Are you still able to manage the stairs okay, Grandma?"

"Of course, I am. I just took them, didn't I?" Her words hissed like a snake.

He suspected she had been using the sofa as a bed, but there was no point in pushing the issue. Instead, he turned his gaze to the faces in the framed photos on the octagonal end table next to the sofa. Facial characteristics helped identify the spirits from the past. There was Granddad Jacob as a young soldier, and another of Larry in his uniform looking about the age David remembered when his parents divorced. A black and white eight by ten photo of a beautiful young woman sat next to the others, most likely high school graduation from the formal headshot and the simple, curled-under hairstyle. Edna, perhaps. He doubted it, the hairdo didn't look like the early 1900s. His mind flashed back to Bernice. This picture may well be the last formal picture ever taken of the woman who would have been his aunt, had she not died so tragically in a car accident at twenty-one years old.

Light breathing tickled David's neck. Edna standing over him caused him to turn away from the shrine of her family. "They're beautiful pictures, Grandma." There was no point in drawing her into the past. Not with the memory of burying her last child still fresh in her mind. He needed a brief reprieve and Jean had been noticeably absent for some time. "I'm going to get some water, may I get you some?" David hurried into the kitchen where Jean stood hands on hips, looking flushed and sweaty.

"I couldn't find her vacuum, so I tried to sweep the dining room carpet." Jean held out an old worn corn stalk broom and pointed to the metal dustpan piled with dirt. "I don't mind helping clean the house, but ... I'm not getting rid of the spiders." Jean grabbed a dingy dishtowel from the counter and wrapped it around the bristles. Snatching a rubber band from the counter, she wrapped it around the broom handle holding the towel in place and held it out to David. "Here, I'll keep Grandma occupied." Jean lured Grandma into the dining room. "I see you have some beautiful carvings." Jean stood in front of the over-sized china cabinet with interest.

"Oh, yes. Larry brought some figurines from Japan and Korea, others I bought when I took Alicia with me to Asia after she graduated from high school." Edna opened the glass cupboard, lovingly gazing upon a jade dragon figurine as she withdrew it.

David watched to make sure the show and tell was underway, then cringing, he headed for the living room curtains faced with the icky task of destroying the minute arachnids. Lifting the broom handle high and pulling the curtains back, the spiders' nests were gathered onto the towel and taken out the back door to be disposed of. After half a dozen trips outside, David brushed away the creepy sensation and some remnants of silky web. He gave a massive sigh and took a final glance at the arachnid-free walls and ceiling. He'd done his part.

Over the next hour, David and Jean swapped roles keeping Grandma out of the way and entertained while the other cleaned. With the kitchen sinks scoured and scraped, the toilets scrubbed, the cupboards wiped down, and dog scraps and messes wiped up, David reminded Jean about the long drive ahead. They stashed the few cleaning supplies they'd managed to rummage and faced Edna.

"It's getting late and we've got to get going. Our kids are waiting and Jean's sister has to get home to spend some time with her own family."

Grandma looked at the floor. Her spirit, which had lifted during their brief visit, plummeted when she realized they were leaving. David stopped at the door. His left brain screamed of the responsibility which lay in his future, but his right brain fought back with a twinge of guilt as he hugged Edna goodbye. The kiss on his grandmother's cheek betrayed her emotions. David wiped her salty tear off his lips. "We'll see you soon." David took her gnarled hand, freckled with age spots and held it for a moment. His head hurt facing the reality the past twenty-four hours was only the beginning of how his life was going to change. Attending his father's funeral pushed him into the position of assuming some responsibility for his grandmother. He didn't know to what degree. For the moment, he had no desire to pursue a relationship with Alicia or Lorraine, but he knew his relationship with his grandmother somehow was just beginning.

Chapter 7

For the first few weeks after Larry's funeral, David called his grandmother weekly. After all, she was family, and it was the right thing to do. But as the calendar flipped past fall and the rituals of everyday life with his hectic work schedule and family responsibilities, the once-weekly calls stretched out. Eventually, the calls became another required task to squeeze into his life, out of obligation more than love. Grandma sounded in good spirits when they spoke and she informed him Barbara and friends from the garden club dropped by often. David convinced himself there wasn't much to worry about. Once in a while, he wondered how she was doing and vowed he would call more often, but he had a life and a job and family. If Grandma needed anything, she knew she could call him.

Before he knew it, Christmas had come and gone, and the new year brought a schedule as busy as the year he'd left behind. David's only private time in the evening found him in front of the computer keeping up to date on the news, the economy, and checking his modest investments. His promise of keeping in touch with Edna had become a faded memory.

One evening the phone ringing drew David's attention from his computer. Surely, Jean or one of the kids would get it. The continued ringing reminded David he was home alone. Turning away from the screen, he retrieved the telephone from the bookshelf in the den.

"I'm so lonely. I miss Larry so much."

Grandma's tired voice caused David to regret his neglect. He reflected on her situation and wondered what his life would be like if Jean, Rachel and Emily, even Nathan, were dead. His chest tightened at the thought. With no excuse for his behavior, he stammered a weak apology for not calling while at the same time attempting to diminish his guilt. "Are you still getting visitors?"

"Alicia visited a few weeks ago. She even brought me a lovely spinach and noodle casserole. It's much more than I can eat by myself, though."

David wrinkled his face at the mention of the spinach casserole. A sarcastic comment popped into his head. He squelched it. "Alicia's been by? That's nice. Does she visit often?" His interest was piqued, perhaps he had misjudged her. Maybe the whole seating arrangement at the funeral was all Kora-Lee's doing. Maybe there was hope his stepsisters would maintain contact with the woman they had called Grandma for nearly forty years. He took in a calming breath, at least Alicia was there to see to some of their grandmother's needs.

"She's been by a few times. It's so nice when she brings Lacey with her. Lacey reminds me so much of my Bernice. But, Alicia makes me so angry trying to convince me Larry wanted to be cremated. I know that's a lie. When am I going to see you again?"

David flinched at the sorrow in her voice and the question he couldn't evade. He mumbled a feeble excuse about his work schedule and promised to try to visit sometime soon. Saddened, and draped in guilt not wholly deserved, David said a reluctant goodbye, promising to call her again soon.

Chapter 8

The parcel delighted Edna when the postman arrived at her door. She recognized the return address. Excited, she scurried to the living room to open the box. The microwave beeping announced her tea was ready, but she ignored it with a new priority at hand. With brown paper torn aside and the treasure removed from the white box, Edna ran her fingers over a yellow photo album, its cover decorated with a childlike drawing of a family under a big tree. Edna traced the large black lettering that read *OUR FAMILY*. She flipped through the first pages. Her eyes welled seeing the black and white polaroids of David and Nathan as young children. As she continued to turn the pages decorated with stickers and carefully scripted calligraphy lettering with glitter pens, Edna got a glimpse into David's life, the life she'd missed for so many years. She paused as she studied David's school photos, his high school graduation and his wedding day all cut in various shapes with special scissors leaving decorative borders. She allowed her mind to insert herself into these key events. She grinned ear to ear seeing photographs of David's children whom she couldn't wait to meet. She pondered what her life might have been like had she been there to share the happy times with her grandson and his family. Tears formed, she brushed them aside along with the imaginary life. Her clock chimed two o'clock. Edna startled at the sound, not realizing how quickly the day had gone by while she was lost in the precious images of a past of which she should have been a part. Her forgotten tea water had long gone cold, but she no longer cared. She rose and called Fred and Marge. She desperately wanted to show off the gift.

Edna waited until after dinner before tapping out the large penned numbers on the dial to call David.

"Grandma? What are you doing up so late? Is everything okay?"

"I wanted to wait until after dinner hour." Edna glanced outside. The sky was dark. It couldn't be that late could it? "What time is it there? Are you in a different time zone?"

"No, we're the same time, but it's almost ten at night."

Flustered, Edna stammered. "I'm sorry, I only wanted to thank you for the lovely gift. It was so nice to receive the photo album of your family."

"I'm glad you like them. The girls had fun picking out the pictures which weren't too embarrassing."

Edna caressed the album in her lap. "I'll call you in a few days, Dear."

"No. That's okay. I'm going to be up a while yet."

Edna wasn't sure if David was saying that to be polite, but she was eager to talk about all the events she had missed. "It looks like you and Jean had a lovely wedding." Edna ached for all the years lost. Her thoughts returned to the present. "When will I see you again and meet my grandchildren?"

"I'm sorry. I've been putting in a lot of overtime, plus its basketball season. Emily has games most weekends and I'm one of the coaches."

"I know you're busy, I understand." She forced a smile in an attempt to hide the disappointment in her voice.

"Maybe we can all make it this weekend. I don't think Emily has a game on Saturday."

Her heartbeat quickened and her mood brightened. "If you're sure it's not too much trouble?"

"No, Grandma, It's not too much trouble. You're a very important part of my life right now. I have to talk to Jean, but I think we can come for a quick visit. I'll let you know on Friday. Okay?"

Edna wiped a lone tear as she hung up the phone. She called to Missy who tramped down the hall and begged at her feet. Edna bent over, tore off a crust of toast and held it out to Missy, and with long slow strokes, pet her only companion. "David and his family are coming this weekend. Isn't that wonderful?"

Chapter 9

David rummaged through his tools in the garage. He tossed selected screwdrivers, wrenches, and pliers in a plastic bucket. Once stashed in the trunk of the car, he returned to the house, eager to hit the road. "How's everyone doing?" He peered into the kitchen. Jean busily gathered assorted rags and cleaning supplies.

"I'm about done." Jean stood at the bottom of the stairway and called Rachel and Emily. "Are you ready?"

"We've been waiting to meet Grandma." Rachel tramped down the stairs. "Hurry up, Emily. Don't forget the CD player and your CDs." Rachel headed out the door with her music and coat in hand.

"Are we leaving or what?" David stood, arms crossed, by the door.

"Someone has to check the doors." Jean hurried through the house, pausing once more at the stairs. "We're leaving, Emily. Dad's waiting."

Right behind, Emily flew down the stairs and out the door. Jean checked her purse, loaded her arms with her cleaning supplies, and with the rest of the family and the overnight bags in the car, took a deep breath and closed the door behind her.

"Does everyone have everything?" David sat behind the wheel. Last-minute forgotten items were inevitable with a family of women. He glanced in the rearview mirror as all parties gave a thumbs up. Armed with enough repair and cleaning supplies for every possible situation, David turned the key in the ignition and the family headed out to visit Edna and, with a little luck, attack the condition of her home.

"The kitchen and bathrooms have to be a priority." Even before the car left the neighborhood, Jean had a pen and paper in hand already scribbling her list of chores - sinks, toilets, tub, cupboards, and floors. "Did you remember the vacuum?"

"Yep, I also brought the shampooer. I'll fix the leaky faucet and see if there are any other repairs, then hopefully I can convince Grandma to let me shampoo her carpet."

With the plan roughed out, they sat back and enjoyed the drive away from Seattle's drizzle and traffic to the dry, less hectic, side of the mountains.

"Remember," Jean glanced over the back seat and looked at her daughters. "I warned you what the house looks like. I don't want to hear any remarks--even away from Grandma. If we all pitch in and put in a full day today and a few hours tomorrow, we can head home early afternoon, stop for dinner in Ellensburg, and still have a relaxing Sunday evening. You can get some homework done if you need to. Maybe we can make the house a little more presentable."

David looked in the rearview mirror to see Emily's head bobbing with the music. "Are you girls listening?"

Emily pulled the earbuds from her ears. "I heard her. We can help clean. I can vacuum and dust."

"We'll see, I think it'll be better if you keep Grandma busy and talking so your dad and I can clean."

Rachel unplugged her earpiece. "I don't understand why she doesn't want you to clean. I'd love it if someone cleaned for me."

David shook his head. "From the looks of your room, I'm not sure you know what clean is." Another glance in the mirror and David saw Rachel shake her head before responding.

"Ha ha, very funny."

From the corner of his eye, David noticed Jean shake her head. "You're not old Rachel, sometimes older people are too proud to have others clean for them. We'll have to play things by ear when we get there and see how it goes."

David glanced at Jean. "Let's stop on the way and eat so we don't have to worry about eating there if you know what I mean. I'm thinking something quick like a burger or deli. We need to get there and get as much done as we can this weekend."

After a brief lunch stop, and with the eastern Washington sun beating down, David pulled the car into his grandmother's driveway. David glanced at the carport as he pulled next to her car. The door to the tool shed at the end of the carport had what appeared to be a new dent. "It looks like Grandma forgot to stop in time and ran her Buick into the shed again. I wonder if I should ask her about it?"

Jean shook her head. "Not today. We have enough on our plate. Perhaps sometime though we should express our concerns about her driving."

David agreed. "Okay, let's try to work until six or so, then we can take Grandma out to dinner before we call it a night and head to the hotel. Leave everything in the car until we've visited a while. We don't want it to look like we only came to clean."

David led his family through the gate and into the small front courtyard littered with old faded, webbed lawn chairs, a rusty metal table, and a broken patio umbrella. Missy's yapping announced their arrival as Grandma opened the door and they stepped inside. David stiffened at the odors that hung in the stagnant air. In his months of absence, David allowed himself to forget the condition of his grandmother's home. He couldn't comprehend how Alicia or his grandmother's friends hadn't taken steps to improve her life. Maybe they tried to clean and Grandma resisted? Based on his brief experience with her, he guessed his last thought was most plausible and he abandoned his preconceived notion of Alicia's neglect. This weekend though, David knew he would have to try to keep his grandmother's home from being either a health hazard or a danger to her, and maybe go the step beyond and restore a resemblance of clean.

"We made it." David embraced his grandmother.

Rachel and Emily stood beside their father. He put his arm around Rachel. "Grandma, this is Rachel. She's sixteen." He looked across to Emily and put his hand on her head. "And Emily is thirteen."

Though tears had begun to flow, Grandma's smile lit her whole face as she bent over and hugged each granddaughter. "Gracious, look at how big you girls are. I had no idea how lovely you were. You're even prettier than your pictures."

Jean winked at Rachel.

Missy's constant yapping made talking nearly impossible. An animal lover, Emily squatted down to pet the mutt, but after burying her nose in the dog's fur, she made a face and pulled back. No doubt the dog was still sorely needing a bath. "Emily, how are you and Rachel at bathing dogs?"

Jean steered her daughters toward the living room, then leaned in toward David. "It's going to be like opening Pandora's box."

"Come on Grandma, let's go sit down." Emily led the way with Missy plodding behind wagging her tail and hoping for another pat on the head.

David followed Jean into the dimly lit kitchen. Crumbs and scraps of food on small saucers invited pests. The stench of urine from the carpet crept into his nose and muddled his other senses. Food crumbs littered the carpet, uneaten, was ground underfoot as Edna apparently didn't see well enough to pick up any remains. David took a deep breath. He hated to upset his grandmother, but the home needed some serious TLC. The trick was how to do it without upsetting her.

Jean stood shaking her head. David sensed she felt she was in over her head. "I'll get started while you chat with Grandma for a while. Maybe send Rachel or Emily out to help bring in some of the supplies."

David joined his daughters in the living room where Edna sat between her granddaughters on the sofa.

Rachel squatted and stroked Missy.

Grandma smiled and patted her dog on the head. "Do you like Missy? She's such a wonderful pet."

At the mention of the dog, David fought back his disgust. He watched Rachel pet the dog, repeat Emily's face, and wipe her hand on her jeans. He chuckled under his breath.

Suddenly excited, his grandmother looked at David. "Would you like something to eat?"

"We're fine, we ate lunch on the way."

"You shouldn't have done that." She gave David a stern look. "I would have made you something."

"Goodness, where's Jean? Is she all right?"

David sprang from his chair. "She's freshening up after the long drive and then she was going to start some tea. You stay seated and I'll check on her." Raised brows focused on Emily, reminding his daughters to keep their grandmother occupied. "Why don't you tell Grandma about your school and sports."

"Sports? Gracious, I admire young girls who play sports. I was quite athletic myself., but it wasn't so popular in my day for girls to play sports." Grandma grinned and positioned herself to listen to Emily.

David bobbed his head in appreciation, then hurried into the kitchen where Jean was hunched over the sink. He snatched a cup from the cabinet, filled it with water, and set the timer on the microwave for sixty seconds. "I told Grandma you were making her some tea."

Jean looked up from scouring and wiped her bangs from her forehead with her arm. "It's a beautiful day. Why don't you have her show you the yard? That way I can at least run the vacuum."

It was the perfect diversion. David rummaged in the canisters for a tea bag, steeped the bag for a minute or so and carried the cup into the living room.

He handed her the cup. "Here you go."

Grandma looked at the cup. "Is there sugar in it? I always have one teaspoon of sugar with my tea. Not two, just one."

Emily started to giggle. David shot a glance at her and returned to the kitchen for the sugar. Returning in a flash, he handed his grandmother her tea and went to the window. "It's such a nice day and we haven't seen your yard yet, Grandma. I remember how nice it always was when Nathan and I were younger. Why don't we take a walk outside and you can show us your plants? Jean will be out in a few minutes."

Grandma set the teacup on the table and beamed as she brought her hand to her face. "I am a master gardener, you know." She pushed herself off the sofa and walked to the side door which opened into her small back yard. David led his daughters outside as Jean entered the room.

"Are you coming, Dear?" Grandma turned and looked at Jean.

Jean sneezed and dabbed at her eyes. "I wish I could. But my allergies are acting up today."

David noticed his grandmother's frown and downcast eyes before she shrugged and turned away. He'd have to stretch out the tour of the yard as long as possible.

The small garden, almost certainly well-maintained at one time, now lay overgrown with ground cover climbing over other plants, and bushes long overdue for pruning. The pleasant sweet fragrance from cherry and apple blossoms hung in the cool crisp air. After the winter weather, most plants were dead or dormant. David could see though every square foot of her small backyard had been planted with bushes, trees, ground cover, climbing roses and other plants he couldn't begin to identify. "What's this?" David leaned over some purple and green leaves with small purple flowers.

"That's Ajuga, it grows like a weed, anywhere you put it. Would you like some? I have so much."

"We have a long bank that would be a great place for it. Do you have a shovel?"

"There's one in my shed. You can dig it up right before you go home."

"How about this?" David pointed to a large bush with whitish-pink flowers.

His grandmother's eyes twinkled. "That's a viburnum." She gently touched the plant. David heard the vacuum start up. He knew Grandma's hearing wasn't the best, but still, he steered her toward the farthest corner of the yard toward some trees growing along the six-foot-tall, battered, wood fence separating her small yard from the condo unit behind her. "These are my fruit trees." Edna pointed to the larger one. "This is a mulberry tree."

Rachel fingered the leaves. "I've never eaten a mulberry before. What do they taste like?"

Edna spun around and giggled. "They're quite tasty like a dried fig, but I'm afraid you won't be eating any today either. The magpies tend to favor the fruit and it's so difficult for me to pick it. I keep the tree for the birds." Edna turned and headed to the opposite corner and pointed to a smaller tree beginning to bud with early spring growth. "This is my cherry tree." Edna pulled a low branch down and frowned. "I've tried everything I could think of, but the starlings and robins always beat me to this, too." She ambled up and down the two sides of her sixty-foot by twenty-foot, yard pointing out all the trees and flowers.

Fascinated by her knowledge regarding plants, David still remembered the pride she had in her garden at her old house, the last time he'd seen her. The yard overflowed in a showcase of flowers, bushes, and grapes, in overabundance, draped across sturdy old wooden pergolas, resembling a Monet painting. It amazed him how Grandma could name every one of her unique plants, none which he would remember even minutes later. The hum of the vacuum still resonated from inside the house. Grandma showed no awareness of the sound but her steps slowed and her breaths came with more effort.

"Your yard looks nice, I like these. What are they?" Emily leaned in and fingered a delicate rose-colored blossom tinged with green, which drooped over large pointy leaves.

Grandma bent down; her smile as delicate as the flower. "That's a hellebore. It's my favorite. I bought the plant at a garden show."

David straightened and turned toward the house. The vacuum cleaner fell silent. David waited a minute or so, then motioned to Emily. "Your yard is beautiful, Grandma. Let's go finish your tea. We can dig the Ajuga later."

Inside, Grandma cozied herself back onto the living room sofa. Jean was still breathing heavy from her mad dash running the vacuum around both levels of the house. David noticed the ground-in food and crumbs were gone. The room looked more presentable, though the persistent odor still permeated the place, burning his nasal passages.

"Jean, didn't you say the girls needed some supplies for school?" He looked with pleading eyes toward his wife.

Taking her cue, Jean smiled and nodded at her daughter. "Rachel, wasn't there something you needed?"

Rachel jumped up. "Oh yeah, I need some poster board for my science project."

Jean grabbed her purse from the end table and looked at Grandma. "Is there anything you need at the store while we're here? The girls need a few things for school. How about you join us?"

Grandma looked at her worn, slip-on, once-white canvas shoes. "I could use some new shoes. What about you David, aren't you coming?" Edna stared at David with hands on her hips.

"No, I want to get the sink fixed. It'll only take a minute, but maybe I'll see if there's anything else that needs a quick repair. You guys take your time. I'll be fine."

His grandmother eyed him with suspicion but she appeared eager to escape the house for a bit. She went to the closet and shuffled after Jean to the door wearing a navy-blue quilted coat with a ripped hem and clutching her purse.

Jean whispered to David. "We'll be back in a couple of hours. Will that do?" He held the door eager to have the place free to get some work done. With his family out of sight, he heaved a big sigh and looked around.

With Missy safely at Fred and Mabel's for a few hours, David maneuvered the upright carpet shampooer, also filled with a healthy dose of scented pet urine deodorizer, across the living room floor. After nearly an hour and a half of strenuous pushing and pulling, lifting and scrubbing, in the living room, dining room, and kitchen, Missy's odor diminished markedly. David breathed the clean spring breeze smell, as promised on the shampoo bottle. He straightened his back and relaxed his shoulders surveying his effort, wondering how long the improvement would last. Cleaning Grandma's house would certainly be an ongoing struggle. There had to be other options that didn't involve bi-monthly trips across the state. A cleaning service was the obvious answer, but even that would bring problems. David could already imagine his grandmother's protests. With the final attachments by the door and the empty soap and disinfectant bottles in the outside trash bin, David wiped his forehead with his sleeve. He glanced over at the still unrepaired leaky faucet and snatched a wrench. He replaced a rubber washer and tightened a few bolts. Exhausted and thirsty, he opened the refrigerator hoping to find an unopened cold beverage. A cold Coke sounded like heaven about now. Inside, next to eggs and milk, assorted condiment jars hid a jumble of uncovered aging leftovers. He wrinkled his nose and pushed bottles away. Instead of a soda, he found old dog food and a set of keys. Deflated, he trudged to the living room sofa for a much-needed breather. As he started to doze off, the sound of a car pulling into the drive jolted him back awake.

"The place smells and looks great." Jean's welcome voice validated his efforts.

David forced his aching body off the sofa and greeted his family at the door.

Jean held a grocery bag and lowered her voice to David. "I bought a few things so we can make breakfast here tomorrow."

Emily followed, carrying a bag from a discount shoe store and set it next to the table. She inhaled deeply. "It smells a lot better, Dad."

David watched as Grandma entered and looked around without much emotion. Oblivious to the efforts directed at her carpeting, she eyed the kitchen and asked if the sink had been fixed.

The carpet needed several hours to dry and David's stomach craved real food. He looked at the wall clock and figured it would be a good time for an early dinner. Everyone piled into the car.

"Is there any place in particular where you'd like to go for dinner, Grandma?" David sat posed behind the steering wheel awaiting a clue on his destination.

"There's a lovely place where I go with Barbara sometimes. They have the best mashed potatoes."

"That sounds great, just tell me the name and which direction to go and I can find it."

Sitting next to David, his grandmother grinned as she peered out the window. David reached across the seat and took her hand. "Grandma, can you tell me where the restaurant is?"

Grandma shot a glance at David. "Of course I know where it is. I've eaten there many times. It's on Columbia Drive."

Although there was a touch of sarcasm, David couldn't help but smile at her wit. He turned the car onto Columbia Drive, knowing at least there would be numerous dining establishments from which to choose should Grandma's memory and sense of direction fail her. Luckily, she spied the green tiled roof with the big yellow letters on the sign for *Shari's Restaurant* a little way down the street on the right.

David was happy to see her hearty appetite as she downed a huge mound of mashed potatoes smothered in extra gravy, as requested. Though she managed to finish her turkey and spuds, a lone biscuit remained and Grandma insisted on a doggy bag. David cringed, knowing full well where the biscuit would end up.

At home, even before she removed her coat, Grandma pulled off part of the biscuit and tossed it to Missy who yapped, begging for food. As expected, Missy sniffed the bread, turned up her nose, and pattered away without touching it.

"Grandma, you can't be feeding the dog off the rug. Put the food in a dish. Besides, it isn't good to feed animals food intended for people, it could be bad for them."

His grandmother looked at the morsel on the ground. "I know. Mother always told me not to feed my Boston Bull puppy anything but dog food." She bent over and plucked the ignored morsel from the floor and stared at it before she continued. "One day when I was in first grade and Mother was out, I gave him part of Mother's homemade doughnut. My poor puppy choked and died. I felt so bad. Daddy never stopped teasing her about how dry her doughnuts were."

David didn't know whether to be serious over her puppy's death or laugh over the comment about the doughnut. "Well, then you know what I mean." He held his laughter at her story pulled so easily from over eighty years earlier.

"I won't feed Missy any more scraps." Edna cast her gaze downward, avoiding David's stare.

Jean tapped David on the shoulder and pointed out the time. He put his arm around his grandmother. "It's getting late, we're going to head to our hotel now. We'll be back in the morning."

Grandma wrung her hands. "Oh, you. Do you have to leave? I thought you were spending the night here."

David shook his head thankful for the built-in excuse. "Maybe another time. With the girls here with us, it's better to get a hotel since you have only one bed."

"I've hardly had a chance to talk with my granddaughters." She reached out and motioned to Rachel and Emily to come closer.

"We'll see you tomorrow." Emily stepped forward and hugged Grandma.

"I wish you could stay."

"We'll be by in the morning and have breakfast together." David ignored his grandmother's pout as they headed for the door and a much-needed good night's sleep.

Grandma was already seated at the dining table eating a slice of toast when David and his family arrived the next morning. David sat next to his grandmother while his daughters followed their mom into the kitchen. "I was thinking Jean and the girls could make breakfast for us this morning so we have a chance to talk."

"Oh. I don't know about that." Grandma's eyes shot a glance over to her kitchen and she pushed off her chair to stand. "They won't know where anything is."

"They'll be fine. Let's you and I go into the living room and relax. You can pretend we're in a restaurant again and let someone else wait on you."

David's remark brought a smile. His grandmother hobbled beside him down the hall to the living room. "Come, sit down." David plopped onto the grimy sofa, abruptly aware a new odor emanated from the furniture. He wished he had thought about shampooing the sofa and love seat too. Maybe next time.

"Grandma, Jean and I have been thinking about how much you have to do by yourself with Larry gone. Most people your age need a little help. You, however, are doing remarkably well getting around as you do." David justified his forthcoming white lie as an incentive for his grandmother. "Even though we're able to care for our home ourselves, we prefer to use a cleaning service." Watching for any reaction, David hoped his fib would encourage her to give a housekeeper a chance. "There are other things we'd rather do with our time, so we have a lady come in once a week for the regular cleaning. We'd be happy to pay for someone to clean for you."

Her voice rose as she squinted at him. "Oh you, I don't need a cleaning service. And you can't trust other people to come into your home. I'm perfectly able to clean my own home. I just don't like to. I can do my own laundry, too. I've cared for myself all these years."

Not surprised by her resistance, David still winced at her defensive tone. Her clothes were stained and carried the odor of dirty water. David had seen and smelled the dishcloths and towels which had been put into drawers, stiff and dingy from air drying. While shampooing, he had surveyed the small clothes drying rack in Edna's bedroom displaying towels and undergarments seemingly washed by hand and hung out to dry. "At least think about it."

The aroma of bacon floated into the room. "It smells like breakfast is ready. I hope you're hungry, Jean makes a great breakfast."

Emily came in all smiles, standing like a doorman at a high-class hotel. "Breakfast is served, and I made the pancakes."

Edna came alive at the table surrounded by her newly-found family. She barely stopped talking to eat. But as the morning wore on, the reality of the approaching work and school week loomed over them.

David looked at his watch. "It's late. We need to leave soon so we can get home by evening. The kids have school tomorrow."

Rachel and Emily rose and gathered plates and silverware from the table. Within twenty minutes, dishes were hand-washed and put away, counters were wiped, and leftovers wrapped and stowed in the fridge with a reminder to Edna to eat the leftovers within the next few days. New sponges, scouring pads and sink cleanser were stashed under the sink. It may have been a futile move, but David hoped they would get at least some use.

"You girls be good, and come see me again, okay?" Grandma hugged them each before she turned to David. "Are you sure you can't stay?"

Her dejected look caused a stitch of sadness for David. "We have to get going. I'll see you in a few weeks." He reached out to embrace Grandma. She clung to him like a drowning victim clutching a lifeline. Smiling weakly, she dabbed a tear as David and his family turned and walked out the door.

Chapter 10

Monday afternoon David sat at his desk reviewing charts from test data. Still tired from the full weekend and long drive, his mind wandered. With his grandmother's living conditions etched in his mind, he couldn't shake the image. Surely, there was something he could do to improve her situation, without constantly traveling across the state to do the work himself. He wanted and needed his weekends for more than driving and doing chores for his grandmother. Maybe it was selfish, but good God, he hadn't asked for all this, and he was busy enough before Grandma's situation. There was no way he could take time off work during the week to go to eastern Washington. Not with the tight scheduling he faced. He looked at his watch, tomorrow's scheduled test flight was in the morning and people were waiting for his input. He forced himself to focus on the task at hand. With the revised plan signed off, he delivered it to the test director and pushed his way out the door to take on the traffic. Driving home, he mulled over the situation considering the few options available to him. Grandma was adamant about not having strangers in her home, but something needed to be done.

Jean was in the loft, busy designing an ad for her business when he finally arrived home.

He pulled a chair next to her. "I've been thinking about what to do about Grandma's house. It seems wrong nobody seems to notice how she's living except us. No one else seems to care."

Jean glanced up from her work. "Maybe she scares everyone off. You've seen how she can be. Even we had to do our cleaning behind her back."

"You're probably right. Alicia is at least a familiar face. If we could convince Grandma to let her come in and clean, then her concern over having strangers in would no longer be valid."

Jean lifted her open palms in a shrug. "It's worth a try, but Alicia hasn't exactly been involved in her life since Larry died. Besides, it sounds like your grandmother isn't exactly on good terms with her or the rest of the family. What are you going to say to Alicia to convince her to clean Grandma's house? That is if Grandma agrees to it?"

Shaking his head, David grimaced. "I don't know. I get the feeling she won't do a whole lot without there being something in it for her. And I don't feel right asking Grandma's friends to help out any more than they already do. I'm sure they do plenty for her already. I can't think of anyone else. It's worth a try for our peace of mind, isn't it?" David pushed his desk chair back and went downstairs to grab a beer. His grandmother's situation was causing him major stress. His neck and shoulders tightened every time he thought about it. Ideally, Alicia wouldn't have to be coerced to assist in their grandmother's care, but his dealings with her and the rest of her family thus far were a galaxy away from how he had perceived caring and concerned relatives to be. He had to deal with the situation as it presented itself, and Alicia was the only one he could approach. There was no other alternative which Grandma would even consider. Prepared to offer a bribe, if necessary, and with resolve, he thrust his doubts aside and marched to the phone. Taking a deep breath, he blew out his frustrations and grabbed the receiver. The phone was answered right away. Alicia's eagerness to chat was a good sign, so David jumped right in and explained his plan.

"I don't know why you think Grandma will let me clean her house for her. I've tried before. I took a shampooer over once about a year ago and tried to clean her carpet. All she did was nag about how I was doing it wrong and how it was going to make the place feel damp. Anyway, she's still pissed over Larry being dissected as she called it, and cremated."

Though Alicia's explanation certainly was believable, David's patience was seeping away. "Look, I know it's tough. But doesn't it bother you she's living in such conditions? Jean and I spent our whole weekend cleaning and driving back and forth. It would sure help me out, not to mention improve Grandma's environment."

"I don't think she minds the mess. I think she likes things that way."

Hearing her resistance, David found himself counting to ten mentally. "Do you think it's good to allow her to live like that?" He pictured Alicia rolling her eyes during the silence before her reluctant reply.

"Well, I can see if she'll let me." She paused. "I'll try."

Relief washed over him. It was a near-perfect solution to ease his concern, and perhaps it would renew the damaged relationship between his grandmother and Alicia. He hung up and grabbed another beer from the fridge before retreating to the living room and joining Jean on the sofa. He shrugged, "I'm not going to place any bets, but at least she said she'd try. We'll see what happens." Grabbing the remote off the coffee table, he tapped the volume button up a few notches and tuned to the six o'clock news. He took a swig of the cold ale, allowing his frustration to seep away. Still, he couldn't brush aside the nagging sense a storm was brewing off on the horizon.

Chapter 11

Edna couldn't wait until Sunday to hear from David. Instead, she called him on Thursday evening a few weeks after their last visit. "Someone stole my silver set." She struggled with the words through her anger and her sobs.

"What kind of silver are you talking about? A tea set?"

"No. My silverware. It was real silver. Eight place settings, plus serving pieces. They were in a lovely wooden case." Edna pursed her lips. She couldn't believe David didn't understand what she was talking about.

"I'm sure it will show up. Where did you last see it? Maybe I can help you figure out what happened to it."

Edna scowled. She resented David's condescending tone. "It was hidden in the living room. You remember my sofa end tables with doors. It was inside one of them. It's been there ever since I moved into this home."

"Is it possible you moved it?"

"No." Her hands shook. She raised her voice. David obviously wasn't hearing her. "I paid over two-thousand dollars for it. I'm sure someone stole it."

"Did anyone else know where you put it?"

Edna thought for a moment, she had told only two people where the silverware was kept. "Only Barbara and Alicia."

"Well, I'm sure neither one would have stolen anything from you. Is anything else missing?"

Frustrated by David's persistent questions, Edna took a deep breath. She emphasized her words. "Nothing else is missing, only my silverware. I know Barbara would never steal from me, she's my dearest friend. She even takes me to church with her." Her eyebrows raised at the notion which flashed in her mind. She had doubted Alicia's character in the past but believed her bad habits were behind her. Besides, she had been the only one in Larry's family who had called and visited her since Larry died. Buried bitterness and distrust resurfaced and began to overwhelm her like a small tremor before the devastation of a larger quake. She shuddered at the thought, but it was the only explanation. She whispered, "I think Alicia stole it."

"Grandma, Alicia wouldn't steal from you. She loves you. Why would she do anything so spiteful?"

David's naiveté didn't surprise her. "You don't understand. You don't know her the way I do." Edna paused as she recalled Alicia's rebellious years. She didn't like to gossip ... however, David was family. He needed to know the truth. "She probably stole it for drug money."

"What makes you think that? She doesn't seem like someone who would get involved in drugs. She's got a daughter. I can't believe she'd do something like that. I'm sure there's another explanation."

Edna shook her head. David didn't know about Alicia's troubled past. "She used to be quite a handful for Larry and Kora-Lee, she was even in trouble with the law." Edna didn't want to share too many details, although she felt compelled to warn David. "Be sure you never loan her money. She's borrowed money from me, and I've never seen a cent. Believe me, it's only a matter of time before she asks you for money."

"When was the last time Alicia came by to see you?"

Edna contemplated the question for a moment before she remembered Alicia's visit. "I don't know when it was ... last week sometime. That must be when she stole it. She came by with a vacuum cleaner and said she wanted to do some cleaning for me. I didn't want her to, but she insisted. I don't know what got into her. I should have known she was up to something."

"We don't know that. I'll come over this weekend and we can look around. I'm sure it will show up."

"We'll just see about that." Edna stewed. "I'm not going to have Alicia in my house ever again." She banged the phone down. No one could convince her the silverware had been misplaced. She knew it had been stolen.

Chapter 12

Hanging up the phone, David buried his face in his hands to squelch a scream. Even as his inner turmoil was about to boil over, he chuckled to himself at the irony of the situation as he went to the living room to tell Jean the latest breaking disaster story.

"You're never going to believe this." He sat back in his recliner and raised the footrest. "Grandma apparently had some silver flatware, real silver, worth around two grand. She says it's been stolen. And, here's the clincher, she says Alicia stole it."

The last bit of his story drew Jean's intense attention. She straightened on the sofa and faced him, eyes staring unbelievingly. "What? Are you serious? Do you think Alicia could do something like that?"

"Grandma's serious. I'm not so sure. She probably moved it and forgot where she put it. You know how we've found things in odd places." Through a forced smile, David sighed, "I guess I know what I'm doing this weekend."

From the loft over the kitchen, David heard the phone ringing. He ignored it, doubting the call was for him. Grandma called only the previous day and he needed at least a few days' break before facing the long drive again. Downstairs, Jean's footsteps scurried to answer it. Her short terse words rose in volume as she spoke. She stopped speaking to the caller and yelled to David to grab the extension. "It's Alicia, and she's mad."

He clutched his head with both hands while he thought about what to say. Answering from the phone on his desk, he extended his stepsister his best warm-welcomed greeting.

Alicia didn't bother to acknowledge his greeting. She started right into her hissing. "That's the last time I clean house for that woman. I never should have listened to you. Now Grandma's accusing me of stealing from her."

David took in Alicia's angry words. Jean had scampered upstairs and stood next to him to listen in on the conversation. He focused on calming Alicia down. "I'm sorry. Grandma called me, too, last night. I didn't know she was so suspicious."

"She called you and told you about her missing silverware? Great. I can only imagine what kind of crap she spewed about me. I don't know who the hell you think you are, waltzing into her life, telling me what I need to do while you sit at home in your own little world and Grandma tells everyone she knows that I'm a thief."

Defenses now on red alert, fanned by the venom in Alicia's voice, David chose his words carefully. "Hold it, Alicia. I don't know why you're mad at me. I only started looking out for Edna because it was obvious you and your family stopped giving a damn about her. You can't seriously think her living conditions are acceptable."

"What the hell do you know about me and my family? You weren't around to see how Grandma treated Mom and Lorraine and me, how much she belittled Dad for marrying a woman who was with child, as she put it. Don't pretend to know about how we treated her. Even though you and Nathan were never around, all we ever heard from Grandma Edna, when we were growing up, was how precious her two grandsons were."

The pot had been stirred; the aftermath now unavoidable. David's anger boiled over. "Whoa. Don't put that on me. As you said, I wasn't around. Remember, we didn't get to see our dad while we were growing up. Your mother made sure of that. And, from what I saw, and the vibes I got at the funeral, your mother still resents us."

"You don't have a clue. Grandma always considered you and Nathan superior to Lorraine and me because you were her only *real* grandchildren. She never considered us as her grandchildren. Maybe that's why we find it hard, after so many years, to consider her family."

David slunk in his office chair stunned by this shocking revelation about his grandmother's bias and bitterness. He couldn't fault Alicia's fury. "I'm sorry, Alicia. I can't help how she treated you and Lorraine, or what she said about me and Nathan. I didn't know. All I know is, right now, at her age, she needs someone to make sure she's not living in a sty. If you and your family can't bring yourselves to correct that, someone needs to."

"Well, I guess that proves the old gal was right. You're so much better than the rest of us. Have fun with her. It won't be long before you see what she is really like."

When the phone slammed down, David flinched. He pulled the phone from his ear as the boom resonated in his ear. End of discussion. He turned to Jean. He knew she'd heard enough to piece it together.

Jean smiled and tried to lighten the mood. "Well, it sounds like she's not volunteering to plan Edna's next surprise party."

David laughed. "It's funny, though." He paused and thought about the conversation for a moment. "She never said she didn't take the silver."

Chapter 13

David and Jean pulled into Grandma's driveway before noon the following weekend. Upon opening the door, her eyes widened and she stammered. "Is it that time already?"

"We're a little early." David greeted her with an embrace. His grandmother held onto him until he pulled back and hinted, she should save some hugging for their farewell. Letting go, she flung the door wide and they stepped inside. David immediately noticed the odor from the dog had diminished since he shampooed the carpet on his last visit. Still, the stagnant hot air was stifling upon entering the dining room. Why were old people afraid of fresh air? Missy bounded around the corner. David ignored the dog and its annoying yapping as he went to the living room. He cracked open a few windows, taking time to look into the corners and check for cobwebs or worse. At once a cool breeze poured into the room. Eyeing the mangy, black-haired creature plodding after him, David looked around for dog messes.

While Jean took a seat in the rocker, David nosed around the house for possible spots where his grandmother might have stashed her silver. Not sure he entirely trusted Alicia, he didn't believe she would steal from her own grandmother, besides, after hearing Alicia's side of the story, it sounded like there was plenty of resentment from both sides. "You mentioned you had a few chores for me.

"My kitchen window doesn't open and I need to do some shopping for dinner tonight. You are staying for dinner and spending the night, aren't you?"

David exchanged a glance with Jean. "No, Grandma. We can't. The kids are home and we need to get back and get our housework done. We can't spend the night this time."

Grandma frowned, furrowing her brow. "I wish you could stay. You have to eat anyway."

"I'm sorry, maybe next time. Jean can help you make a shopping list." He winked at Jean before continuing. "I can do a few repairs before we go to the grocery store." He rummaged around the card table and handed Jean a pen and paper, his eyes pleading. A pencil drawing caught his eye, a youngster's depiction of three females holding hands. Two of the figures had long jet-black straight hair, the last figure wore short white hair. The artist's signature, Lacey, was carefully written in cursive across the bottom. "This is a nice picture of Lacey. Is it new?"

Grandma's frown and tight face shifted immediately. Her eyes sparkled as she scampered to David's side. "Oh, yes. We colored together while Alicia vacuumed my carpet. Lacey is such a nice young girl. She reminds me so much of my Bernice at that age." She took the drawing from David before flip-flopping again to a frown. She shook her head. "It's too bad her mother is so troubled and steals from other people."

Convinced Alicia had no role in the missing silverware, David knew he and Jean had to find it today to put the whole misunderstanding to rest. He headed for the kitchen and shuddered at the familiar sight of counters covered with crumbs, spilled food, and the dog dish filled with rotting table scraps. David groaned, afraid what he would find when he opened the door of the harvest gold refrigerator straight from the '70s. Leftovers sat on plates and in bowls, uncovered and dried up, resembling some ancient find from an archeological dig. He wrinkled his nose at the foul odor, but sighed with some relief no green fuzz was growing, yet.

After a glance around to make sure his grandmother wasn't watching, David removed a few plates and bowls. He tossed the contents in the garbage and glanced at the empty matching gold dishwasher. He guessed, in spite of the appliance, he would find no dishwashing soap and guessed she washed dishes by hand, so he quickly grabbed the dish soap and scouring pad Jean had purchased earlier. With the few dishes washed and dried, he returned them to the cabinet. Sure, she'd miss the food, and accuse someone of doing something behind her back, like stealing it, but it was the lesser of the evils. He couldn't risk her eating anything that might make her sick. He brushed aside a few jars, checking for hidden spoiled goods. Instead, he spied Grandma's reading glasses lying next to the mayo and ketchup bottle. Removing them, he chuckled and put them on the counter, remembering the misplaced keys from his earlier visit. "Are you missing your glasses, Grandma?"

She wandered in, spying the glasses on the counter, she snatched them up and slipped them into the pocket of her sweater.

David grinned at her. "I found the glasses in the fridge. You must have accidentally put them in the refrigerator with the food." Noticing her scrunched expression and rutted brow, he knew he was in trouble. Nonetheless, he forged ahead. "Do you think you might have misplaced your silverware accidentally, too?"

"Oh, you. I would remember. It was in a big wooden box, not like these glasses. Anyway, I've already called my insurance man and told him about it."

Her face reddened before she stomped off. David returned to the refrigerator and pulled open the produce drawer. A plastic bag of dark green mush, once a member of the lettuce family, lay at the bottom in a wet slimy puddle. He pulled it out with his thumb and forefinger and tossed it in the garbage under the sink, leaving a slimy trail across the floor.

"Damn." David watched the slime meld into the brown indoor-outdoor carpeting knowing full-well ripping out the dirty and germy carpet would have to be among his next projects. Disgusted, he picked up a wet dishrag from the sink. He flinched at the rancid smell and feel of it as he carried it at arm's length to the washer and called to Jean for help.

"I think it's time to do some laundry again. Do you mind gathering Grandma's clothing and towels while I'm gone? I'll wipe down the fridge, and then take her to the store." David pulled a rag from the drawer. He cringed at the stiffness and odor of the replacement rag, and returned to the laundry room once again, allowing the washing machine lid to slam down. Grabbing several paper towels from the roll, David wet them, made a futile attempt to wipe the carpeting, and returned to the refrigerator.

"What are you doing?" Edna stood in the doorway, her hands on her hips. She stepped over to the trash can and peered in. "Why are you throwing away perfectly good food?"

David felt like he did when he was six and pulled a chair over to the counter to sneak his favorite gingersnaps from the white ceramic cookie jar only to discover his grandmother watching from behind.

"Just a bit of lettuce that has gone bad, that's all. See." In haste, he gathered the white plastic liner and lifted it from the garbage can.

Grandma scowled. She moved to the refrigerator and nosed around inside.

He rolled his shoulders to ease the increasing tension. With the trash bag full, David escaped outside and dumped the evidence of his crime in the dumpster.

When he returned, Grandma stood by the entrance to the kitchen, her hands on her hips. "I guess I'll have to buy more produce, too when we shop. Can we stop at the Public Market?"

David glanced at his grandmother. "Where?"

"The Public Market. I always prefer to buy my produce there. Mother always bought her produce at the outdoor market in Seattle. It's much fresher."

He dreaded making another stop for produce, but then decided it was simpler than trying to convince her the produce at the neighborhood grocery store was plenty fresh. "Sure, Grandma, if you like." Grabbing his keys, he mumbled to himself. "Just what she needs, more produce to spoil in her refrigerator."

"Okay, I have to get my purse. A young lady never goes anywhere without her purse." She hobbled off toward the dining room, returning with the battered tan purse she carried everywhere.

"Aren't you coming?" Edna looked back at Jean.

"No, I think I'll do some reading, and relax while you're gone if that's okay?"

Edna sulked. "You know I don't like having strangers alone in my house. Look what happened with Alicia." She looked over at David and began to protest.

"Jean's had a long week. If it's okay with you, let's let her stay." David noticed her hesitation as she considered the request.

"You are David's wife, I trust you. You can stay if you like my dear."

With his grandmother out of the way, David knew Jean could scout the house for places the missing silver might have been stashed. He hoped when they returned the mystery of the missing silverware would be solved. He shooed Grandma out the door and turned back to Jean. "Good luck finding the silverware."

"I hate to snoop, but we can't accuse Alicia of stealing something that hasn't been stolen."

"I know. Sorry you're missing out on your girls' night out."

Jean shrugged. "Bring me a cold Coke when you come back. I have a feeling I'm going to need it."

David kissed Jean on the forehead and turned to see his Grandmother waiting by the car her arms crossed at her chest.

Insistent on pushing her own cart, David flinched as Edna maneuvered the cart like an insecure six-year-old on her first two-wheeler, veering one direction, over correcting, then nearly running into the produce tables. Remembering the shed at the end of the carport, he imagined her ability to drive a car was severely deficient by now, also. He dropped the question as casually as possible "Are you still driving, Grandma?"

She shot an accusatory glance his way. "Of course, I am. How else do you think I can get around? I certainly can't walk now, can I? And, I'm not going to ask my friends to drive me everywhere I need to go."

Not having any choice, for the time being, David gritted his teeth. "You're right." It was a touchy subject, but for everyone's sake, a subject he would have to address soon. A bite of bitterness gnawed at him. He hadn't asked for this responsibility and now Alicia made it sound like he wanted to take charge. Hell, if others only gave a modicum of awareness, he wouldn't have to do everything.

Grandma cocked her head, rolled her eyes like a teenager, and wheeled her cart around the corner out of his sight. Stopping at every produce display, she held each variety close to her eyes, rolled the fruits and vegetables in her hand, and sniffed them. "I miss not being able to buy fresh produce every day." She reached the plump fresh berries heaped in plastic bins, plopped one of each kind into her mouth, and, seeing David watching her, smirked like a playful chimp stealing a banana. She lifted a green plastic basket of red morsels and grinned as if they were precious stones.

David's mouth watered at the sweet scent. His stomach growled its realization it needed nourishment.

"I remember when I used to make jam every year. Have I showed you the freezer filled with jam I have in my shed?" Grandma snatched another berry.

The idea of a freezer full of homemade jam sent a tremor down David's spine. He wondered how many years' worth had accumulated, and mentally, added another item on his growing list of things to check. He shook his head as Grandma put plastic bags holding lettuce, onions, and apples into the cart. She seemed to have forgotten about the produce stand, which was fine with him, though he suspected most of this week's produce purchases would be next visit's spoils.

Grandma leaned in close, eyes squinting at the price signs. "I remember when lettuce was ten-cents a pound. Now look at the price of things."

David walked beside his grandmother, reaching out periodically to help her steer the wobbly cart around the corners and through the aisles filled with late Saturday afternoon shoppers.

"It's been so long since I've had such a leisurely time shopping. I enjoy it so much."

David glanced at his watch. He found no enjoyment strolling through the grocery aisles for over half an hour and still being only halfway through. Rounding the corner, the aroma of hot bread oozed from the back counter where bakers busily prepared the "guaranteed fresh every hour," bread. His stomach growled as he thought about fresh hot bread topped with lots of butter. Edna gawked at the center display, where assorted baked goods enticed buyers. She squeezed and pawed at the packages. "When I'm feeling stronger, I want to start baking again. I used to make bread and cinnamon rolls every month, I'm an excellent cook, you know? There's nothing like fresh home-baked bread and rolls."

David agreed. Edging the cart quickly away from temptation, he moved it quickly down the next aisle. Stopping, he reached for some toilet tissue knowing there were only two rolls left.

"Oh no, Dear." Edna's quick frown stopped David. "I have plenty of tissue paper."

"I checked under the sink and you're about out. You might as well buy the things you need for a few weeks while you're here since it's hard for you to get to the store these days."

"Oh, you." Grandma gathered her brow and pouted as she snatched the cart back and started down the aisle again. David grabbed a four-pack of tissue paper, and caught up with her, placing it in the bottom of the cart. "Is there anything else you need?"

"Oh, I almost forgot. I have to get baking powder; Mother is having the Rebekahs over for tea this evening. She's been a member for so many years you know, ever since Father became a member of the Independent Order of Oddfellows. Have you ever been to one of their meetings?"

Though David had heard of the Oddfellows, he had never heard of the Rebekahs. He guessed the group was the woman's equivalent to the men's fraternity. He turned around and studied his grandmother's face, wondering how many years in the past her mind was at this moment.

Grandma continued on her way. "Mother is going to make her baking powder biscuits with her homemade raspberry jam. She asked me to pick up some baking powder."

"I don't think your mother needs baking powder." David hoped his words would bring her back to the present day.

Edna huffed and glared at him. "Of course, she does. How would you know?"

David followed her, nervously checking his watch again, predicting a longer day than expected. He took in a deep breath. "Let's go get some baking powder, Grandma." Uncertain where to find it or even what it might look like, he searched several aisles before he finally spied the red can next to the flour and sugar. Grabbing one, he handed it to her. "Here you go, one can of baking powder."

"What's this? What do I need baking powder for? I have some already and I don't do much baking these days." Grandma waved him off like a pesky gnat.

David took a deep breath, reminding himself her age allowed for erratic behavior. He sighed. "Of course, I don't know what I was thinking," and placed the can back on the shelf.

Pushing the cart to the car, David wondered about the planned stop at the Public Market. His grandmother hadn't mentioned it during the past hour. He was certainly not going to bring it up if she didn't. He quickly put the groceries into the car, settled Grandma into the seat, and headed back to her home. As he expected, she'd long forgotten about the stop at the Public Market. With a sigh of relief, he managed the quick drive to her home and pulled the car into the driveway.

Armed with groceries, David pushed through the door. As Grandma made her way to the kitchen with a small bag, Jean stopped David. "I peeked inside every drawer, cupboard, and closet. There's no sign of the silverware. I managed to find some white vinyl LP's from Betty Crocker and broods of dust bunnies, but there are no silver place settings in this house."

Looking over his shoulder to the clanging in the kitchen, David shrugged. "Maybe there is no silverware. It might be something she's remembering from years ago." He shook his head. "I don't know what to think at this point."

Jean tipped her head toward the back yard. "I changed her bed and did a load of laundry. I also washed her mohair sweater in the sink. It's outside drying. Don't forget to remind me to bring it in before we go home this evening, or we'll be in trouble."

Grandma shuffled out from the kitchen. "You are staying for dinner, aren't you?"

David and Jean exchanged glances. "I'm sorry, we can't. We need to get home. Jean can help you get dinner started if you like before we leave."

Her eyes cast downward. "I wish you could stay."

Not willing to go on a guilt trip, David changed the subject and went to unpack the groceries. "What do you want for dinner?"

His grandmother filled a cup with water and placed it in the microwave before she cast a disgruntled look in his direction. "Can Jean make meatloaf?"

Chapter 14

"**I** can't find my sweater anywhere. Someone has stolen it." Grandma's distraught tone accosted David and Jean when they returned to visit two weeks later.

"Why would anyone want to steal your sweater?" David stole a glance at Jean as he considered all the earlier phone calls to him, regarding missing items.

"My favorite mohair sweater is not here; it's been missing for weeks. I've looked everywhere. Who would take my favorite sweater?"

Without warning, Jean bolted from the room. The rear screen door banged open and closed. Seconds later Jean returned and sidled next to David. Turning slightly, she showed David the sweater hidden behind her back.

David bobbed his head and ushered Grandma to the sofa. "Why don't you sit down while Jean and I look around to see if we can find it?

In the hall, Jean's eyes relayed her panic. "I left it outside drying the last time we were here. Tell her I'm looking for it. We'll have to concoct a story about finding it."

A few minutes later, Jean reappeared with a wide smile and the sweater draped over her arm. "It was in your bedroom closet."

Grandma's eyes narrowed. She snatched the sweater away and began caressing it, first with her fingers, then by rubbing it next to her cheek like a small child with a favorite blanket. She stopped and sniffed the sweater, then pulled it away, her eyes glistened.

"Someone has washed it. This is a mohair sweater, it has to be washed by hand. Who would do this?" She started to cry.

Stunned by her dramatic reaction, David was happy Jean stepped in and sat next to Grandma. "I'm sure it's okay." Jean patted her hand. "May I see your sweater?" Jean brought the sweater to her nose. "I'm sure it was hand-washed. It smells exactly like the soap I use at home for

76

handwashing." "No." Grandma snatched her sweater away again. "It's ruined, feel it. It's not soft like it was."

David reached across and gently took the sweater from his grandmother. "It looks fine. It's clean. That's good, isn't it?" The sad irony of the situation struck. A filthy sweater covered with sweat and food stains from years of wear was preferred to the clean, fresh-smelling garment. Perhaps the clean smell gave it away because she obviously hadn't seen the dirt that had covered the sweater.

Jean looked at David and held her hands out questioningly. She mouthed the words. "Should I tell her?"

David shook his head. Confessing would only upset her more.

"Do you know how much I paid for this sweater? Edna's eyes glared as the sharp words spit off her tongue. "Twelve dollars. Now I'll have to buy another."

The idea seemed absurd, but his grandmother's grief was real. David attempted to calm her to no avail. There was no need for Jean to feel guilty about her good intention. At least Grandma would be wearing something clean and fresh for a change. That is if she would still wear it now. It was best to drop the subject and wait until she forgot about it. And with her ever-diminishing memory, David expected it would be soon.

Chapter 15

Edna trudged into the kitchen and opened the refrigerator, revealing near-empty shelves. David hadn't been by for a month, and Barbara was visiting her daughter somewhere out of state, Edna couldn't recall where. She didn't feel hungry but she knew she had to eat something. The produce bin held a few old lettuce leaves, a mushy tomato, and a few withered peaches. She closed it and contemplated her prospects for dinner, shrugging off the idea of settling for canned soup. She could never get used to the taste of canned soup, not after having made her own for so many years. Perhaps eggs and bacon, she thought. Yes, that would be perfect, and not too much trouble.

She promised David she wouldn't drive anymore after he asked her about the dented storage shed. With Barbara gone and Fred caring for Marge during her illness, Edna had no other option. Surely David would understand the necessity. Confident and smug with her ability to drive, Edna grabbed her tan handbag and keys and sauntered to the car. She turned the car onto Columbia Drive for the three-mile jaunt to the market. At the sound of the siren, Edna panicked and straightened in her seat. Uncertain where the sound was coming from, she shot a glance in the rear-view mirror. She squinted through the glare of the burning sun. A white car with flashing blue lights had pulled up behind her. Edna's heart raced as she steered the car off the road to the shoulder. An officer marched to her side and motioned for her to roll the window down. Her hands trembled as she clutched the window knob, finally getting it to cooperate.

"May I see your license?" His no-nonsense words came sharp like a drill sergeant as he thrust his hand out awaiting her license.

Edna fumbled for her wallet. Unable to withdraw the small laminated card, she attempted to hand the wallet over to him.

"I'm sorry. You will have to remove your license yourself."

Flustered, Edna struggled to free the license. The glassine window held it tight, refusing to release the precious authorization to drive, as if not wanting to reveal its hidden secret.

"Do you realize you could have hurt or even killed someone when you ran that stop sign?"

His words shot like bullets, shattering her confidence. She knew there was a stop sign on the corner, how could she have missed it? "I would never hurt anyone. I just didn't see the sign." With shaky hands, Edna finally freed the license and handed it to the stern-faced officer. Her eyes gushed as she reached for a tissue from her purse. She dabbed her eyes as the officer examined her license.

His eyes narrowed. He shook his head while handing the license back to her. "Do you realize your license expired over six years ago, Mrs. Pearson? I can't let you continue to drive. The law requires you to pass a driving test to get your license renewed since it's been over six years."

His glare forced Edna to look away.

"At your age, I'd consider parking the car for good."

Edna pouted. She knew he was going to make a fuss about her age, and the expired license, but what did he know? After all, she had driven for over seventy years and had done fine. "I didn't remember about my license, but I'm perfectly capable of driving." She used her most convincing tone while watching him scribble out the citation on his clipboard before turning it toward her.

"Sign here."

Edna took the clipboard and stared at it through her resentment.

The officer pointed to a line at the bottom.

Edna's unsteady hand relayed her frustration as she inked her name on the line. Waving off the officer, she returned her attention to starting the car again.

"You don't understand, Mrs. Pearson. You can't drive. I can take you home, or you can use my car phone to call someone to get you."

"But the market is less than two blocks away." Her hands still trembled as she stuffed her wallet and the ticket, inside her purse.

"It doesn't matter if it's a half block. You can't drive. Do I make myself clear?"

Her temples throbbed. "I need to go to the market. Can you take me to the market? I'll call my neighbor from there."

79

The officer helped her into the squad car. "Be sure to have someone move your car as soon as possible. Remember, no driving until your license is renewed. You might want to consider finding another way to get to the market in the future, perhaps you've been driving long enough."

When the officer pulled into the entrance to the market, Edna couldn't wait to free herself from the tension engulfing her within the squad car. She knew it was proper to thank the officer, but she scowled as she opened the door and stepped unsteadily out. She stomped toward the wide glass doors of the grocery store, stopped partway, and looked back with a stern glare as the officer pulled away. She pooh-poohed the idea of calling Fred to get a ride home and somehow arrange to get her car home. The whole idea was absurd. With the officer gone from sight, she spun around, and trudged back in the direction of her car, without the bacon and eggs.

Edna stewed all the way home. Safely in her driveway, she mumbled about the nonsense of having to take a driving test. Imagine, she had been driving for longer than that young officer's father had been alive, possibly even longer than his granddad. She slammed the car door and went into the house to make a can of soup.

Fred offered to drive her to the Department of Motor Vehicles in Richland the following Tuesday for her driver's exam. Though she still resented taking the exam and having someone driver her, she knew better than to arrive for her test alone. Her anger and resentment still fresh, Edna climbed into the passenger seat of her Buick. She fumbled for the seat restraint after Fred reminded her it would be required before even starting the vehicle for the exam. During the fifteen-minute drive, menacing clouds loomed overhead and light rainfall danced across the windshield. By the time they arrived at the red brick, single-story building with the American flag fluttering in the gusty wind, dark clouds blanketed the sky. Fred followed Edna inside. He pointed out the correct line for those taking the exam and informed Edna he'd wait for her in the back of the room.

On shaking legs, Edna approached the counter and pulled off a ticket. Relieved there were few other customers, she took a seat next to Fred.

With all the nervousness of a teenage girl applying for a license for the first time, she clutched her purse and checked the clock.

Ten minutes later a dour-looking woman hollered, "Number twenty-two."

Nervous, but with Fred's encouragement, Edna shuffled to the counter. The female Department of Motor Vehicles clerk behind the counter never looked up, only pointed to the vision testing machine and barked orders. Edna placed her forehead against the bar, bumping the glasses she was not used to wearing. Flustered, she pressed herself to focus on the blurry characters she knew were the key to her being able to drive in the future. She stammered the letters to the woman who glowered back, mumbled she had passed, though barely, and moved her along to the next attendant. Edna breathed a little easier and her neck muscles loosened. Without a hint of pleasantry, a middle-aged woman dressed in a light brown uniform approached with an order to move her car to the front parking spot. "I'll be right out to begin your driving test."

Palms sweaty, Edna pulled her car in front of the building to the posted position. She shuddered at the thought of driving in the constant rain, but there was nothing she could do now. She gripped the steering wheel, ready to show everyone she was still capable of driving.

The examiner marched over to the driver's side window and motioned for Edna to roll it down. With the window unrolled, the examiner snapped orders at Edna as she sauntered around the car. "Please start the car and turn on your turn indicators."

Edna's gnarled hands shook as she turned the key and focused on hearing the directions over the vroom of the engine, and the falling rain. Edna flipped the turn signal up and down, twisted knobs and switches to turn on her lights and stepped on the brakes. The unsmiling female with eyes of steel circled the car and inspected the tires. Edna's stomach churned watching the woman maneuver around the car, finally opening the passenger door and slamming it behind her, sending a spray of water across the seat.

Reaching across, the examiner fastened her seat belt and glowered at Edna. "Is your seat belt secure?"

Edna tugged on it, smug she had it in place.

"If you are ready, you may start the car." The snappy abrupt tone relayed indifference and impatience. There was no concern for the examinee, it was simply a job, all business.

Edna puzzled over the nonsense. "Imagine, after driving for over seventy years, you make me take a driving test. I never needed an exam to drive when I first started driving." The car lurched forward.

"Pull into the street and head toward Riverside Boulevard."

Startled, Edna glanced across the seat. She couldn't remember where Riverside was. She turned the car right and considered all the cars speeding past. When she was a young girl, there weren't many cars. Mostly she and her mother used streetcars, or the bus when they went downtown to shop.

"Turn right, Mrs. Pearson. We're heading to Riverside, remember? Now, turn left at the next intersection."

With each new order to turn right, turn left, and make sudden stops, Edna's heartbeat quickened and her hands trembled on the steering wheel.

"Mrs. Pearson, you need to pick up your speed a bit, stay with the flow of traffic."

Edna shot a glance across the seat. She seethed at the condescending tone.

"Okay, Mrs. Pearson, I need you to turn right at the next light, then pull into the outdoor market a few blocks down the road, on the left. Park the car in one of the diagonal parking spots behind the stand."

The orders were flying too fast. Edna didn't understand. It wasn't right to put her through all this. "You're making me nervous." Her fingers clenched the wheel. A dull thud banged in her chest. "I'm perfectly capable of driving, but I don't know where all these cars came from."

"The traffic is fairly light, Mrs. Pearson. Are you sure you're comfortable driving?"

"Don't tell me about the traffic. There are cars everywhere. The last time I came to Seattle there were hardly any cars."

"We're not in Seattle, Mrs. Pearson. We're in Richland."

Confused, Edna glanced over at her passenger. An unfamiliar woman stared back at Edna, her mouth agape. Flustered, Edna returned her gaze to the road. "I don't understand. I recognize the old stores and the outdoor market where Mother and I use to shop." Her mind was in a haze. She wanted to be done with all this nonsense.

"Watch out. There's a stop sign."

A loud voice screeched from next to Edna, alarming her. A loud horn blasted. Panicked, Edna slammed on the brakes. She lunged forward, restrained by the seat belt shoulder strap. The car skidded to a sideways stop on the slippery street. Her pulse raced and her breathing was shallow. A black shiny car swooshed by in front of her. She blinked momentarily from the glare. Her mind spun like tires on the wet pavement.

Edna gazed in awe at the black shiny metal, reflecting sunlight as it bumped along the street. Her eyes widened. She had never seen a car before. Everyone on the street was running out for a look. Soon the whole street was lined with people.

"Isn't it pretty? See the lights, like little chandeliers, hanging from the side?" Edna giggled like all six-year-olds do, as the car with its little wheels tried to get through the crowd that had poured into the middle of the cobblestone street. Sometimes, in wet weather, Edna had seen the horse-drawn carriages lose their footing and slip on the smooth stones.

"Mrs. Pearson. Are you okay? Are you hurt?"

Dazed, Edna turned and studied the woman next to her. She smiled and clambered down from the trolley she was riding in, and hurried over to the sidewalk. "Come on, we have to hurry." Edna looked along the street. She could see people gathering at the outdoor market. She was surprised by the cement walkways though. They weren't made from wooden planks that went *squish* on rainy days. They weren't even covered with an awning, like the sidewalks she and Mother followed on their way to the Public Market downtown.

"Mrs. Pearson, stop, you can't walk away like that." A stern-faced woman scurried alongside.

Edna dashed along the street. She wanted to see the Indians who had slept on the sidewalks the night before. Early in the morning the market always came alive with the Indians selling brightly woven, colored, handmade, blankets and baskets. Edna loved to watch as the Indian women wove the reeds of different colors in and out and wrapped them around to make such beautiful and useful baskets. A firm grip took hold of her arm. Edna turned and pleaded. "Please can't we buy a basket? I like them so much."

"What are you talking about, Mrs. Pearson? We need to get back to your car. We can't leave it in the middle of the street."

Edna yanked away and wandered down the street against the woman's protest, then melted into the crowd. The damp crisp air chilled her and she tightened the red scarf, which her mother crocheted, around her neck. She was thankful Mother was with her to keep her from becoming lost in the maze of sellers and buyers.

"Mrs. Pearson, please, we have to go back."

Edna ignored the urging tone at her side. She looked at the woman next to her. Mother was nowhere in sight. She puzzled over where her mother had gone and wondered who the bothersome woman was.

As Edna neared the market, the sweet aroma of fresh sweet melons, spicy herbs, and fresh flowers filled the air. She squeezed through the people gathered in front of the first few stalls. The Farmer's Market was one of her favorite places. She especially loved going in the mornings when the farmers backed their wagons up to the wooden stalls and unloaded their produce and dairy goods. Edna liked to browse, but Mother kept insisting they get going. She turned around to face the impatient tone, not at all like her mother's.

"Mrs. Pearson, please. We have to get back in the car. It's blocking the street."

A large hand encompassed hers, and a comforting arm wrapped around her shoulder as she was led from the produce stand. She blinked and stared at the uniformed gray-haired woman. "Where's Mother? What happened to Mother?"

"Mrs. Pearson, your mother's not here."

The firm voice confused Edna. She didn't understand why this unfamiliar woman appeared so angry.

"I think that's enough for today. We need to get back."

Edna turned with questioning eyes. "Where are we going?"

"Mrs. Pearson, you're disoriented. We need to get back."

Edna brought her hands to her warm cheeks. Flustered, she looked around at the gawking crowd, shaking their heads. She didn't understand where she was. The woman led her away from the crowd to a big white car parked in the middle of the road.

The woman opened the door and helped her into the passenger seat. The unfamiliar woman climbed behind the steering wheel and drove her back to a large brick building with a sign, "Department of Motor Vehicles."

"Come on inside. Is there still someone waiting here who can take you home?" The woman's voice softened. She approached and offered her arm.

Edna pulled away and frowned. "What about my license?"

Shaking her head, the examiner delivered her message. "We can't give you a driver's license in your condition. Have your friend take your car home, Mrs. Pearson, sell it."

Edna didn't understand what had just happened. What did the woman mean, *her condition?* She shuddered at the thought she was losing her driver's license. Imagine, being told she couldn't drive. What was she going to do? Edna scowled. Too proud to admit her failing, she crossed her arms. "I don't want to drive anymore anyway." She was so mad she could chew coal.

Chapter 16

As the last of the mulberries shriveled on the tree, the final berries eaten by birds, and the blossoms on the perennials alternately bloomed and wilted, Edna could scarcely believe nearly a year had passed since Larry's death. Her bills and paperwork piled up, and with it, her frustrations. Things she normally handled with no apprehension were now the bane of her days, causing increasing angst. She surveyed the clutter in her living room. An avalanche of white envelopes and magazines covered the card table like snowdrifts after a blizzard. She always managed without difficulty in her younger years. Even when she was married, she'd taken responsibility for all the financial affairs, writing every expense and cash entry into a small accountant's ledger. In these past few years when things become overwhelming, Larry helped out. Now, without him, she had no one to handle her financial affairs.

Edna plodded to the brass pole light, flipped the switch on, took a deep breath, and sat at the card table. How did everything pile up so quickly? She pushed aside coupons for pizza, dry cleaning, windshield repair, and gutter cleaning, shaking her head at the absurdity and waste. So much mail she didn't want or need. She sorted through the piles of envelopes, pulled out the bills and pushed the occupant mail to the side. Her fingers fumbled with the contents of a white envelope with green bars at the bottom and a label printed in red, reading, FINAL NOTICE. Unfolding it, her eyes strained to scan the fine print at the bottom of the correspondence from the electric company for a clue. She thought about fetching her glasses to make out the wording more clearly but wasn't sure where she'd last put them and didn't particularly like wearing them anyway. Her heart raced as she labored to read the enclosed letter. "Services will be disconnected." She didn't understand, she had always paid her bills on time. Indignant, she fought to contain her frustration, though she couldn't control her quivering body. Her left arm brushed against the pile of junk mail, sending a flurry of envelopes and advertisements drifting to the floor. "It's not right getting so much garbage." She selected a few more envelopes and ripped them open, studying the contents, confused by the columns of numbers and rows of type. How come everyone was making things so complicated? Frustrated, she conceded defeat. She needed to be rescued from the paperwork which buried her, but she didn't know who she could trust to handle such a responsibility. Her pulse speeding up, Edna snatched the phone and dialed Barbara's number.

Hot tea and Barbara's favorite peanut butter cookies were waiting when Barbara arrived.

"I appreciate your help, Barbara. I know it takes time away from Robert." Edna pulled out her checkbook and recent bank statement and handed them to Barbara. "I don't understand how they can cut off my power. I paid the bill."

Barbara flipped through the canceled checks and read the letter from the power company. "It looks like you paid only $10.71 Edna, not the $70.71 you owed."

Edna snatched the bill. "Let me see that. How can my electric bill be so high?"

Barbara laughed. "Everything is more expensive these days. I'll call the power company and get this squared away. Let's look at the rest of your bills while I am here and make sure everything else is okay."

With Barbara's help, the useless mail was tossed, checks written and signed, and envelopes stuffed, sealed, and stamped. The clutter on the table disappeared.

Barbara reached across the table and held Edna's hands. "You know I don't mind helping you, but you need to find someone who can help you with your bills on a regular basis."

Edna tightened the grip on her friend's hand, frightened of the reality bearing down. She had to accept she wasn't getting any younger and her tasks were becoming more difficult than she could have anticipated. "You're right." Silently, she cursed the circumstances that left her feeling alone. Defeated, Edna admitted it was time to find someone to handle her affairs permanently. "I don't know who I can trust."

"You could ask Alicia.".

Looking up, her mouth dry, Edna's voice came scarcely above a whisper. "I can't trust her, even if she was willing."

Surprised, Barbara looked at Edna with questioning eyes. "I don't understand why you don't think you can trust her. You used to be close to Alicia. What happened?"

Edna frowned. Barbara was a dear friend, but Edna didn't like to share too much of her personal affairs with others. She paused for a moment, then explained how her silverware set had disappeared. "I think Alicia stole it."

"I can't believe that. Have you asked her about it?"

Edna raised her voice to Barbara, which she seldom did. "I'm certainly not going to ask her. She would just deny it anyway."

"What about David? He's been helping you this past year. Maybe he'd be willing to help you."

Edna had debated for some time about burdening David with her financial affairs, but there was no other person with whom she felt comfortable. "Yes, that's what I need to do." Even as she sensed her independence ebbing away, a wave of relief swept over her.

Chapter 17

Accustomed to a new calamity each week, David wasn't surprised at all by his grandmother's mid-week phone call and latest lament.

"Someone stole my egg beater."

Remembering her glasses stashed in the refrigerator, he guessed the egg beater, along with other missing items she'd called about, like casserole dishes and old tennis shoes, had found some new, totally bizarre, temporary location. "Are you sure you didn't put it somewhere else, Grandma?"

"No. I always put it in the third drawer by the pantry. It's not there. Someone stole it."

David inhaled deeply, a reminder to be patient with her increasing age and signs of dementia, which he knew he would have to address. Soon. "Why would anyone break in and steal your egg beater? I'm sure it will show up. We all forget where we put things sometimes."

"Oh, you. You think I misplaced it, don't you? But you never found my silverware either."

David silently acknowledged the silverware was still a mystery and noticing the tremor in her voice, he didn't want to upset her any further. "It's okay, we can replace it easily enough. I'll check your doors and locks the next time I visit, okay?"

"I want you to call the police."

His neck muscles tightened like the overstretched strings on a guitar. "Why don't we wait until I can check things out first? I love you. I'll call you in a few days."

"You don't believe me." Grandma sighed loudly. "You'll see."

Before he could respond, the line went dead.

The next evening, an unknown number from eastern Washington appeared on the caller ID. He'd long ago come to recognize not only the phone numbers of Fred and Barbara but also the Tri-Cities Fire

Department. Every phone call it seemed, especially unknown numbers, brought only frustration and stress. David tensed and took a deep calming breath before picking up the receiver.

"Mr. Bryant, this is Officer Schwartz with the Richland Police Department. Edna Pearson gave us your name and number. She called yesterday to report a burglary. This is her third call to us in the past few weeks. Our visits to her home revealed some damage to the door frame and window, but nothing substantial enough to believe there's been a break-in. But we thought we should bring it to your attention in case you want to do some upgrades and make her feel more secure and maybe then she'll stop calling us."

David thanked the officer and hung up, already tired from the next trip he faced, now only days away instead of several weeks as he dared hope during his last visit.

Weary from not nearly enough sleep and his frustration flowing like molten lava, David waved goodbye and headed out the following Saturday. After so many trips, his mind and body were on auto-pilot. Grandma's car still sat in the driveway. David knew as long as the car sat right outside, her stubborn defiance, along with the presence of the car, was trouble waiting to happen. He'd have to shift selling the car to the top of his other chores.

Barely inside, Grandma started right in on the most recent burglary, immediately pointing out the side window. "See." She struggled to slide the window open. "It's off the track." She showed David where the wood was chipped away on the outside. "Someone tried to break in."

"Are you sure it hasn't been like this for a while? Maybe you didn't notice it before."

"No. It happened when I told the police about it last week. I told you on the phone. You never believe me. The officers were so nice to come right out and take a full report from me."

David forced the glass back into position on its old metal frame, wiped the frame with a rag sprayed with WD-40, then grabbed his screwdriver. With the latch tightened, David stepped back. "Now it won't be so easy to break in. I'll buy a wooden dowel to place on the window frame for extra security, and replace the deadbolt lock on the door." Leaving the window open a bit for ventilation, David went to the back door. The small kitchen reminded him of a sauna filled with men wearing old sweat socks. Dark rings spotted the carpeting. He suspected the once wet areas now lay as host to mold and mildew. He opened the window behind the sink and checked the lock on the rear entry door.

Grandma smiled as she surveyed David's handiwork. "Thank you. I feel much safer now."

"Grandma, what do you think about taking out your kitchen carpet? It's damp from your leaky faucet, and frankly, it smells like Missy has used it more than once." At the mention of Missy's name, the dog ambled around the corner. David forced a weak smile for his grandmother's sake, and then gently shooed the dog away.

Scrunching her face, she hesitated. "I like the carpet. It's much more comfortable to walk on."

At the risk of upsetting her further, David nonetheless pushed on. "Let's at least see what's under the carpet. It would be much easier to clean a linoleum floor than shampoo a carpet." David pried the dark brown molding away from the wall.

Grandma stood outside the kitchen, arms crossed. "Are you going to be able to fix it if I don't like it?"

"Don't worry, I'll make sure you're happy." David held his breath as he peeled back mildew-infested urine-drenched carpeting from the floor, leaving remnant black rubber particles stuck to the flooring beneath. He blew out a slight breath seeing the exposed linoleum. "What do you think, Grandma? I think it looks pretty good. Why don't you come over and take a closer look?" Standing, arms crossed, David breathed easier and analyzed the newly exposed outrageous gold and brown toned geometric design straight out of decades past. It was dirty, though only slightly worn.

Grandma bent down to see what he had uncovered. A smile replaced her pout. "It's exactly what I would have selected for myself."

David smiled at the comment. From her gold velour sofa to the tweed brown dining room carpet, he didn't doubt this floor was to her liking. "Good. Let's hope the rest of the floor is in good shape and we don't have any surprises." He continued to pull the carpet up, stopping to get a small red hand truck from his pickup. He moved the refrigerator to the center of the room and freed the last few feet of carpet. "Well, Grandma, it looks great, doesn't it? The room sure looks brighter."

With his grandmother's blessing, he hoisted the old carpeting onto the hand truck, and with a big heave, he flung the carpet into the dumpster outside. With a well-worn scrub brush, a bucket of water and ammonia, and a hefty serving of elbow grease, David put one more dreaded chore behind him.

Taking a breather on the sofa after his exhaustive task, David joined his grandmother for some tea. A large mess of envelopes and mailings spread across the table. "Are you doing okay with your monthly bills, Grandma?"

She hesitated. "Nathan and you are the only family I have left. It's too bad Nathan isn't around."

"I can help you, you know that. What do you need me to do?"

Though she averted her eyes as she spoke, David saw her flush with embarrassment while she explained how difficult it had become to pay her bills.

"I need someone to handle my finances for me. I get confused by the bills lately."

"I don't mind helping, but have you asked Alicia? You know her a lot better and she lives closer so it would be much easier on you."

Grandma shifted in her seat. "You know I don't trust Alicia."

"I know but I live so far away. You'd have to mail the bills to me along with some checks, then I'll have to send everything back to you so you can sign them." He paused, knowing as he said it, the idea was ridiculous and the only easy answer was one he'd rather not think about. "The best thing to do is have all your bills mailed to me and designate me as your power of attorney."

"I could do that. I already have a living will. I can name you a power of attorney for my health care matters, too."

David sighed. His voice betraying his brain's unyielding protest. "Okay."

A slight smile crossed her face. "Are you sure it's not too much trouble?"

"You're family, Grandma. Do you remember how much you and Granddad did for Nathan and me when we were little? Now it's my turn to help you."

Rummaging around on the card table for a pen, his grandmother made out a list of her monthly bills. "Let's see, there's home owner's association dues, phone, electric, and medical bills. Make sure you pay these. Of course, there will be more."

"I want to know whenever you pay a bill and the amount. Be sure to call me. I need to record the expenses." She reached for her tan handbag, perched atop the bundle of current bills, and searched for the checkbook. "I guess you'll need this."

"Do you have any extra checks? This book won't last long."

David followed his grandmother to the closet and watched as she rummaged around for a few minutes before she retrieved a small box. With it in hand, she clutched it like a treasure chest for a moment before turning it over to David. "Don't forget to let me know when you pay the bills. It will be such a relief not having to worry about the paperwork."

Her weak smile erased any doubt of him taking on another chore, though his senses told him things weren't going to be all that simple.

Chapter 18

Overwhelmed and burning out, like the last rays of light that filtered through the large windows in the loft, David poured over the bills and bank statements from his grandmother. She kept remarkable records, especially for her age, but her method of organization was unconventional. To ease his task, he created a spreadsheet to track her monthly expenses based on the past year's records. He hoped to identify her financial stability based on her current retirement income. He fumbled through the musty wooden trunk she sent home with him, along with two crumpled shoeboxes filled with canceled checks and old bank statements. Her most important papers, as she considered them, were kept in a nine by twelve, worn, purple and pink cloth handbag, with round plastic handles. David had seen it often, laying on the card table in the living room, amidst her paperwork. He rummaged through the handbag and found old passbook savings accounts, her ancient social security card, now sandwiched in yellow laminate, and oodles of lists. She had lists of all her debtors and their addresses, lists of funeral arrangements to be made when the time came, and a list of dates and names of everyone to whom she had ever loaned money. With one exception, this list included everyone in Larry's family.

Jean came up the stairs with a cold glass of cola, setting it on the corner of the desk. She shook her head as she turned on the desk lamp. "We have a light. Why don't you use it? You're straining your eyes."

David mumbled he could see fine, took the glass from Jean and gulped his cold caffeine-free drink. He didn't need the caffeine. The stress of dealing with Grandma's affairs was plenty enough to keep him up at night. "Can you believe Grandma has loaned money to everyone in Larry's family, including Larry? Here's a promissory note from almost twenty years ago. She loaned him twenty-thousand dollars. I remember her saying she had paid for Lorraine's college."

Jean leaned in and looked over his shoulder. "That's probably what it was for."

David shook his head. "She loaned Lorraine and Alicia each a few thousand dollars too. It looks like the only debt ever repaid in full was the money she loaned to Alicia's ex-husband."

Jean walked around behind his chair and began to knead his neck.

"That feels good." David stopped staring at the expenses he had totaled for a moment and turned to Jean. His tension eased somewhat, he tipped his head back and rolled his shoulders. "I can't figure how come her expenses last year were so much higher than this year. I guess I should go through the canceled checks and see if anything jumps out. Maybe there were some unusual medical expenses, like hearing-aids or hospital bills."

"You should take a break." Jean rested her hand on David's shoulder.

"Not yet." David patted her hand, maintaining his focus. "I don't understand how come she has so many different accounts at different banks. Must be the mentality of the Depression era." He laid the statements out across the desk. "She must have thought her money was safer if it were placed in different banks."

Jean glanced at the statements "I guess. Or, she simply forgot she opened some accounts and kept opening new ones. How else do you explain three different accounts at Bank One, alone?"

David conceded the possibility and continued to review the previous year's bank statements. He noticed, on two separate months, check numbers were written, and cleared, out of sequence. One check for nine-hundred eighty dollars, and one for thirteen-hundred dollars.

He retrieved the returned checks corresponding to the statements from the shoe boxes. Thankfully, in spite of the unique filing system, the checks were at least grouped by month. The payee name in both cases was Alicia Sykes. "What do you make of this?" David held the check out to Jean.

"It is interesting, isn't it? Maybe it was for a gift, or, it's part of another loan she didn't write down."

"They're odd amounts for a gift." David squinted and cocked his head. "If they're a loan, why would the check numbers be so out of sequence? Grandma didn't continue the sequence from these books until months after these checks were written." David turned them over to study the bank endorsement. "They were both cashed the same day they were written." David laid both the checks out, next to several other returned checks. Grabbing his reading glasses, he compared the signatures. "Do these signatures look the same to you?"

Jean adjusted the desk lamp, shining more light on the blue checks. She leaned over to study the penmanship. "No. The writing isn't as shaky and unsteady." She looked up. "You don't think Alicia forged these checks?"

"I don't know what else to think at this time. It doesn't make sense Grandma wrote one check from a book then put it away and used another book, does it? I think I need to keep checking her past statements."

He couldn't fathom Alicia stealing, but the missing silverware still nagged at him. Surely there was another explanation. He again checked the amounts against his grandmother's list of loans. He didn't see any notation of the odd large amounts. "I don't know what to do about this." David leaned back in his brown vinyl desk chair and stretched. "Do you think I should ask Grandma?" He looked toward Jean for a clue as to his next move. He wasn't prepared to confront Alicia, but he couldn't ignore what he had found.

Jean pulled up a chair, studied the front of the check, and then turned it over to view the endorsement. "Look at this. It looks like the check and the endorsement are both written with the same blue pen, doesn't it?"

David examined the second check and compared it to the one Jean held. "You're right. There's no point in upsetting her. I think we already have the answer." He paused. "Remember when Grandma's silverware was stolen? She believes Alicia may have been responsible. Makes you wonder now, doesn't it?" David sat staring at the checks, talking to himself more than to Jean. "I don't understand how Alicia could do something like that." The veins in his neck bulged in anger. "I should have insisted Grandma put away her personal papers in a safer place."

Jean rubbed David's shoulders. "It wasn't your fault. Alicia wrote these checks long before you became involved in her affairs. Besides, we had no reason to suspect her of anything like this."

Pushing the checks aside, David gathered the rest of the statements. Perhaps his grandma was correct in distrusting Alicia. David brought his hands to his temples, hoping the massaging action would keep the inner explosion at bay. "What kind of hatred makes someone do something like this, especially to a family member? Getting involved with her family has caused me nothing but grief."

"If you hadn't gotten involved, where would your grandmother be now? Who would be caring for her?"

David sighed. Jean was right. There was no one to look out for her at this time except for him. Maybe in time, Nathan would be back home and able to assist. This thought would have to be enough, for now, to keep him going. With his resolution strengthened, David took a deep breath before returning to his search for further discrepancies.

Chapter 19

E dna hurried to the door to welcome David and Jean when they arrived Saturday before noon, as promised.

"Come on in, my dears, it's been so long since I've seen you."

"I'm sorry the holidays are busy and with all the snow and terrible pass conditions and frequent closures, we couldn't risk the drive." David placed his bucket of repair tools on the floor and embraced Edna.

"You must be hungry after your long drive." Edna released her grandson and smiled at him.

"We're fine. We grabbed a bite on the way."

"Oh, you. You know better than to eat on the way. Let me make you something anyway, I have plenty of food here." Edna scurried to the refrigerator and began rummaging through its contents.

David peered over her shoulder. "Grandma, it looks like that's spoiled." He pulled out a small white dish. She saw him wrinkle his nose. "See, it's turning green. You can't possibly eat this." David pulled the dish out. "It needs to be tossed."

Edna frowned as David dumped the spoilage in the trash can under the sink. "That food was perfectly fine. I could have scraped off the little bit of mold. You young people are so wasteful." Edna resented David's interference. He was always after her for something when he came over. "You think I don't know how to keep my house clean, and you think I'm dirty." Her pulse quickened and tears formed.

David put his arm around her shoulder. "You're ninety-three. There's nothing wrong with needing help with some things." He opened the kitchen window, pushed it open, then pulled off several paper towels and began wiping her counters.

Edna eyed him like an eagle. "You don't understand. I can clean my own house, but I don't much like doing it. And, I'm certainly not going to pay someone to clean it. Besides, my house is fine as it is." Edna glanced around the kitchen, suddenly self-conscious of the cluttered counters.

"You never know if you can trust strangers coming into your home. I've already had my silverware stolen." Though Edna loved having her grandson and his family in her life, she disliked the goings-on behind her back. It was insulting how her own family seemed displeased with how she lived. "You think I don't know how everyone is always cleaning things behind my back, but I've seen it."

"Grandma, you know we're only trying to help make your life safe and comfortable."

David's attempt at an explanation didn't appease her. She crossed her arms, firm in her resolve to make him understand. "I'm perfectly capable of looking after myself and my home. You make me feel incompetent." She fought back the burning sensation in her eyes. "I have always been able to do my chores, even when I was a young girl I had chores. I didn't care much for dusting, but Mother insisted. She also taught me to iron and darn socks when I was only eight." "Father always said, 'You darn a pair of socks better than anyone, including your mother.'" Edna laughed at her voice which she made deeper, in an attempt to imitate her father. "Mother always got upset when he said that to her."

Jean took a dishtowel off the counter. "How about while I'm here I help you throw in a load of laundry?"

"Oh, you," Edna frowned, "I just washed that." She snatched the dish towel from Jean. "I prefer to wash my clothes by hand like Mother did when I was a young girl. You young people today are so spoiled with modern conveniences."

"Some things don't get clean when you wash them by hand. Some things need to be washed by machine. I can help you wash a small load of undergarments and bath towels."

"It's nonsense to waste all that water and electricity when I have so few things to wash. Anyway, the washer is too confusing to use." She hobbled through the house, gathering her dishcloths and a few washcloths. She handed the bundle to Jean. "Here, put these in the sink. I'll show you how to do the laundry."

Edna stomped up the stairs, fuming. Frustrated, David trudged after her. She collected some undergarments from her bedroom, carefully tucking them under her arm, away from David's sight. Returning to the kitchen, Edna pursed her lips. "See, this is all there is." She placed the items next to the sink. She turned on the faucet and reached inside the cupboard under the sink for her washing soap.

"Have you ever used Fels-Naptha?" She held out a large yellow bar of soap for Jean to see. "This is the only kind of clothes soap Mother ever used." With the water still running, Edna held the bar under the faucet for a few minutes, enough to produce some suds, then she dropped the bar into the water, and turned the knob off. She grinned as she swooshed the soapy water and the gentle floral scent filled the room. As the pile of bubbles rose, a few glistening orbs floated in the air. Edna swatted them and giggled as she had all those years ago.

Hearing water running, Edna was excited to help her mother. It was Saturday, wash day. Mother smiled at her. Edna looked around the kitchen. "Where's my stool?" Edna shrugged, confused she couldn't find her stool. Mother always put it to the right of the big washbasin so Edna could use it when she helped Mother with the wash. She didn't notice the empty pot on the woodstove. Mother must have already emptied the boiling water into the heavy metal sink attached to the wall. She liked how her nose tickled from the soap bubbles, and she reached up to scratch it.

Across the room was Mother's oak Hoosier cupboard, with two shelves for the jars of sweet and pungent spices. Edna, remembering the stick she always used to stir the clothes, scurried over to a long drawer and clanged around, searching for it. "Here is the stirring stick." She proudly held out a long-handled, wooden spoon for her mother to see. Then, Edna gently pushed the items around in the sink with the stick. She glanced over at her mother. "See, I can do a good job." Edna giggled with the joy of helping.

"Yes, you're doing a good job." Edna smiled at the woman who handed her a few dirty towels.

"See, everything must be washed in progression, just as you told me. First the dish towels, then my undergarments, finally the other dirty clothes." Edna removed the towels and dishcloths. She wrung out the now-clean items, over the pot. Then she went to the laundry room, grabbed her wicker basket, and placed the damp clothing into the basket.

Next, she threw in her undergarments and repeated the process. "We need to go outside now." Edna lifted the wicker basket and carried it outside to the old circle-shaped clothesline, which sat on a platform above the ground.

"Do you need help hanging the laundry on the line?"

Startled by a male voice, Edna turned to see who was asking to help her. Mother had left already and her grandson, David was there. She didn't understand where Mother went but straightened and reached for the first item in the basket. "No, I prefer my way. I have never forgotten the method Mother taught me. Mother and I will remove the clothes later when they're fresh and dry. Tomorrow is ironing day."

Chapter 20

Edna answered the knock at the door.

The postman, already dressed in his springtime shorts, handed her a parcel. "Sign here, please."

She glanced at the return address, but couldn't decipher the writing. Only two days from her birthday, her excited hands trembled as she thanked the postman and closed the door. Sitting at her dining room table, she examined the package, running her fingers across the brown butcher paper. She noticed 'FRAGILE' stamped in big red letters numerous times across the front of the package. Edna ripped at the paper with the enthusiasm of a child and removed the lid from the sturdy, white box. She lifted out a dark, oak-framed, eight by ten portrait. Salty tears formed. Though she hadn't seen Nathan for several decades but there was no mistaking the soldier in his dress blues. David must have told him her birthday was approaching. She recognized the stripes of Sergeant First Class and beamed with pride while her heart yearned to see him again.

Gazing upon the picture, Edna's breath caught at the resemblance to his grandfather, Jacob, when he was in the army. Her thoughts drifted to how handsome Jacob had been in his army uniform. She loved the military life, though the excitement of being the wife of a soldier had worn off fairly early as she faced its realities and uncertainties. Moving around was tough on the children. She was grateful they were so young when Jacob was an enlisted man. She was also thankful he had insisted on requesting a post in the states as the change was less traumatic for Bernice and Larry. Edna wondered if that was why Nathan had stayed single. Edna knew military life could be such a stress on a relationship. She carried the photograph into the living room. She scooted over the other framed photos on the end table, to the right of the sofa, and sat Nathan's picture among Bernice's graduation photo, and photos of Larry, and Jacob, in their uniforms. She stepped back, hands on her hips and gazed upon the three generations of enlisted men.

The next evening as Edna prepared her dinner, Missy's yapping caught her attention. The dog ran from the living room to her. She marched down the hall and caught the sound of the phone's incessant ringing, she snatched it up in frustration.

"Hi, Grandma. Happy Birthday."

Edna brushed her hair away from her ear and strained to hear the voice on the other end. "Gracious. You're a little early, but that's okay. I wasn't expecting you to call until tomorrow."

"Did you get the gift I sent?"

Edna plopped in the rocker next to the phone, confused. "I thought the gift was from Nathan. I didn't know you sent it, David."

"Grandma, this is Nathan."

Edna's heart skipped a beat. She brought her hand to her face. "Is it really you?" It had been over a year since Edna became reacquainted with David. Now, Nathan had surprised her with a phone call. Her heart swelled at the realization that now she could get to know her other grandson.

"I'm sorry I haven't called earlier. I don't have a lot of free time with my current assignment and it's even tougher with the time zone difference."

Edna blinked back the tears. "When will I be able to see you? It's been so long."

"I'm hoping sometime next year. I won't know for sure until it gets closer to the actual transfer. The army doesn't always give a lot of notice."

Edna sighed. She knew the routine. She remembered her own move across the United States with her two young children. "I remember when Jacob was ordered to Fort Monmouth, New Jersey, we were allowed only one-week notice."

"When was that?"

Edna pondered for a moment. A slow smile came at the long-ago memory of Jacob's life in the service. "I think it was 1935. I remember both Larry and Bernice were quite young." She reached across to the end table and removed Nathan's photo and gazed upon it again as she listened to her grandson.

"I bet it was quite a long trip for you."

"I should say. Jacob knew our old Ford would never last through the two-week trip across the states, so we traded it, along with five-hundred dollars, for a new, shiny, blue Chevrolet. It was the classiest I had ever seen."

"So, what did you think of New Jersey?"

"I loved living on the east coast, although Jacob was seldom home and never adjusted to the lifestyle." Edna sighed deeply, remembering the antique stores, the dances, and socializing with the military wives. Her head swayed as she started humming an old Bing Crosby tune that resonated through her head. *Where the Blue of the Night Meets the Gold of the Day.*

Words crackled with static across the phone line. Edna stopped humming so she could make out the voice and the words. "It's difficult getting used to a life so far from home, and so different. It's hard to be happy away from those you love. At some point though, you need to return home."

Stunned, Edna closed her eyes. She couldn't believe what Jacob said. The words echoed as if she heard them only yesterday. She bristled.

"I've requested a transfer to Washington, to Fort Lewis."

The words shocked Edna as if she'd been struck. Her face warmed with anger. Once again Jacob had betrayed her. She knew she shouldn't be surprised; Jacob had hinted now for over a year of his dissatisfaction living in New Jersey and he always had to have something to complain about.

"But I, like the other army wives here, and the children have friends, especially, Larry. He's finally adjusting so well with the other children his age." It didn't matter though. Jacob was miserable. If Edna wanted to continue to live with him in peace, she was expected to honor his wishes. She had long questioned her decision in marrying this man, but now, there were the children. She and Jacob agreed to stay together and make the best of the situation, for the sake of the children.

"Grandma. Are you okay? What are you talking about? You're not an army wife anymore and your children are both gone now."

"Bernice and Larry are gone? Where did they go?" Edna shook her head. She brought her hands to her temples. Her heart throbbed in her head and a dull pain thudded in her chest. "I don't understand. What happened, Jacob?"

"I'm not Jacob, this is Nathan, your grandson."

Edna detected frustration in the tone across the line. Weary from all the aggravation, she squeezed her eyes shut.

When she opened her eyes, Edna studied her surroundings. She was not in her home with the crystal prism chandelier hanging over the large mahogany table, where she had entertained so many of the ladies from the base. The surroundings seemed simple and disorganized, not at all like her. "I'm sorry, I don't understand."

"This is Nathan, your grandson. Do you remember? I called to make sure you received the photo I sent for your birthday."

Edna gripped the color photo of the uniformed officer that lay in her lap. She whispered to herself. "Nathan." Her breathing returned to normal. "When am I going to see you again?"

"Soon, Grandma. I'm sure I'll see you by your next birthday."

"That's too long. I might not live that long." Edna's voice drifted off as she returned the phone to its cradle.

Chapter 21

With Rachel's high school graduation approaching, David called his grandmother with an invitation to spend the weekend and attend the up-coming baccalaureate ceremony.

"It's been a long time since I've been to a graduation or formal church celebration." Grandma's excitement danced across the line, spanning the distance between them.

Arriving the following weekend, Grandma's brown, brocade, overnight bag stood positioned by the door, a welcome sign of her enthusiasm.

"It looks like you're all ready to go." He cast a glance at her once again forlorn appearance. Her navy blue knit pants, as well as her blue and red floral pullover, had seen better days. Jean would definitely need to do some mending, and perhaps they would do some shopping, before taking her back home after the weekend.

Missy yapped, running to the door. David still cringed at the sight of the mangy dog. He stepped inside to the faint aroma of bacon grease, grimacing at the thought of Grandma cooking on the stove, and the hot grease. "Are you sure you should still be using the stove? Your eyes aren't as sharp as they used to be." He had wavered over broaching the subject, but the recent call from the Tri-City Fire Department regarding the smoke detector concerned him enough to worry about her, and her neighbors. "I understand you accidentally set off the smoke detector the other day." Grandma's glare cautioned David. He would back off for now, rather than risk upsetting her before the four-hour car trip with her.

"Oh, you. I can see just fine. Besides, I don't use the stove much anyway."

Watching her disappear into the kitchen, David shook his head seconds later when pans clanged and cupboard doors closed, a likely attempt to disguise or hide evidence of her morning breakfast, most likely, cooked on the stove. She startled when David appeared in the kitchen.

"Is there anything I can help you with before we go?" David observed the food crumbs and fresh spills on the counter. He poked his head into the laundry room and checked for fresh dog piles. Without the kitchen carpet, the room no longer smelled sour and unpleasant. At least the newly exposed linoleum could be easily swept and scrubbed. David grimaced at the fresh spills on the stove and made a mental note to address his concern over her cooking when they returned on Sunday.

David secured the lock on the rear door and pulled the blinds halfway. Missy continued her incessant barking at the empty dish by the door. David groaned. "What about Missy? Do you have someone coming to take care of her?'

Edna shuffled into the kitchen. "Fred has a key. He's going to stop by later and pick her up."

David found the dog food beside the dryer and quickly filled the dog bowls with nuggets and water. To save time, he'd call Fred from the road and verify his task. Grandma headed for the door; head held high. She passed her overnight bag and the screen door slammed behind her. David followed, picking up the small overnight case, pushed the lock button, and followed his grandmother down the driveway.

"Gracious. It's been a long time since I've been to Seattle. Did you know I attended high school there?"

"I remember that. Maybe, we'll take a drive to your old neighborhood. Would you like that?"

Her eyes twinkled. For a moment, David imagined a young woman helping her mother in the kitchen and walking to school along the once-narrow streets of Capitol Hill. He reached for his grandmother's frail arm and aided her into the front seat. Setting the small overnight bag in the back, he climbed in.

"That would be nice. I remember my home in Seattle and one somewhere by a lake where I taught for my first few years. I can't remember much. It was so long ago." Her voice trailed off.

David glanced at his grandmother as he pulled away from her townhome.

She looked straight ahead, but her mouth relayed her joy. "I can't wait to see your home again, Dear."

"You've never been to my house before."

"Oh." She brought her hand to her cheek. "Are you sure? I thought I'd seen it before."

To ease her discomfort, David reached across the seat and patted her hand. "I'm sure Jean sent you pictures Grandma, and that's what you remember."

She turned. A broad smile replaced the wrinkled brow of concern on her tired face. "It's a lovely home." Her soft voice trailed off.

Not sure how long his grandmother would be comfortable, David drove slightly over the speed limit for most of the way. "Let me know if you need to make any stops. There are plenty of places we can take a break."

Fortunately, the drive was uneventful. With pleasant chit chat and no more flashes of confusion, David relaxed as he pulled off the freeway exit for the final stretch home. Pulling into the long front drive to his house, Grandma's eyes widened as she surveyed the expansive lawn and wooded acreage. He helped her out, and, grabbing her bag, led her to the front door.

Inside, Jean stood by the door and took the overnight case from David.

Grandma sniffed the air and edged her way toward the kitchen. "I just realized I haven't eaten since breakfast, and I'm starved. How long until dinner?"

David peeked inside the oven. His mouth watered as the smell of cheese and sweet basil escaped through the open door. "I hope you like lasagna?"

His grandmother grinned like a child. "Oh my. I can't remember the last time I had lasagna."

After freshening up, Edna walked to the door and grabbed her overnight bag. "Where's my room?"

Her directness caught David off guard and he smiled. "It's downstairs. There's only one bedroom on this floor. If the stairs are too difficult, you can stay in our room for the weekend."

"The basement is fine. I prefer not to be a bother or be in your way."

David puzzled momentarily over his grandmother's words and tone, wondering if he detected a trace of martyr in her voice. He helped steady her as she stepped cautiously down the stairs to the small mother-in-law apartment, complete with fridge, sink, stove, and microwave. In her bedroom, David and Jean watched her unpack the entire contents of her bag, carefully placing her clothing in the dresser before putting out her shoes, making herself quite at home.

"This is a lovely room. I could live in this much space. I don't need more than this to be comfortable." She marched across the room, shoulders back, making herself at home, and pulled back the lace curtains. "It's nice you have enough room where someone could live, even for a long time, and not be in the way."

David glanced sideways to Jean. He stopped short of a full eye-roll, considering it a dismissive gesture. He didn't want to guess what she might be implying. "Yes, it is very nice. The bathroom is right across the hall. There are fresh towels and soap, shampoo and conditioner are in the shower. Let us know if you need any help with anything."

After his grandmother surveyed her accommodations for the weekend, she flipped the light switch off and stepped slowly up the stairs with the rail for support.

"Hi, Grandma." Rachel and Emily greeted her at the top of the stairs. "We're glad you're coming with us tomorrow."

"I didn't know we were going somewhere. Where are we going?"

David led her to the sofa. Once seated, he reminded her of the baccalaureate service preceding Rachel's graduation.

"That's nice. I wish I had known. I didn't have a chance to get a gift."

Rachel sat next to her. "Nobody's bringing gifts. It's only a small religious service."

Ready to sit and relax, David was happy when the timer on the oven beeped and the oven door clanged shut. His stomach rumbled. "It smells like it's dinner time. I hope you're hungry, Grandma." David escorted her to the table. Rachel and Emily emerged with the last utensils and took their places while David scooped a serving of meaty and cheesy noodles onto Grandma's plate.

Before pushing her plate away, she downed two healthy-sized servings. "This is wonderful. I haven't enjoyed a meal like this for so long." Edna grinned from ear to ear. "I wish I could stay longer."

The next morning, David went downstairs to check on his grandmother. Already dressed for the evening ceremony, her dress showed years of wear and the frayed hem drooped on one side. She shuffled out in ratty slippers. Dismayed, he hoped he could convince her to change clothes, so Jean could get the dress washed and mended. He laid out the family's plan for the day. "We're not leaving for the church until after dinner, why don't you put on some slacks for now? They might be more comfortable for walking in the yard."

"I'll be fine." She turned her back to him and started up the stairs, remarking how well she slept. "This is so nice. I could live in a place like this. Maybe you could build a place like this for me." She paused and fumbled for words. "Not here, of course. I wouldn't want to be in your way. It could be somewhere nearby, like next door."

David bit his tongue and led her into the kitchen.

A few minutes later, Rachel appeared. She hugged Edna. "Good morning, Grandma. After breakfast, we're making peanut butter cookies for the reception after the service. Do you want to help?"

"Mmm. Peanut butter cookies are my favorite." She clapped her hands like a little girl.

A former teacher, college-educated in the late '20s, at a time when many women didn't attend college, Edna took a great interest in education. Her eyes brightened and she spoke excitedly, questioning Rachel. "Have you decided where you will be attending college?"

"I'm still waiting to hear. I've applied at the University of Washington, Western Washington, and Central Washington University"

"How exciting for you. Will you be joining a sorority?"

"I might join a sorority. I haven't decided yet. It depends where I get accepted. Neither Central nor Western has sororities."

"Oh, my." Grandma shook her head and frowned at Rachel. "I don't much care for sororities and fraternities. They encourage so much drinking. My daughter, Bernice, was killed in a car accident coming home from a fraternity party with some of her housemates. She was only twenty. They suspected the young fraternity boy driving may have been drinking." She shook her head and fell silent.

Rachel glanced at her mother. Jean rushed over. "Well, Rachel still isn't certain what she's going to do. She still has a lot to decide."

Noticing the pot had stopped percolating, David rose and poured some coffee for himself and his grandmother.

Edna looked in the cup, wrinkled her nose, and pushed it away. "You know, Dear, I do prefer tea in the morning. Is that okay?"

"Of course it is." David sighed, poured the coffee back into the pot, and started a cup of water in the microwave. Jean popped bread in the toaster and fried some eggs and quick sausage links. Minutes later, Emily joined the family, greeting her grandmother with a quick shoulder squeeze.

Drinking his brew, David savored the rich full-bodied buttery flavor, breathing in the robust aroma and praying somehow the strong coffee would morph into an inner strength for him to make it through a day of activities that would keep his grandmother engaged. After breakfast, remembering her love of gardening, he guessed a walk outside in his spacious yard, could easily fill most of the morning. The garden tour delighted her to no end, and once more her knowledge about the various plants and shrubs astonished him. Her face brightened when David pointed out a bank planted in Ajuga from the starts he had dug from her yard months earlier. It was thriving in the damp soil, making the bank a striking mass of purple spires. Mid-afternoon, Jean gathered the playing cards. After a few attempts at various games failed, Jean quickly shoved the cards back into the box and stashed them away.

David rested his chin in his hands. "What shall we do now?"

Jean shook her head. It appeared she was out of ideas to entertain Grandma. "How about we get the cookies started?" She opened the cupboard and found a large glass mixing bowl and gathered the ingredients while Rachel grabbed the mixer and placed it on the kitchen peninsula.

Edna shuffled in. "I like my peanut butter cookies chewy, not crunchy."

"Then we'll make them chewy." Jean smiled, making room at the breakfast bar for everyone and moving a stool over for Edna.

"I'm quite a good cook myself." Edna grinned, waiting with a fork to make the crisscrosses on the cookies before sprinkling them with sugar. "I won plenty of cooking contests and awards."

The sweet scent of warm peanut butter cookies enticed everyone. Jean poured milk and placed the first batch of cookies on a plate.

Edna smacked her lips as she chewed. "These are soft and chewy, just the way I like them."

Cookies baked, and on a large serving plate for the reception, David arrived with a take-and-bake pizza. While the pizza cooked, Jean prepared a quick salad. Grandma looked content, even tired as she went to the living room and sat down. Jean wiped her hands and dashed out of the kitchen to dress for the church service.

David joined his grandmother. His forehead wrinkled in concern. "Do you want to take a coat? It gets chilly in the evenings here." Downstairs, he found her navy blue, quilted coat. It carried the faint scent of her home before it was cleaned. He immediately regretted he had suggested it but carried it upstairs.

"She's not wearing that." Jean shook her head, meeting David at the top of the stairs.

"I was hoping it would look a little nicer than what she's wearing."

Edna shuffled over and snatched her garment before David could stop her. "Mother bought me that coat years ago."

Though the worn and stained coat looked old, David doubted her mother, who had passed away nearly thirty years earlier, had purchased it for her. He called to Rachel and Emily. They ran down the stairs. "Do either of you have a sweater Grandma could borrow?" He narrowed his gaze. They detected his urgency and tromped up the stairs, returning with a tan, loose-knit, baggy cardigan. "Thanks." David carried the sweater over to his grandmother. "Let's see how this fits." He held the sweater out.

"That's not my sweater." Grandma pulled away and eyed David.

"I know, but it's a bit chilly, and I'm afraid your coat will be too warm once you're inside." He shot a glance at the girls and Jean who were waiting by the door with the plate of cookies in hand.

Edna hesitated, then her expression softened. She allowed David to drape the sweater around her shoulders, then help her into the sleeves. "I need my hat. Did you bring my hat?"

David scurried back downstairs and fished through the drawer where she'd put her clothes, searching for her brown fake fur hat. He chuckled thinking the hat looked like a Russian ushanka hat. Returning upstairs, Edna placed it triumphantly on her head. She walked out the door, arm in arm with David to attend Rachel's baccalaureate.

Chapter 22

Edna stepped slowly toward the entrance to the church. She couldn't recall if she had ever been to a baccalaureate service. The soft scent of the purple hyacinth floated on the breeze of the late spring evening as David led her by the arm down the sidewalk. Vibrant yellow and orange zinnias and white and red geraniums lined the walkway.

Nearing the church, Edna warmed with the sunlight that glistened off the arched orange and yellow stained-glass windows of the old-fashioned brick church, reminding her of a building from long ago with its pillars and arched columns.

"This is a pretty church, isn't it, Grandma?" Rachel reached over and took her free hand. Edna smiled and a surge of happiness overtook her. She strutted like a peacock on show, proud and happy to be included in her great-granddaughter's event. Flustered by the growing size of the crowd, Edna was pleased David was there to guide her through the sea of spring-colored pastels, and flower print dresses, worn by the large crowd milling around outside. She brightened seeing the smiling faces of the students wearing dress clothes for their special occasion.

Escorted through the oversized double doors into the vestibule, Edna glanced at her clothing and smoothed her soft fabric. She smiled, feeling appropriately dressed for the day in her outfit.

"Have you ever been to a baccalaureate service, Grandma?" Rachel leaned in with a soft voice.

"Oh, gracious, no. I haven't been to any graduation ceremony in quite some time." With failing eyes, Edna strained to make out the figures outlined in the vibrant, colored glass windows. She puzzled over which Christian saints they might be. Rich chords of music bellowed from the dozens of gray pipes of a majestic organ, dominating the space behind the altar where the white-robed choir stood. Stepping inside the already packed church, Edna glanced around. She never imagined there would be such a crowd. David helped her into the wooden pew. The high, open ceilings filled with the choir's strong voices singing "Amazing Grace." Edna strived to remember the words from her youth, her lyrics hesitant and faltering as she sang along with the choir. Her voice cracked with the dryness of age. She smiled as memories of her youth flowed through her mind.

Edna sat swaying in time to the music until it stopped and the minister instructed the congregation to be seated. He began by congratulating the new graduates, then introduced the first speaker.

"Can you hear okay?" David patted her hand.

She flung a quick smile, but sat silent, engrossed in the ceremony.

The speaker took the podium. "Too many people define themselves by what they do as a profession, rather than the type of person they are."

Edna sat poised on the edge of the pew, contemplating the inspirational words as if they were directed to her.

"When you graduate and leave here, what kind of person will you be? When you look back on your life at the end of the road, what will you see, what will you remember?" His words echoed in Edna's head. "What will you remember?" Her mind strained to remember.

Edna looked down, beaming with pride at her long, fitted, gray wool skirt, that her mother worked on so hard, for her graduation. Mother always loved sewing for her youngest daughter. Daddy was such a dear. He bought her a black, felt, hat with a wide rim and a silk fuchsia sash to match her mohair sweater. Edna put her hand to her head to feel the new hat atop the long blond braids wrapped around her head. Feeling so grown up in her new hat, she looked over to her father. "It's just the fleas' ankles." Smiling smugly, she looked out of the corner of her eye and saw several members of the graduating class turn their heads to look at her. She had finally made it to her high-school graduation day. She shifted to the edge of the long wooden bench as she listened eagerly for the school president to announce her name. A lone tear trickled down her cheek, and her chest swelled over her achievement. The crowd applauded.

The thundering applause startled Edna. She gazed toward the front of the large building. Her eyes widened at the size of the crowd and her shrill voice broke. "Where did all these people come from?"

Next to her, a kind voice reassured her. "Grandma, these are all the graduates and their families."

"But the graduating class is only twelve. I don't remember so many people coming to watch me graduate." A sudden flush overcame her. She looked around. The fashion was not the same on these youngsters. She didn't recognize the classmates surrounding her, with short skirts, tight tops, and clunky shoes. She looked down at her mint green, flowered, double-knit dress with brown slip-on shoes. She touched the top of her head. There were no braids wrapped around her head, and no wide-brimmed hat with its fuchsia sash, only fine, thinning hair, pinned in place underneath a fur cap. "David, where have all these people come from? What am I doing here?" Her voice cracked.

David leaned over and put his arm around her. She was comforted by his smile as he hugged her. "It's okay, Grandma. You just forgot where you are. It's a ceremony for Rachel's graduation, her baccalaureate."

Edna glanced over at her great-granddaughter and smiled weakly. Rachel smiled back. Edna fumbled in her purse for a tissue, then dabbed her eyes. She wiped away a small tear for all the years that had passed.

Chapter 23

Edna lay on the floor. She didn't know where she was, or what happened. Though beams of sunlight streamed through the windows, her mind blurred with veiled memories. She tried to move her right leg and arm to push herself up, but they failed her. Her heart raced. Sweat formed on her forehead and dripped down her cheeks. She could taste the salty drops. Across the room, a mylar balloon floated freely attached to a long blue ribbon. She recognized the balloon Barbara had given her. When was that? Yesterday? Last week? Longer? When Barbara brought the blue balloon adorned with white stars and red and white stripes, and the words, *Happy 4th of July*, the balloon hugged the ceiling. Now it floated mere feet off the floor. Memories floated back into her mind, the strawberry pie and going to the 4th of July parade with Barbara. She guessed a few weeks had passed since that day. Now, the balloon, once full and flying high, was deflated and barely hanging on, much like her life, empty and drifting without purpose. Panic gripped her. No one would hear her cries for help.

She lay on the floor for some time before the phone rang. Missy yapped and ran in circles in front of her. Edna fought to push herself to stand, or even crawl to get to the phone to answer it. There wasn't pain, only numbness down her side. Missy quieted, then strutted over and lay next to her. Edna slowly reached out her left hand and stroked the dog's black fur. She wondered how long she would lie alone like this, helpless as a baby. A short while later, the phone rang a second time. Edna waited, praying to hear someone come to check on her. She gazed at the old antique clock on the bureau, she blinked several times to clear her blurry vision unable to make out the time. For a few minutes, she concentrated on the tick-tock of the wooden pendulum as it swung back and forth. Then, came the pounding from somewhere. She listened, wondering if her ears were playing tricks on her. Hearing the pounding again, Edna turned her head toward the door. Her breathing relaxed, realizing someone was knocking. She tried to yell "I'm here. Help me," but her tongue, uncoordinated and unwilling to form words, only allowed a weak sound from her dry throat. A man's voice came from outside. She guessed it was her neighbor, Fred.

"Edna ... are you here?"

The knock grew louder, then a key turned in the door. He called out again as he walked in. "Edna. Are you okay?" Seeing her on the floor, Fred stooped, and awkwardly raised her to a seated position.

"Thank God you're here. I can't move." Her voice cracked as she reached out with her hand that worked and clutched Fred's hand, afraid to let go.

Fred gently released her grip. "You'll be okay now; I'm calling an ambulance."

Edna's muscles relaxed, knowing she wasn't alone. She sat dazed as she looked at her leg that didn't feel a part of her. A few minutes later, sirens wailed louder and louder, finally cutting off outside her home. Missy bounced around with a constant high-pitched yapping, ratcheting Edna's tension level up. She snapped at her dog, which she rarely did. "Quiet, Missy."

Fred met the emergency crew at the door and led them into the living room. Bending over her, one of the EMT's carefully lifted her and carried her to the sofa. They were quiet as they raised her eyelids and shined a light. They pumped the black cuff of the blood pressure monitor so tight Edna thought her arm would snap like a frail tree limb. Her heart thumped fast but unsteady like a poorly tuned engine.

"What are you doing?" Flustered, as they talked around her and passed things back and forth, Edna called out. "What's happening? Talk to me." Her words sounded strange and slurred.

"It will be okay, Mrs. Pearson, we are checking you out. Do you have any family nearby who we can call?" One of the men looked at Edna, then turned back to Fred as the other technician held his radio and called out numbers. A voice cracked across the line.

"Nathan. I want you to call Nathan." Edna's voice broke with fear.

Fred bent over her. "Edna, don't you want me to call David? Nathan is out of the country."

"No, I just spoke with him, he said he was coming home."

117

"I know, for now, let's let David know you're going to the hospital. He can call Nathan, okay?"

Edna pulled away from the hand that held her down. "I don't want to go to a hospital. I just need to rest for a few days." She struggled to speak clearly enough to catch the attention of the emergency crew. "Why are you taking me to a hospital?" Edna's heart pounded like a drum against her chest, tight from the rage swelling inside.

The lone female EMT turned her attention to Edna, speaking softly, but with authority. "I'm sorry, Mrs. Pearson; you've likely suffered a stroke. Resting in bed isn't going to do it. We need to take you in for observation, and some more tests. "Do you know how old you are, Mrs. Pearson?

How ridiculous, of course, she knew how old she was. "Ninety-two ... no, wait ... ninety-three."

"Do you know how long you were out before your neighbor arrived? Do you remember what happened?"

Too many questions bombarded her all at once. They didn't make any sense. How could she possibly know how long she was out? She frowned and turned away from the woman, and mumbled, "I don't remember what happened. You can't expect me to remember that."

Lifted onto a stretcher, she was hooked to a machine that beeped in time with her heart. The ambulance pulled out with lights flashing and sirens blaring for all the neighbors to notice. Before she knew it she was wheeled through the double doors of Good Samaritan Hospital.

"Please, someone. Call my grandson for me. Is anyone listening?" Edna stared into the hall as a dash of white coats and machines rolled by.

Chapter 24

The nurse directed David to Room 304, bed B, the farthest from the door. He knocked before he edged inside. The last rays of sun filtered through the gauze-like curtains, casting light on Grandma's distant and frightened eyes and sunken face. David bent down to kiss her cool cheek. He immediately forgot about his long drive as he gazed at her, helpless, in the stark dreary hospital room. "How are you doing, Grandma?" David winced at the beeping of the machines and the wires which snaked around her, overwhelming her frail body.

"Oh, David, I'm so glad you're here. When can I go home? When can I leave this terrible place? No one tells me anything."

His grandmother's voice strained over nearly unintelligible words. David grabbed a chair by her bed and slid it over. "You had a stroke. I just got here and haven't had a chance to talk to the doctor yet." He took a seat and held her cold, clammy hand, forcing a smile to avoid expressing the agony he suffered sitting in a hospital room, breathing in the stagnant, antiseptic odor. "I'll see Dr. Smith later today. Why don't you rest? I'll let you know what the doctor said after I speak with him." David stroked his grandmother's hand, and it began to warm. "I'll be back to see you in a little while." David patted her arm, turned, and left.

His call to the doctor before leaving home had allowed him time to consider the options he knew were going to be presented for his grandmother's care. Continuing to live without some sort of help was not going to be one of them. After a short drive to the medical center, David rode the elevator to the fifth floor to search out Dr. Smith. He knocked on the open door as he announced his arrival. "Dr. Smith? I'm David, Edna Pearson's grandson."

"Come on in." Dr. Smith waved David in and motioned to a chair opposite him.

David took a seat in front of a large, cherry wood desk piled with papers and files.

Dr. Smith immediately set about discussing Grandma's situation. He fumbled through papers and scribbled notes as he spoke. "It's a good thing your grandmother's neighbor checked in on her. She might have laid helpless for days. She's suffered a mini-stroke. By itself, I wouldn't be worried, but I suspect she's had a number of these over the past few years. They're called Transient Ischemic Attacks, or TIA's for short. She's at risk of having a more serious stroke in the future. With her advanced age, I strongly suggest assisted living arrangements or having someone come to her home several hours a day, at a minimum. I also suspect she is suffering from early to mid-stage dementia. My best guess would be Alzheimer's Dementia, which will worsen with age."

David nodded at the doctor's direct words. He had suspected as much with her increasing forgetfulness and bizarre words, reactions, and tales. Still, he felt a spasm of pain in his chest, another indication his body was reacting to his ongoing stress. His worry over his grandmother's safety had grown over the past months, after two visits by the local fire department for a fall, and a minor stove fire. This meeting merely confirmed his earlier concerns. With this latest stroke, Edna's ability to continue to live on her own again was only a fantasy. How could he possibly find caregivers who would tolerate her difficult nature? He knew he would be blasted with her full wrath if he told her she needed to move to an assisted care facility. David's gut twisted as he slinked further in his seat at the thought of the upcoming confrontation. "I know my grandmother will have to accept help cooking, cleaning, and bathing as per doctor's orders, but I still am not looking forward to breaking the news to her."

Dr. Smith chuckled. "I understand. If you, or your grandmother, have any questions, let me know. I'll be more than happy to talk to her."

David stood and thanked him, then with a sigh and hesitant steps, he returned to the car to face Grandma's fury. During the short drive, David decided to ease into the doctor's orders, when he spoke to his grandmother. The limited movement and slurred speech caused by the stroke, along with memory issues, would improve with time. The Alzheimer's would only worsen. He'd address these issues separately as she adjusted to the changes forthcoming in her life.

A few minutes later David guardedly poked his head into his grandmother's room. He looked into her eyes for some indication of her mood, before he edged inside.

She narrowed her eyes and glared. "David, when can I go home? I don't like it here and nobody's telling me why I'm here. I want to go home."

"Grandma, you know why you're in the hospital. You've had a stroke; your doctor says you can only go home if you agree to have someone come and help you with cooking, cleaning, and bathing."

"That's okay, Dear. I'm sure Barbara can come to help me out until I get stronger again."

David shook his head. "No, you don't understand." He guessed his Grandma already understood his message but was too proud and stubborn to admit it. "He means professional help, a trained nurse or nurses' assistant. Barbara is a wonderful person, and I know she's a dear friend, but she can't do it. She isn't a certified caregiver." For all the relief David felt knowing she would be better cared for, and less danger to herself or others, he recognized his grandmother's resistance and resentment. She didn't see her lack of personal hygiene and how she appeared to others, nor did she comprehend how her home had fallen to such dreadful conditions in such a short period. He now wondered if the disease made her unaware or unable to care for her home, and her pride prevented her from asking for help. "Your bedroom and bathtub are upstairs and you won't be allowed to take stairs by yourself any longer."

She shot a quick response even before hearing him out. "I don't need the bed; I sleep fine on the sofa and I can wash using the downstairs bathroom."

David took a deep breath and began counting to ten slowly in his head. "Grandma, that's not enough. Your glaucoma is worse, and it's dangerous for you to cook. You need to bathe, and the downstairs sink isn't adequate. You need help." He punctuated his final words with a firm gaze.

"I don't need help. I can wash myself with a cloth. And I told you I don't want strangers in my house."

Responsible for her humiliation and anger, David decided to try a different approach, one which would appeal to her need for socialization, and not make her feel helpless. "Wouldn't it be nice to have someone to help you with chores, and to talk with throughout the day?"

Her glare, like daggers, relayed her disagreement.

"I'm sorry, Grandma, you have no choice other than staying in the hospital, going to a retirement facility, or having someone come to your home."

"No. I want a second opinion. This doctor doesn't know what he's talking about." She struggled to sit up in her bed, fighting the wires and restraints that held the monitoring equipment in place.

The proud woman had been independent for most of her life. David, sitting by her bedside, stroked her forehead and long thinning hair. "Dr. Smith has been your doctor for years. You've always seen him."

"Oh, you." Grandma frowned from her squinty eyes to her pursed lips, like she'd bitten into a sour lemon. "I want another doctor's opinion."

Her command came without allowance for anything but obedience. Reluctantly, David agreed to find another doctor to meet with her the following afternoon. "Goodbye, I love you, I'll be back to see you tomorrow." David squeezer her shoulder, about her only body part not hindered by wires and gadgets. He waved and headed out to leave a message for Dr. Smith at his office. If Grandma wanted a second opinion that was her prerogative. Surely an associate of Dr. Smith could offer a second opinion, which would undoubtedly confirm the original diagnosis.

David didn't want to be deceitful, but he was entrusted with her care. He would do what was right even if it meant upsetting her and facing her fury. If he had an option, he wouldn't hesitate to turn the job over to someone else. Alicia had managed to stay mostly absent since Larry's death, especially since her attempt at cleaning failed. With questions still looming over him about Alicia's honesty and motives, it was probably best she remain absent. And, Nathan was still out of the country. David, once again, found himself at Dr. Smith's door to request an appointment with one of his associates.

Grandma scarcely finished her breakfast when Dr. Armado arrived in her room the next morning. She shooed David out with a dismissive hand flick. "I want to talk to the doctor alone."

David left, knowing full-well stories would be fabricated and embellished to portray her ability to care for herself and maneuver around the house, especially on the stairs. He also had confidence in Dr. Armado's ability to see through her fantasy. David had done all he could to lessen the risk of harm to his grandmother, or others. He already had tripped the fuse to her stove, forcing her to do all her cooking in the microwave and set back the temperature on the hot water tank. Besides Fred having a key, several neighbors and friends had emergency contact numbers. All throw rugs and footstools had been removed to avoid tripping. There was no doubt, for Edna's safety, it was time to take her living arrangements to a more controlled level. Grandma's frantic high-pitched voice penetrated the hospital door and spilled into the hall.

For the doctor's sake, David opened the door and poked his head inside. "Is everything okay here?" David approached her bedside, glancing at the doctor for a sign. Dr. Armado looked back with a slight shake of his head and a shrug. Her tense face informed him the news hadn't been well received.

"I don't want any help. I don't need it." Sharp, bitter words spewed like hot steam released from an old over-heated jalopy.

David flinched, half expecting something to be thrown at him.

"As I explained to your grandmother," the doctor fixed his gaze at David, "My recommendation is for a health-care worker to come to her home at least during the day." He watched his patient out of the corner of his eye, before continuing, "The alternative is to find a full-time care facility."

"Do you hear that, Grandma? You need to accept help." Sympathetic to her plight, David kept an even measured tone to not relay a sense of giving orders. "It's the best thing for you." She half sat, half lay in bed, draped in a hospital-issued blue, cotton robe, her eyes brimming and blinking away tears. David's impatience softened. The fragile, defeated woman made him regret the situation he imposed upon her. He reached for her hand. She pulled it away without a word. Her expression showed pain and anger. The doctor slipped out the door, leaving David alone to reconcile with Grandma and try to salvage the damage he had done to the relationship he worked so hard to forge. "Grandma, you know this is for the best. This way, you can still stay in your own home, and you can give me some peace of mind knowing you're safe." Her expression relaxed a bit, but she refused to indicate any indication she accepted his argument. "I'll interview some caregivers. Think of them as companions who will be there to offer friendship as well as assist you with grooming and such." David heard his condescending tone. He knew she hated it and regretted his tone as he bent to kiss her cheek.

Edna's face reddened. She tugged at the tubing restricting her movements. "You can't know what it feels like to be old." She adjusted her hospital gown and rolled to her side, facing away from David. "I will not have anyone see me naked."

Chapter 25

After three days in the hospital, Edna stood at her front door, clutching David's arm. She smiled as wide as she did the first time she'd seen her dorm room at the Normal School. The numbness in her right leg was gone, and her words came with ease and clarity. Struggling with her new stability cane, at David's insistence, Edna hobbled into the house, flipped on the light switch, and glanced around, smiling at the familiarity and independence it signified. She shivered and rubbed her arms for warmth for a moment before shuffling to the thermostat and cranking it up all the way.

"Where's Missy? Why isn't she here to greet me?" Edna 's eyes darted around searching for her lone faithful companion.

"Fred took her for a few days. Why don't we get you settled and then I'll walk next door and get Missy?" David placed her vintage box-shaped overnight case at the foot of the stairs.

Edna immediately grasped the handrail and started up the stairs.

"Wait, Grandma, let me help you." David rushed over and grabbed her arm.

Edna frowned and pulled her arm away. "I'm perfectly capable of taking a few steps myself. I'm not an invalid. I can put my own things away."

"You know what the doctor said about stairs. You're not supposed to take them by yourself. Your caregivers will be here to assist you during the day and get you to bed safely. Do you understand?"

Edna shot a glare at her grandson. "I don't need any help, and I don't like being talked to in that tone."

"I'm sorry, Grandma," David rose his voice, his tone firm. "You have to start listening to the doctor and the caregivers."

She couldn't believe how stubborn he could be. She scowled.

David grabbed her suitcase with his right hand, and using his left arm for support, he assisted her ascent. She stopped at the landing. Taking a few deep breaths, she paused and looked at her dried flowers, before continuing to the top of the stairs. Once in her room, David placed the overnight case on her chenille bedspread. Edna flipped the latch and removed her white bed jacket, camisole, and under-garments, hiding her lingerie from David's view. She pulled open the top two drawers of the white and gold bureau and nestled her things inside. Grabbing her other personal items, she took them into the bathroom and set them out. "I must have forgotten my hairbrush. It isn't here." Edna stepped into the bedroom. "David, we need to call the hospital. They have my hairbrush."

David double-checked the suitcase. "I'm sure we picked it up. I remember putting it in your bag."

Edna put her hands on her hips. "It's not here. Why don't you believe me?"

David looked around the room. "Did you put it away already?" He turned his back to her and went over to the dresser.

She eyed him with suspicion as he opened the top drawer.

"I didn't put my hairbrush in there." She reached across to stop his intrusion into her personal garments.

Avoiding any facial response, David held out the missing hairbrush. "Look, it must have gotten tangled in your clothing."

Without a word, Edna snatched the brush and stomped to the bathroom, banging the cane hard on the floor. Ambling out, she marched straight to the top of the stairs and stood at attention with a scowl, until David took her arm to assist her down the steps.

"We only have a few minutes before your new caregiver arrives. Let me get you some tea and then I'll go get Missy."

Seated on the sofa, Edna fluffed the throw pillows. "I still don't understand how come I have to pay for services I don't want or need."

"We've been through this already, Grandma. You need to have someone help you around the house and with the stairs so you don't hurt yourself." David patted her hand and walked out leaving her alone with her resentment.

A few minutes later the microwave beep signaled the water was heated. She sulked at the realization her freedom to do things her way, had been vanquished. Her life would no longer be the same. David placed the cup on the small end table. She scowled. Steam rose from the ceramic mug. David always made it too hot. She stirred it for a minute before grasping the cup by its handle and taking a sip. Sipping her steaming, yet satisfying, beverage, she envisioned her last bit of pride gobbled and gulped down into the belly of a big fish. She sunk into the sofa cushion as David disappeared out the door to fetch her only solace.

Moments later, the door banged closed and a high-pitched bark brought a smile. Missy rounded the corner and pounced onto Edna's lap, licking her hand. She stroked her dog, then buried her nose into her fur. "Gracious, has Missy been bathed?"

"Yes, Fred said he had her groomed."

Pulling away, Edna straightened. "I hope he isn't expecting me to pay for that."

Avoiding an outward display of frustration, David shook his head. "He did it as a welcome home gift. I'm sure he isn't expecting to be paid."

Edna cast her eyes to the floor. She used this ploy with her father as a young girl, often with a favorable response. "I don't want anyone in my home, and I don't need anyone. Besides, how do you expect me to pay for it?" She had saved prudently for years. Her income from her teacher's retirement and social security was sufficient, but there were bills to be paid every month. "I don't like throwing away my hard-earned money to pay people to do things I'm perfectly capable of doing myself." Somehow, she would find a way to prove to David she didn't need help.

"Don't worry, you have enough money. I've been over your books and you will be able to live comfortably for many years." David squatted next to her and patted her hand. "There's nothing for you to worry about."

Missy yapped, jumped down, and trotted to the door before it chimed.

"I'm sure this will work out fine for you." David headed toward the door.

Edna sat fixed and erect. She disliked David's condescending tone and him telling her about what she could afford. It wasn't his place. For a moment she regretted her decision to put him in charge of her affairs, after all, she was still able to think on her own. The doctor and her grandson could force her to have someone come into her home, but she was not going to enjoy it. Edna couldn't make out the murmurs from down the hall, but she knew they were talking about her. Agitated, she tapped her foot on the floor until David and a tall woman with greyish hair appeared in the room.

"Grandma, this is Mabel." David's eyes narrowed, hawk-like, awaiting her response.

She recognized the warning in his eyes, like she'd seen in her mother's eyes all those years ago, eyes that warned Edna to behave, eyes that didn't need words. She forced a smile before her gaze met Mabel's.

Mabel extended her hand to Edna. "Pleased to meet you, Mrs. Pearson."

Edna ignored the greeting as she looked her over. Not overly made up, but appearing professional. Judging by her large round stature, it appeared she at least knew how to cook, which was something Edna always favored.

"I've heard so much about you."

Edna's eyes shot an accusatory glance at David. She wondered what kind of talking had been done behind her back.

Mabel quickly continued. "Your grandson has told me how knowledgeable you are and what an interesting life you've led. I look forward to hearing some of your stories."

Still skeptical, Edna softened her gaze but sat firm still unwilling to befriend Mabel.

David left Edna seated on the sofa. "You'll have time to get to know each other after I show Mabel around." He led Mabel down the hall. He pointed out the bathroom then headed to the kitchen. Edna pushed herself off the sofa and trudged along behind them feeling the part she had so often in her childhood, the tag-along little sister on Pearl's dates. She didn't appreciate being left out of the conversation and certainly didn't appreciate them talking about her. Following the perpetrators of her misery into the kitchen, Edna stood hands on hips, listening.

"Make sure she knows you're in charge of the meals and cooking." David handed Mabel a folder.

Edna glared at David and Mabel as they swung around, caught in their plotting. It had only been a few minutes, and Edna was already a non-being in her own home.

David led Mabel upstairs. Edna knew David would scold her if she attempted the stairs and he didn't invite her to join them. She tottered shakily back to the living room with her cane, and sat down, bringing her hands to her warm flushed face. Missy trotted behind and pounced on the sofa next to her. Edna stroked her best friend and whispered how she was lucky to have the little dog, the only thing in her world that hadn't begun ordering her around.

Returning, Mabel smiled as she sat next to Edna. "Well, the setup is workable, but the stairs and bathroom are going to be challenging. I'm sure we can handle it. We'll do fine, won't we, Edna?"

Determined to set the ground rules early, and not appreciating Mabel's humiliating tone, Edna glared at this stranger in her home. She clipped her words. "I prefer Mrs. Pearson."

"Remember, we talked about the stairs, Grandma?" David's eyes narrowed with a direct gaze at her. "You must not take the stairs unless Mabel or your other help is here. Mabel will make sure you're in bed for the night, and Sarah will be here first thing in the morning to get you dressed and make your breakfast. You can take the stairs only after Sarah arrives in the morning to help you. Do you understand?"

Edna's anger swelled, but she knew better than to say anything now.

David's tone softened. "I've got to get going."

His comment brought her anger to the surface again.

"I told you I could only stay for the afternoon."

Emotions engulfed her as they had when she was younger and she had to say goodbye to her father as he left for the week to go to work on Vashon Island.

"I'll see you soon. I promise." He leaned over and kissed her cheek. A moment later he was gone.

At the sound of pots and pans clanging in the kitchen, Edna pushed off the sofa and marched to the kitchen to find Mabel rummaging through the cupboards. Frustrated, Edna stamped her cane on the floor. "What are you doing?" She resented the intrusion into her home, especially her kitchen.

"I'm going to make us some dinner. That's what I was hired to do."

Hired. The word struck Edna like a blow. A grown woman, independent for her entire life treated like a child, who required a paid babysitter. "Well." Edna stormed over to the stove. "I've been cooking most of my life and have even won awards for my skills. If I need any help, I'll ask." Spying a grocery bag on the counter, she reached into the bag and pulled out some canned goods and bread. "What's this? This is not the type of bread I buy." Lettuce, onions, tomatoes, apples, and broccoli spilled from plastic bags. "I prefer to buy my produce from the farmer's market. It's much fresher, you know?" Edna inspected the tomato, rolling it around in her hand, to ensure it was not overripe, before placing it back on the counter.

Mabel took her hand. "Maybe next time I go to the market you can come and help me select the produce." Her smile warmed. "Do you like cornbread and chili?"

Edna sniffed the air. Her stomach churned from the smell of the strong onion and garlic. Chili wasn't particularly to her liking, but the fresh cornbread sounded good. She resigned herself to the fact as long as Mabel was there, the house was no longer hers. Besides, she would make what she wanted once Mabel was gone.

Early the next morning, Edna woke with a sense of dread. Mabel had reminded her a different caregiver, Sarah, would be arriving at nine o'clock to make breakfast and do some laundry and cleaning. Edna didn't want a different girl. She didn't want any girl. It wasn't fair having to pay for services she didn't want or need. She pouted as she pulled on a beige linen top with orange poppies and purple forget-me-nots. She grabbed the brown knit slacks from the wooden garment drying rack by the window, stepped into her slippers, grabbed her cane and shuffled to the stairway. She paused remembering David's orders. Straightening her posture and her resolve, she gripped the stair rail tightly, and using the cane for balance, she stepped down the stairs. With each step her confidence rose, further confirming she didn't need anyone to assist her. Safely reaching the kitchen, she filled a pan with water for her oatmeal and spoke to Missy who sat awaiting her morning food. *Hmmph.* I'm not going to wait until nine for my breakfast. I'm hungry now." She carried the pan to the stove and turned the front knob. She heated some water for tea in the microwave and dropped a slice of bread in the toaster. Hearing the toaster click down, Missy bounded around the corner and yapped for her morning treat. Edna hunched over and stroked the dog. A few minutes later, the water sat in the pan still unsettled, with no indication the water had even started to heat. Edna fumbled with the knob, then tried the others. She stomped. The stove was broken. Mabel must have broken it last night. Edna bristled, now she'd have to make her mush in the microwave. She hated how it always tasted gooey and sticky cooked that way. The toast popped and Edna smiled at Missy as she tore off a corner and held it out. In begging stance, Missy greedily snapped at the toast. Edna barely had time to finish eating before the doorbell rang. She glanced at the clock. At least Sarah was prompt. Edna hid the evidence of her dishes in the dishwasher before scurrying to the door at the sound of the knob turning. Edna pursed her lips at the realization complete strangers had keys to her house.

Sarah looked surprised when Edna opened the door. "Oh, I see you are already up and about, Mrs. Pearson. I'm Sarah. I'm happy to meet you. Just to remind you though, I'll be by every morning this week to help you get dressed and assist you with the stairs."

Edna eyed her, waiting for the lecture she guessed would follow about the stairs. Instead, Sarah smiled and extended her hand. Edna looked at the dark purple nail polish which adorned Sarah's long nails. Edna shook her head. Sarah looked barely out of school, maybe twenty-one at the most, her hair with a bad dye job, pulled back into a childish ponytail. She didn't even look professional in her tight jeans and tight-fitting top. Edna stood firm in the doorway. She couldn't imagine this young girl having much experience caring for anyone, let alone being a certified nurse assistant or whatever David had called her.

Sarah pushed the door wider and slid past Edna with authority. She set her purse and a folder on the dining table. Missy bounded around barking at her ankles. "Your grandson told me you had a dog." Sarah squatted and patted the dog's back. "How are you, Tessy?"

Missy eyed Sarah, took a few steps backward, and growled.

Edna frowned. "Her name is Missy, not Tessy."

Sarah shrugged off the correction, grabbed her things, and walked into the kitchen. "Your grandson has set a schedule for cleaning, laundry, and shopping. First, let's have some breakfast." Sarah looked around. She turned the front knob on the stove, waited a few seconds, then turned it off.

Edna crossed her arms, watching for a response from Sarah regarding the stove.

Instead, Sarah looked through the papers in her folder then smiled weakly at Edna. "Why don't you relax and have a seat in the living room? I'll look over our schedule and let you know when breakfast is ready."

Edna didn't want breakfast. She was satisfied, but she couldn't very well tell Sarah. And she certainly didn't need a schedule. She wasn't one of the children she used to teach. She turned grudgingly toward the living room and sulked on the sofa. Missy pounced onto her lap. Edna punched the buttons on the television remote and flipped through the blurry images dancing across the screen. She had forgotten to have David check the T.V. "The darn thing never works right." She clicked it off, sat back, and listened to Sarah banging around in the kitchen. Feeling helpless, Edna fidgeted with some magazines and straightened the framed photos on the end table before the smell of bacon wafting into the room brought an unintended smile. David must have told Sarah how much she liked bacon. Not one to be chased away, Edna stomped back to the kitchen and peeked in. "Is the stove working?" Edna eyed Sarah.

Not looking up, Sarah mumbled it was working fine. Edna glared at Sarah's back. Someone was up to something.

Seated at the table, Sarah wrapped something around Edna's neck. "This should help keep your lovely shirt clean."

Edna looked down at the brown dish towel pinned like a bib draped in front of her. She buried her face in her hands and struggled to fight off the burning anger and shame that simmered. She wasn't a helpless toddler just learning to eat. Her plate looked appetizing, scrambled eggs and bacon, but the bacon wasn't crispy like she preferred it and how her mother always made it when she was young.

Edna pushed the food around with her fork although she knew her mother hated it when she played with her food.

"You're not eating. Is everything all right?"

"Yes, Mother- I'm just not hungry. May I go to my room now?"

"What's the matter? I thought breakfast was your favorite meal. David said bacon was your favorite."

Edna closed her eyes to hold back the tears. Daddy hated it when she cried so Mother had encouraged her to try not to cry so easily. "I'm sorry, Mother."

Firm, comforting arms draped across Edna's shoulders. "It's okay, Edna, I'm not your mother. My name is Sarah. I'm your new friend."

The concern in the soft voice made Edna feel better. Struggling for self-control, Edna raised her eyes from the plate. It wasn't her mother squatted next to her. Confused by the stranger, Edna's tears released like a spring downpour.

After breakfast, Sarah ran around the house like it was hers. She wiped and dusted, and rearranged things to her liking. But Edna was certainly not going to stand for the intrusion. Sarah went to the living room window and drew the blinds back. Edna squinted to shield her eyes from the brightness of the day. Sarah bent over Edna's gold metal planter filled with African violets. "These are incredibly healthy violets, but it looks like they need a little water." Sarah removed a pot from the planter box.

Edna scurried over and snatched it away. "I can take care of my plants myself. They have to be watered from underneath, you know." Edna placed the pot back in its proper place. "You get the water, I'll water them." She fingered the delicate purple and pink blossoms, plucking the dead ones between her thumb and forefinger, and dropping them inside the planter. Sarah returned with the water and Edna demonstrated how to correctly pour the water into the tray underneath. "This is how the watering must be done." She stared at Sarah, assuring her directions were clearly understood.

As the day wore on, though she didn't want to admit it, Edna enjoyed her time with Sarah, sharing stories about her family, her many friends, and her numerous travels especially to Thailand and Korea. Sarah listened with genuine interest. Still, Edna should have expected it was too good to last. At eight o'clock Sarah announced it was time to get ready for bed.

"I'm not a child, and I never go to bed this early." Edna's rage spewed like steam from her tea kettle. She sat resolutely on the sofa to no avail.

Sarah approached and took her hands. "I'm sorry, but I need to leave at nine o'clock, and your grandson wants you in bed for the night before I leave." She supported Edna under the arm and helped her up the stairs.

Edna scowled with each step until they reached her bedroom.

"Okay, where are your pajamas?" Sarah looked about and headed for Edna's dresser.

Edna hurried over. "I'm perfectly capable of getting them myself."

"I'm sorry, of course." Sarah stepped back. "Your grandson wasn't sure if you were using protection at bedtime or not. Do I need to get anything for you?"

"Protection?"

"You know, for accidents in your sleep."

"Oh, you." Edna fumed. How could she understand? Edna sat on the end of her bed.

"My instructions indicate tonight is your shower night." Sarah reached out and began to pull Edna's shirt over her head.

Edna jerked away. Her shirt, free of her arms, hung draped on her shoulders. Edna covered her chest with her arms. "I don't need your help. I'm not an invalid."

"It's okay, Mrs. Pearson, I'm used to this type of work. There's absolutely no need to feel self-conscious about it."

Edna planted herself firmly on the mattress. Of course, she's used to it. She was not the one being undressed like a small child. She wondered how Sarah would feel if she were in her place. Sarah walked into the bathroom, leaving Edna alone, half-naked on the bed. Her sweaty palms trembled as she wiped the tears from her hot cheeks.

Chapter 26

During the next two months, Edna refused to let those girls think they were in charge. It was still her house, and she was still the boss. She only needed to convince David to talk with the girls and explain things. When David called on Sunday evening, her frustration boiled over. "I don't like it when they send different girls all the time. Just when I get used to one girl another one takes her place."

"I know Grandma, but you have to be patient with them, they're trying their best. Different caregivers keep coming because you scare them off. Also, they are not able to work seven days a week."

What did David know? He wasn't there to see what went on. "I still don't understand why I can't take care of myself. I have to show those girls how to do simple things like vacuuming. I like my carpet vacuumed all in the same direction. My dishes are never put away in the right places, and most of them don't know how to cook properly. My morning girl doesn't even know how to make mush. Even after I showed her, she still doesn't make it right."

"You're going to have to get used to some things not being done exactly as you like them."

Edna pouted. Why should she have to get used to things she didn't like. It was her house. "How come my stove doesn't work for me?" Edna sat erect in her rocker, gripping the phone receiver, determined to get answers. It always worked for the girls who came. She knew David had done something to the stove so she couldn't use it. Though David promised to look at it when he visited the next time, she knew better. She glared at the phone receiver, wishing her glare could travel across the line so David would know she was on to him. She resented the cruelty of aging. She wasn't a spiteful woman, but everyone was treating her like a child. She needed to show David and her caregivers she didn't need their help. She wanted her independence. Unable to receive any satisfaction from him, she cut the conversation short.

Determined to show everyone she could take care of herself; Edna woke Monday morning with renewed confidence. She dressed, paying particular attention to pin her hair neatly. At least Mabel was coming this morning. Edna liked the way Mabel let her talk about the old days. Some of the girls about talked Edna's ear off with silliness about the latest shows on television and the newest music, for which Edna had no patience.

If she hurried, she'd have almost an hour to herself before she surrendered her freedom to whatever schedule was planned for her. Edna slid her feet into her slippers, and ignoring her instructions, she started down the stairs feeling stronger than she had in some while. Halfway down, her legs buckled. She tumbled to the bottom. Landing face down, her right side burned with pain. Her head pounded. She tasted blood on her lip, and the harsh carpet fibers scratched her cheek. She glanced at the short distance between her and the front door, knowing it would be some time before Mabel arrived. Missy trotted to her side. Edna moved her left arm and stroked her dog's fur. With a deep breath, Edna pushed off the ground, wincing at the pain that shot down her side. Giving up, she fell to the ground. Her mind whirled and went dark. When she opened her eyes again, she couldn't understand what was happening. Her surroundings blurred in a whirl of activity.

"What are you doing? Please stop." Edna's voice broke. She looked at the figure that loomed over her.

"It's okay. I'm going to check your vital signs." The male figure bent over her and unfastened her top button.

"No, stop." Edna flung her arms about, waving off his attempt to remove her blouse. Her heart pounded with increasing fierceness. She struggled to bring her arms to her chest and protect her honor.

"Calm down. It's okay. I need to see if you are injured."

Though his voice sounded soothing, Edna knew better. A man is not to be trusted. Jacob's words echoed in her ears from long ago while he held her arms with a tight grip and he tried to insult her virtue. *Damn it, Edna, we're engaged now. You can't be a prude forever.*

"Please, God." Edna pleaded and begged as the male figure groped her body seeking to touch her warm bosom. Numb, she prayed silently for strength. *"I can't be true to myself and give in to the pleasures of the flesh."* Edna closed her eyes to block out the image of violence against her.

A soft hand stroked her forehead. Calm now, Edna opened her eyes. Someone was bent over her, only it wasn't Jacob. Edna lifted her arm to wipe away tears, confused by the stiff gray nylon cuff that encircled her upper arm.

"Where's Jacob? Did you find him? He tried to hurt me."

"No, Mrs. Pearson, there's nobody named Jacob here. Your caregiver found you at the bottom of the stairs. You apparently fell. My name is Ethan, I'm with the Fire Department. We're just going to check you out to make sure you're okay."

Mabel squatted next to her with a cool washcloth and held it to the rug burn on her cheek. "You're going to be all right."

Edna allowed the cold wet compress to help mute the stinging pain. It didn't help ease the humiliation of being nearly forced into a physical relationship against her will by the man she loved. The man whose ring she wore and vowed to marry.

Lying safely on the sofa, Missy yapped and ran around in circles at her feet.

"You know you're not supposed to take the stairs alone." Mabel lifted Edna's head and placed a small crocheted throw pillow underneath the back of her neck.

Edna's eyes and nasal passages burned as she fought off the emotion. She had been defeated. David and the girls had won. She closed her eyes and prayed for patience.

Chapter 27

For the four months following her stroke, any happiness Edna found in life faded more each day like the blossoms in her garden wilting from the extreme summer weather. Her days were now something to get through rather than lived. Barbara's visits became infrequent as she spent more time caring for her husband. Alicia and Lacey stopped coming by long ago after the silverware disappeared. Different caregivers came and went before she could even get used to them. Only Mabel remained a constant presence, a presence Edna had come to welcome in her life. Even David's visits became less frequent and she yearned to see him again.

"After the holidays, we'll have you over again." He told her over the phone.

"What about Nathan? Have you heard from him? He said he'd be home for my birthday, and that's coming up next month."

"He called a few weeks ago, it looks like his transfer has been delayed."

Edna wasn't surprised, she'd experienced such delays with Jacob's enlistment, and Larry's return to the states with Kora-Lee was put off several times.

Depressed from hearing about Nathan's postponed return, Edna let go of her frustration when David called to invite her to his home again for the following weekend. Thrilled to once more be included in his family, and escape the rigid schedules which her girls insisted upon, Edna started packing her things as soon as he called. With the unusually hot weather, even touching a hundred degrees at times, made her home unbearable without air conditioning, she welcomed the cool reprieve from the other side of the state. Finally, the weekend arrived. She sat in her over-stuffed beige rocker, waiting for David.

Like always, Missy announced David's arrival before the doorbell buzzed. Edna shifted in anticipation on the chair as Mabel's footsteps scampered to answer the door.

Edna waited patiently for David to come into the living room. Mabel held the overnight bag. "Here you go, I think I have enough clothes packed for the next two days." She turned to David. "I wasn't sure if she needed a dress for any special occasion."

"Nah. Our oldest daughter, Rachel is coming home for the weekend and I'll be taking her back to school on Sunday. We thought it would be nice to have Grandma over again and give her and you a break." David grabbed Edna's cane and handed it to her. She leaned forward and pushed off her chair as David reached his arm out for support. Walking a few steps to the closet, Edna's joints cracked a bit. She winced in discomfort but was relieved to get her legs moving.

"I can't forget my coat." Edna yanked on the hanger holding her winter coat. The metal hanger clanged to the floor. "I can't reach my hat." Edna fumbled with the cane as she tried to reach the shelf.

Mabel stepped in and found Edna's fur hat. She helped Edna into her coat and placed the hat on her head, carefully tucking her pinned hair inside.

"Don't forget to check all the lights and doors before you leave. And turn the heat down." Edna instructed Mabel before she pushed her way out the door with David following behind. Stepping outside for the first time in several days, Edna was surprised how much the weather had shifted. She loved fall and the welcomed cooler temperatures. But the chilly air stung her ever-thinning skin and she shivered at the thought of the impending winter. Gold and brown poplar and alder leaves already littered the ground around her complex. Edna adjusted her hat, pulling it down further over her ears as she walked to the car, her breath leaving a hint of lingering fog.

Once seated, David stretched the seat belt across her. She shifted her weight feeling uncomfortable due to the restraint that held her chest and body tied to the seat. "I can't move with this thing. Why do I have to wear it anyway?"

Reaching across, David removed her shoulder belt, slipping it over her head, and tucking it behind her. "It's the law." He closed her car door, placed her bag and cane in the back seat and climbed in. He turned on the radio and twisted the knob until he settled on a station playing music that didn't rock the car with blaring lyrics and loud noise.

"Thank you. That's much better." Edna scooted forward slightly and twisted her torso. Relaxed and pleased to be on the way, Edna settled in for the long drive. The barren landscape spread as far as she could see, but Edna liked the dryness eastern Washington offered. It had been her home since her children were youngsters, going on sixty years now. Her heart ached as she remembered her children, her babies, now both dead. She turned her thoughts to her great-grandchildren. "How are Emily and Rachel doing?"

"They're fine. They're looking forward to seeing you again. I'll be driving Rachel back to Central on Monday when I bring you back home. You can see how much your old university has changed since you went to school there."

Edna narrowed her gaze, confused by David's comment. "What are you talking about? I never went to Central. I went to the state Normal School, in Ellensburg. I told you all about that." She shook her head. How could David get things so mixed up?

David laughed, "Central Washington University is in Ellensburg, it's the same college that used to be known as the Normal School, back when it was only a teachers' college."

Edna turned, puckered her brow, and gazed out the window. "Imagine. Well, I should think I knew that, that's what it was named when Bernice attended school there." She smiled, looking forward to learning more about her great-granddaughters, maybe forge a closer bond than she had managed with Lorraine or Alicia, and likely never would with Lacey.

On their arrival, the aroma of sage and rosemary floated to the front porch from the fan's exhaust. Edna's stomach growled, and she flinched in embarrassment. When the door opened, Edna brightened, seeing Rachel and Emily race down the stairs.

"Hi, Grandma."

"My gracious. I had forgotten how tall you young lasses were." She glanced across to David. "Goodness, they do take after their father, don't they?" Noticing her great-granddaughters looked like their father pleased her, and knowing Rachel was following in her footsteps by attending Central Washington University, pleased her even more. She looked forward to teaching the girls some skills she was taught by her mother and grandmother.

Jean motioned toward the kitchen. "Dinner's almost ready." Rachel and Emily went to gather plates and utensils to set the table.

With Edna freshened up and rested after the long drive, David pulled out a chair at the end of the table for her. "You're the guest of honor today, Grandma. You get to sit in my chair."

Scanning the table, Edna looked at Jean. "I must remember to give you my real silver sometime. I never use silver anymore and it would be much more formal for such occasions. I used to enjoy so many formal meals when I was a military wife."

Jean carried out a roasted chicken on an oval platter and placed it in the center of the table. "Real silver would be nice for special guests, like you. Did you find yours?"

"Oh no, of course not. Barbara helped me with the insurance company forms. They were so nice and sent me a check for the set that was stolen. I bought a new set."

Rachel and Emily came in with bowls of potatoes and green beans to pass around. Edna had always delighted in a well-set table. At the sight of the crisp golden bird ready for slicing, her stomach gurgled again and she blushed. When everyone was seated, Jean bowed her head and led the family in grace.

"That was lovely, Dear. I am not used to such habits with Larry's family." Edna recalled the many meals shared with Larry and his family where she always felt like an intruder. She shook off the past, refusing to acknowledge all the things missed over the years with her grandsons. "I wish Nathan could join us. He said he was being transferred. I can't wait to see him again."

"He's still hoping to be here this Christmas." David reached for a serving bowl and plopped a mound of mashed potatoes on Edna's plate. He passed the potatoes around then reached for the gravy, which he knew Grandma loved, and ladled the thick golden sauce into the well Edna made with her spoon.

"*Mmmm.*" Edna's eyes misted watching David's family, her family, across the table filling their plates. She ate with a robust appetite, taking seconds on the potatoes and gravy, and relishing the warm biscuits with butter. "These are nice Dear, sometime I'll have to show you how to make my baking powder biscuits. It's a shame, women today don't spend so much time baking as in my generation. I wish I could see well enough to bake pies again like I did when I was younger." Edna turned her attention to Rachel and Emily. "Do you girls help your mother bake? Mother taught me to bake when I was only seven."

Rachel and Emily exchanged looks. "Sometimes. Today we made the chocolate pie. It was easy, pudding and whipped topping."

Edna frowned. "Mother insisted both my sister and I learn to cook. Her lessons have served me well. I don't think much of the short cuts they have these days, like pre-baked pie crusts and canned fillings, they're not as good as fresh-baked. I could teach you young ladies a thing or two about baking sometime." Edna paused and shook her head. "I tried to teach Lorraine and Alicia how to bake like my mother taught me, but they weren't interested."

David glanced at his daughters; Edna saw him wink at them as they rose and carried dishes to the sink. "Maybe Grandma can teach you something about cooking before you leave for school on Saturday?"

"Would you teach me to make an apple pie, Grandma?"

Rachel's request surprised Edna. She had become accustomed to youngsters not being respectful to their elders these days. It was disheartening. "Of course. But you know I don't see so well these days. You'll have to help me."

"Can you teach me too?" Emily took a break from rinsing off dishes.

After losing Larry's family, Edna felt a hole in her heart. Now that void had been filled with her new family's love and acceptance. Edna smiled and wiped the dampness from her eyes.

The next morning, Edna woke before dawn. She blinked laboring to see through the darkened room. Flustered by the unfamiliar surroundings she took in a few deep breaths. As her mind cleared, her mood brightened. She was at David's for the weekend, visiting with her grandson's family. Pushing herself up, a sharp pain shot down her back. She wasn't used to such a firm mattress. She rose and gathered her grooming supplies then scuffled to the bathroom. She washed her face, and combed and pinned her hair up. At the bottom of the stairs, she took a deep breath, pondering her next step. As she was about to grip the handrail, David called down to her.

"Grandma, I thought I heard you moving around." Meeting her at the bottom he aided her assent. In the kitchen, her mouth watered at the strong rich aroma of fresh coffee.

Jean stood at the coffee pot. "Do you want some breakfast?"

Edna stared at the coffee pot. "I usually prefer tea in the morning, but I don't want to be difficult. Coffee and toast are fine. Do you have any jam for my toast?"

"I like my coffee strong" David warned with a raised cup.

"If that's how you like it, strong coffee is fine with me too, Dear." She took a seat as David carried a cup of coffee over to her. She puckered her lips at the first sip and frowned as David chuckled. She held the cup out to him. "This is much too strong."

Sipping her freshly-brewed tea and buttered toast with jam, Edna smiled when she noticed her granddaughters.

"Do you want to make an apple pie this morning, Grandma? Mom bought a bunch just for a pie."

"In my day, we mostly made apple pies from a tree in our yard." Edna gobbled her toast. "But I suppose these days things are different. I'm afraid I won't be much help with peeling the apples." She held out her hands, fingers knotted and gnarled from age and arthritis. "That's okay, we can peel." Rachel reached for the first apple to peel while Emily held a knife ready to slice. Jean measured out the Crisco and flour. "Do you have a pastry blender?"

Jean shook her head and handed her two knives. "Sorry, I always cut the shortening in with these. Will they do?'

Eyeing the two knives for a moment before accepting them, Edna fumbled with the coordinated effort required to successfully reduce the butter to small pieces. Frustrated, she handed the knives back to Jean. "I'm afraid I'm not as nimble-fingered as I used to be."

Edna sat on the stool at the island and watched the flurry of activity. "Remember to make the crust flaky, only add half the shortening at a time, and don't forget to use ice-cold water."

Jean held up the rolling pin. "Would you like to roll out the pie crust, Grandma?"

Instead, Edna offered to instruct Emily on how to best complete the task. When the crust was in place in the pie pan, Edna proudly poured the sliced apples mixed with sugar and cinnamon, into the completed crust while Rachel plopped the top crust in place. "I like my pie a la mode. I hope you have ice cream."

The sweet smell of apples still filled the entire kitchen and main floor of the house after the dinner hour when Jean set the dessert plates on the table.

Edna's mouth watered. "It looks exactly like the pies I used to make. Did I ever tell you I won quite a few ribbons in my day for my baking?"

"Maybe we can see some of your awards sometime."

"Are you looking forward to seeing your old college again, Grandma?" Rachel asked as she cut the first slice of pie and plopped on a generous scoop of vanilla ice cream before she handed the plate to Edna.

Edna didn't understand. "I didn't know we were going to my old college?"

"I'm heading to college tomorrow morning. I'm going to Central. Your old alma mater."

Puzzled, Edna tipped her head in contemplation, then brightened, remembering what David had told her. She nodded her acknowledgment. "Yes, in my day we called it the normal school. You study hard and don't party too hard."

"Have you been back to the campus since you graduated?" Rachel spoke between bites of warm apple pie with ice cream melting down the sides.

"My Bernice went to college in Ellensburg for a time too, so I visited with her often before she died. She wanted to be a reporter. I think Ellensburg is a lovely town. I can't wait to see it again. It's been so long."

Edna awoke from a restless night and glanced out the window. Smoked hickory and sweet maple scents floated into her bedroom, reminding her how mother took such pleasure in caring for her youngest daughter. Looking across the small room Edna noticed the silhouette of her suitcase on the chair. Excited at finally going off to college after so much planning and saving, she glanced at the illuminated dial of the clock on the nightstand and pulled it closer so she could read the blurry numbers. The bright sun shone through the open blinds informing her it was later than it should be. She couldn't miss the train on this important day. Frustrated, Edna trembled as she dressed in her best dress. She hurried to the bathroom and fumbled with her hairpins until she managed to pin her hair atop her head. Her joints hurt and she found it difficult to climb the stairs as she gripped the handrail firmly for support, and followed the aroma of breakfast into the kitchen.

"Good morning, Grandma. We didn't know you were awake. I see you managed to get upstairs by yourself, but we'd rather you wait for help." Jean was poised over the stove with a spatula. "Are you hungry?"

"Yes. You know I always prefer a hearty breakfast on such important days." Edna didn't understand why Jean was making a fuss about the stairs. She made her way to the table where Jean placed a plate of pancakes and bacon in front of her.

Edna buttered her hotcakes and poured thick syrup over them. She usually loved breakfast, but after a few bites, her stomach rebelled. "We have to hurry or I'll miss the train. How come nobody woke me?" Feeling anxious, she twirled a few strands of long hair that had fallen loose in front of her eyes.

"What train?" Rachel raised her eyebrows.

"The Milwaukee and Pacific. Papa said it leaves promptly at eight in the morning from Union Station for Ellensburg."

"Grandma, there's no train." Rachel cocked her head and looked at her. "We're driving to Ellensburg. I don't need to be there until early afternoon. Then Dad will take you home after that."

Edna's heart beat faster. Her breathing quickened as panic crept in. "Afternoon? That's too late. I'll never get to my freshman orientation in time." She noticed confusion on the faces of the others who had gathered to her side.

Rachel squatted in front of Edna. Taking her hands, Rachel looked into Edna's eyes. "Grandma, what are you talking about? There's no orientation. I started school in the fall, five months ago."

"You don't understand." Edna could hear her voice shake as she directed her anger at Rachel.

David came in and sat down next to his grandmother. "What's wrong, Grandma? You've hardly touched your breakfast. You've always loved pancakes."

Edna looked at her plate, the hotcakes now soggy and running into her bacon. "I'm going to miss you and Mother."

David took her hands in his. "Your mother's been dead a long time, I'm your grandson, not your father."

Jolted by the words, Edna looked around. Everyone sat staring at her.

"It's okay, Grandma. It's been a busy weekend." Rachel led her to the living room and handed her a couple of copies of her mother's cooking magazines. "I'll finish packing so we can leave sooner."

"Okay, I don't want to be late." Nervous about the trip to Ellensburg, Edna skimmed through the pages of the magazines with enticing photos of pasta, salads, and desserts but she found it difficult to focus on the reading material. She turned to see David place her brocade overnight bag by the door next to a plastic laundry basket and a knapsack. She pushed off the sofa, relieved. "Is it time to go?"

"Yes, we can leave now if you like. Rachel's just about ready and I'm sure you're eager to see how much the college has changed through the years."

Edna rose from the sofa. "We have to hurry. The president of the college has agreed to meet me and the other girls at the train station, and personally show us to our dormitories."

David helped her slide into her navy quilted coat. "Grandma, there's no meeting with the college president today."

Her pulse quickened as she fought her growing frustration. "What do you know?" Her voice rose, exasperated. "The president always meets the incoming students."

"That was a long time ago. It's your great-granddaughter, Rachel, who is going to college now."

The words confused her momentarily. She studied the mature slender young woman next to her, her granddaughter. She remembered the photograph book David sent her. Photos of a lifetime of which she was not a part raced through her mind. Photos of small children, her great-grandchildren, growing up. "Rachel's going to college now, not me?" She remembered the baccalaureate she'd gone to a while back. It seemed such a short time ago she herself had said goodbye to her own parents. Now she stood at the door saying goodbye to Jean and Emily to take her great-granddaughter to Ellensburg to begin her own college life.

On the road, Rachel leaned forward and tapped Edna's shoulder. "Grandma, tell me about when you went to college."

Edna struggled against the restraint of the shoulder harness to look over her shoulder. "Oh, my gracious, I'm not sure when that was. I imagine it's been some time, hasn't it? I was a teacher you know, my entire life. What's all this talk about college anyway?"

"I'm going to Central Washington. Dad says that's where you went, back when it was known as the normal school."

David looked across the seat and took Edna's hand. "Why don't you tell Rachel what it was like when you went there?"

Edna straightened in her seat feeling important. Memories of her youth flashed like the old talkies through her mind. She recalled her eagerness to see the dormitory room and meet her roommate. "I hadn't had a roommate since I was seven and shared a room with my sister, Pearl. She was ten years older than me and moved out shortly after I was born. I remember my first day at the normal school. I wasn't prepared for what the dorm mother said when she introduced herself and welcomed me." Edna chuckled at the memory so clear in her mind as if it was yesterday. "She told me my roommate had come down with the measles."

Rachel laughed. "What did you do?"

"I spent a few nights sleeping on a lumpy mattress out in the hall, alone." Her voice drifted off and the feeling of loneliness crept in again. She glanced at David, forced a smile, and closed her eyes, resting her head against the back of the seat.

Rachel leaned in. "I bet the dorm rooms look a lot like they did when you went to school. They probably haven't changed much. I can't wait for you to meet my roommate. Her name's Jessica, she's really nice."

Two hours later, David pulled the car into the large lot closest to the rows of red brick buildings that formed the hub of primarily freshman dormitories. Rachel clambered out of the car and opened Edna's door. Edna's stomach churned as she stepped out and looked around at the strange surroundings. "I don't know this place. Is this the right place? It looks so much bigger than it did when I attended."

Rachel and David urged her on. "It's been a long time. I'm sure they've added lots of buildings over the past seventy years." Rachel grabbed her duffle bag and pushed open the heavy wooden entry door, stepping inside. Edna and David followed. The large window at the end of the hall cast rays of light into the hallway littered with signs announcing meetings and posters promoting upcoming events. Rachel led the way past a small sitting room. A large television screen flashed a scene of a woman dancing in tight-fitting pants and a short top while long-haired musicians playing guitars and drums banged out loud grating music. A group of young men and women sat on the overstuffed couch and floor, cramming popcorn into their mouths. Before they stepped into the elevator, Edna looked around, trying to take in the surroundings. The atmosphere of noise and salty snacks was nothing like she remembered. After a short ride, the elevator doors opened to commotion coming from the dorm rooms on both sides of her. A few students were heading down the hall, bundled warmly and carrying backpacks. Edna turned to look at a boy with longish jet- black hair and a large earring stretching his lobe. She sighed. It was not at all like she expected. She couldn't understand why a boy was in the girl's dorm. This would not be allowed in her day. Rachel inserted a key and turned the knob to open her dorm room. Edna glanced around the room. It was small and she wondered how all of her things would fit. Edna was confused by the unfamiliar girl who stood staring at her.

"Hey, Jessica." Rachel stepped inside and put her laundry basket on the bed. "Grandma, this is my roommate, Jessica."

Edna instinctively stepped back when Jessica approached to greet her. The dorm mother had assured her that her roommate's disease wasn't contagious, but Edna was still hesitant. Slowly, she approached to meet her first roommate.

Chapter 28

Even with extensive engineering experience, sometimes David's head throbbed from the intense attention required to perform his job. It was nearly quitting time and the entire surface of his work desk lay cluttered with wiring diagrams and computer runs. The phone rang, forcing him to click his thinking on hold. He hated interruptions, especially late in the day. Frustrated, he snatched the phone. "Hello."

"David. It's Fred, Edna's neighbor."

David shifted in his seat. His heart skipped a beat or two. He held his breath and dropped all focus from his work.

"I stopped in to visit your grandmother this afternoon. She was outside weeding in the rain with only a short-sleeved shirt and socks, but no shoes. She got angry and began hitting me when I told her I'd come to take Missy out for a walk. I don't think she recognized me."

David's mind raced with memories of his grandmother's confusion during her visit only weeks earlier. He remembered his conversation with Dr. Smith about Alzheimer's progression. "Is she okay?" His chest tightened.

"I called 911. The paramedics insisted on taking her to Good Samaritan. I thought I should call you."

Thanking Fred for his concern, David returned the phone to its cradle. He groaned, pushing aside the paperwork on his desk. Pulling out his cell phone, David doodled on a yellow legal pad as he hit the stored number for the hospital. The emergency room nurse took his name and promised to try to locate Dr. Smith. David listened to the recorded message repeating over and over and over how they knew his time was valuable while continuing to keep him waiting on the line. His neck tensed, but he used the time to make notes of the questions to ask the doctor when he finally answered. David's patience was all but exhausted when Dr. Smith finally picked up.

"Sorry to keep you waiting, David. I just left your grandmother. I have her file here. She's going to be fine. She's likely suffered another mini-stroke, but I don't think there's any permanent damage."

After tolling his head in circles a few times, David breathed a little easier.

"I believe the real concern for us now is her Alzheimer's symptoms are progressing. She's presently very confused."

David continued to doodle on the yellow note pad. "As you warned me during our last visit, I've noticed she's been having increased occasions where she seems to be living in the past."

"That's one of the primary indicators. You need to know, as it progresses it's also likely she'll fail to recognize you, or other family members, and sometimes Alzheimer's sufferers get violent. There are support groups for family members of patients suffering from Alzheimer's. If you're interested, I can put you in touch with one."

David cringed at the thought. Gathering with others affected by Alzheimer's, sitting around sharing their depressing stories, was not something he welcomed. "That's fine, I'll pass, for now."

"I know you're in the Seattle area, and it's difficult for you, but if you are able to take some time off it would be helpful for her to have someone familiar around."

David agreed, assuring the doctor he would schedule time off and would call him to confirm an appointment time when he arrived in town.

Dr. Smith's voice softened. "When do you think you will be here? I can schedule a time for you to discuss her current situation and options for her ongoing care."

David closed his eyes and allowed himself to process the not so subtle message about what options lay in Edna's future. "I'll try to be there tomorrow before noon."

"I'll be in my office most of the early afternoon unless something urgent comes up. You can visit with your grandmother, though I don't think she's fully aware of what's happened to her."

Thanking the doctor, David clicked the receiver, and redialed the admitting desk, tapping his pen on some papers as his call was forwarded to the third floor and then transferred to his grandmother's room. "How are you doing Grandma? It's David … DAVID, your grandson." David strained to hear the trembling voice on the line.

"David. What's happened to me? Nobody will tell me what is going on." Grandma's voice quivered through her panicked tone.

"It's okay. You were a bit confused so Fred called the hospital, then he called me."

"How did I get here? I remember the bus ride, but I thought we were going to a restaurant."

David sighed. "No, Grandma, there was no bus ride. An ambulance brought you to the hospital. How are you feeling now?"

"I'm hungry. I remember the bus, I can't remember where we dined, but I remember they brought me food."

David rested his head in his palms and released his breath like a deflating balloon. His grandmother's life, once full and colorful, had been reduced to empty and faded memories of her former life. "We'll talk about it when I see you tomorrow."

"When am I going to see you? I need to see you."

"Tomorrow, Grandma. I'll be there tomorrow." David hung the phone up and sat for a long time considering his grandmother's heartbreaking reality. Grandma's mind was eroding, along with her quality of life. Little by little, washing away her essence, like the ebbs and flows of the tide, and David was powerless to stop the inevitable destruction. His head spun like a whirlpool, dizzy at the overwhelming decisions he knew lay in his, and more importantly, his grandmother's, immediate future. Helplessness swept over him.

Returning his focus to the drawings on his desk, David forced himself to concentrate. He cursed under his breath at the time. He hated working under pressure, but with the necessary trip to the Tri-Cities looming, he had no choice except to finish nearly a day's work in the next few hours. He called Jean to let her know he would be late and would be leaving in the morning again. "I know you're busy too, but would you order some flowers for Grandma? I don't know her room number, but she's on the third floor at Good Samaritan. I'll see you and the kids as soon as I can."

Though most days his work had tight time constraints with others awaiting the completion of his task, his grandmother needed him, and his priority was to her not to some bureaucratic company. With his request for two days of unplanned vacation completed, David dropped by his supervisors' office with his reports before heading home to prepare for his trip the next day, and to address the difficult decisions he knew he would have to confront.

At home, David rested his elbows on the table, his chin in his hands, and looked across the dinner table. His head throbbed from the frustrations that played and replayed through his mind. He didn't need a blood pressure cuff to inform him his blood pressure was spiking. Already he'd put thousands of miles on his vehicle with monthly or twice monthly trips across the state. There was only one way out. "I'm sure the doctor is going to recommend assisted care. You know it's going to be a battle to get her to accept that."

Jean shook her head. "You have to stop going at the pace you've been going. You need to convince her it's the best thing for her."

"Grandma's been through a lot these past two years. Her physical and mental health are failing and, I hate to say it, but we both know it's only going to get worse. We have to move her closer to us. It's the only thing left to do." David paused awaiting Jean's agreement.

"I know. This past year you've spent every day wrapped up in some detail of her life." Jean took the plate of leftovers from the fridge and put it in the microwave. "I know you're only doing what you have to, but you spend more time with Edna than you do with your children."

With his resolve set, David had only to convince his grandmother moving from eastern Washington, where she'd spent nearly sixty years, was the best thing for her.

"I suppose I should call Alicia and let her know. I think I owe her that."

"How do you think she will take the news?"

Wondering himself, David held his palms up and shook his head. "I honestly don't know."

David groaned at the abrupt annoying beeping. He rolled over and held a pillow to his head before surrendering. He flipped the alarm off. He longed to stay in bed. Six a.m., the same cruel time he normally woke for work. He glanced over at Jean, still motionless. The urge to wake her struck him. He pushed it aside. No reason to disturb her sleep. He rose and plodded to the shower to get ready for the long drive before what he knew would be a long day. Five minutes later, fully awake, he smiled at the aroma of deep roast Columbia beans perking from the kitchen. Jean was awake and the java was brewing. His attitude immediately improved. Jean padded around the kitchen in her sorry pink robe and purple slippers, one size too big. He made a mental note of a gift idea for her approaching birthday. "Good morning." David kissed her and headed for the coffee pot. Removing his toast from the toaster, he forced a smile. "Tell Emily goodbye for me. I only plan on spending one night, but I'll have to see how things are." With his vintage metal thermos of coffee in hand for the long drive, and the spike of caffeine which he knew he would require, David headed out the door for what he estimated was nearing his fortieth trip. His mind whirled with all he had gone through in the past two years. He never would have guessed he had the emotional stamina for such a draining chore. He never even imagined he would be taking on such a chore. He had driven the route so many times his mind went into auto-pilot along with the car.

Chapter 29

The morning after she arrived, Edna shifted uncomfortably in the bed. Through the dim light, something wasn't right. Her surroundings were unfamiliar and her mind disoriented. "What's going on? Where am I?" She called out with a barely audible voice. Her mother must have heard her though because she came in to check on her. Edna struggled to raise herself from her prone position to look around. "Mother? Is that you?"

Her mother took her hand. "It's okay, I'm here."

Edna closed her eyes. Her mind wandered through the many happy memories she'd shared with her mother. "You've been gone a long time. Are we going to have another picnic?" Edna remembered their walks through the woods as the towering trees rustled from the breeze. Edna inhaled deeply the sweet scent of the trees. She smoothed the woolen blanket Mother had laid out for them. "He loves me, he loves me not." She giggled and reached for a small white daisy snuggled in the grass as the river forged its way past them. A comforting and reassuring hand rested on her shoulder. Edna looked up.

"Here, Edna, drink some water."

The cool wetness on her lips quenched her. Her mother pointed across the river to where a patchwork of vibrant wildflowers dotted the meadow.

"Do you see your beautiful flowers? Everyone is thinking of you."

Edna smiled and turned to see the delicate dainty blossoms dancing in the wind. She turned back to her mother. She looked different somehow. Edna couldn't make sense of her hazy surroundings. Her mind blurred with obscure imprecise shapes like someone's feeble attempt at forging a beautiful Monet. Jumbled sounds and a voice floated in and out of her awareness. Her body tightened with agitation. Someone kept trying to interrupt Mother and her.

"Mrs. Pearson? Can you hear me? You need to drink, you'll get dehydrated."

Edna swallowed another sip from the glass held to her lips. She looked around. Her left arm throbbed. She lifted it and panicked seeing all the tubes and wires that ran down her arm to an electronic box that emitted rhythmic beeps and hissing sounds. "Help!" Her voice strained. "Where am I?" Edna turned and shifted about in the bed. A soft blue cotton gown covered her wrinkled frail body.

"It's okay, Mrs. Pearson, you're fine."

The woman standing next to her did not look at all like her mother. Confused, she scanned her surroundings. The field of flowers was gone. A lone glass vase filled with white daisies, purple fragrant lilacs, and bright orange tiger lilies sat on the end table. "Where am I? How come nobody will tell me what's going on?" Edna struggled to pull the covers off.

"You're in the hospital, Mrs. Pearson. I'm your day nurse. My name is Terri."

"I don't understand." Edna's heart raced and her breathing quickened. She didn't remember being brought here. She only remembered Mother. She closed her eyes tight. Her mind reeled with confusion. She didn't understand where her mother had gone. She opened her eyes and stared at the nurse. Fear gripped her. "I must have had a dream. I've been having quite a few lately." Edna's eyes widened as she examined the woman neatly dressed in pink cotton pants and a white and pink printed top.

"Tell me about your dream, Mrs. Pearson." Terri took Edna's hand and rubbed it.

Gripping the loving hand, Edna relaxed. "I was in a beautiful meadow picking wildflowers with Mother. I was seventeen and had quite a crush on Kenneth. It was a glorious spring day and we spread our woolen blanket out and ate a picnic lunch."

"It sounds like a lovely picnic. I'd love to hear if you have any more dreams. I'll be back to check on you after the doctor has been by." Terri turned to leave.

"Where's David? Where's my grandson?" Edna raised her eyes to follow the nurse.

Terri paused at the door and turned. "I'm not sure. The doctor will be by sometime later today. I'm sure he'll be able to tell you more."

Edna lay impatiently, staring at the walls with the impersonal striped beige paper absent of any photos or décor. She wished to be in her warm and cozy home and wondered if anyone had called David.

"Hello, Edna. How are you doing this morning?" Dr. Smith came to her side and took her hand. "Can you squeeze my hand?"

Perplexed, she squeezed her eyes closed and complied with a weak grip of the doctor's hand.

"That's good. Do you know your name?"

"Of course, I know my name. Edna Mooney."

"Mooney?" The doctor's eyes studied her much as one might ponder over an abstract piece of art.

Flustered, Edna labored to understand what was wrong. "No, wait. That was my maiden name. My married name is Pearson."

"How about children?"

"Two. My daughter, Bernice is dead." Her head pounded inside, rebelling against something, maybe the present, maybe the past. "Is that right? No. Larry's dead too." Edna's voice dropped off. Though she was crying, she couldn't lift her hand to wipe the tears away. Frustration rose like an expanding wave ready to engulf her.

Dr. Smith drilled her about her grandchildren and other family members.

"My two grandsons are David and Nathan. Then there's my mother. I'm much too tired. Why are you asking me all this?" Edna pounded the bed with her fist. "I'm not senile you know."

"No, Mrs. Pearson, you're not senile. Sometimes people get a little confused when they get older. You've likely suffered another small stroke. What we call a TIA. It's nothing to worry about. Do you know why your neighbor, Fred called the aide car?"

Edna raised her eyebrows. "Fred? He called? I don't understand."

"He found you outside in the rain confused and disoriented. Do you remember?"

Edna eyed the doctor. "I don't remember that."

"What has me concerned is you appear to be getting confused a lot more." The doctor looked at his chart and flipped the pages.

"I'm not crazy." Edna resented the doctor's implication.

"You're not crazy. Confusion can occur with age." Dr. Smith looked over the rim of his glasses. "Do you remember how you got here?"

Edna thought for a moment. She remembered being at home and now she was in this small room. "I guess Mother brought me in their new car. I remember the ride." Edna ignored the sigh as the doctor moved a chair closer to the bed.

He leaned over and took her hand. "Your heart and other vital signs are strong, but we'll want to watch you for a day or two before we release you."

"What about David? Did somebody call David?"

"Your grandson is on his way. I'll stop by and chat with you tomorrow." Dr. Smith patted her hand with his goodbye.

Chapter 30

David pulled his Chevy pickup into the visitor lot at Good Samaritan Hospital. Now familiar with the layout after several visits, he maneuvered through the halls with ease. He had long ago grown accustomed to the pine-scented disinfectant and alcohol which assaulted him each time he entered the hospital. With apprehension, he stepped inside the hospital room, relieved by the fragrance of a large bouquet sitting on the nightstand next to her bed. Initially, his nerves got the better of him as he remembered his Grandma's confusion during their phone conversation the previous day. But he relaxed when her eyes widened in recognition.

"Hi, Grandma, how are you doing?" Stunned by her frailness, and the wrinkles which set a little deeper in her drawn face, he forced a smile in an attempt to belie the sadness which had overtaken him.

"David, is that you? No one will tell me why I am here."

"What do you remember?" David leaned over her bed, and took her hand in his, halfway expecting to hear about her bus trip. Instead, she told him how she had been visiting her mother.

"I talked to Mother for a while. I haven't seen her in some time, you know?"

"Yes, I imagine it's been a while." David pinched the bridge of his nose. His nasal passage burned and he shut his eyes for a moment to hold back his tears. He recognized his grandmother's increasingly vivid visits with her mother as a sign of the cruelty of Alzheimer's. His research on the internet, and talks with Dr. Smith, had served him well. He knew what to expect with each stage and knew now to accept her reality without attempting to change it.

"Have you seen my new blue and white calico dress, David?" Grandma pushed herself to a seated position. She pointed to the chair next to the bed. "Mother made it for me. Don't you love the cross stitch? I'm going to wear it to the dance at school next week."

David glimpsed the hospital robe that lay across the chair and cracked a smile. "Yes, it's a lovely dress." Looking at the assortment of flowers on the nightstand, he noticed the card stuck in the nearest bouquet and leaned in to read it. Alicia had sent them. His jaw dropped and he pulled the card from the bouquet. After all this time with no contact from her, he wondered how she had found out Edna was in the hospital. Most likely Barbara had called her. "Has Alicia been by?" David held out the card for his grandmother to see.

"Alicia? Oh yes, she and Lacey brought me some beautiful flowers. She's such a lovely girl, and Lacey is so sweet." Edna struggled to stretch her arm out. She pointed to a large machine monitoring her vital signs. "See, Lacey brought that for me."

Taped to the machine was a small "Get Well" card with butterflies and flowers drawn in vibrant colored felt tip pens. Underneath the homemade card hung a small school photo of Lacey. David remembered his mother having him and Nathan print their names on the back of their school photos to send to their grandparents when they were small. He flipped the photo over and read the writing on the back. "To Great-Grandmother, Love Lacey. "This is a nice picture of Lacey, isn't it, Grandma?"

"Oh yes, she looks like her mother, but I can see Larry in her too."

David puzzled over the confusing comment, knowing Alicia was not a biologic offspring to Edna as she so often informed him. But it made sense she longed for a link to her side of the family. He guessed it was only natural wanting to see your lineage passed on, even if only in physical characteristics. "Yes, she does."

Her new sense of peace brought him comfort but he was curiously amused by her new affection for his stepsister. If he had the option of moving his grandmother closer to him or having Alicia and Lorraine step up, he would welcome the reprieve. But he couldn't imagine one visit on Alicia's part indicated such a commitment. Yet it was surprising, and he was certain, uplifting, for his grandmother to have other visitors. He realized too, that he would need to let Alicia know of his plans to move Edna closer to him. He wondered what kind of resistance that conversation would entail. He couldn't think about that right now.

"When can I go home?" The panic rose in his grandmother's voice. "Where's Missy? Is Mother taking care of her? She doesn't like Missy too well you know? She scolds her for jumping on the furniture and doesn't like me to feed her anything but puppy food."

"Your mother isn't ..." David bit down on his lip. "Missy is doing fine, Barbara is watching her."

Grandma either ignored or didn't comprehend the reference to Barbara. Her eyes misted as she pleaded. "I want to see Missy."

David stroked his grandmother's hair. "You're going to have to be patient. Dr. Smith wants you to stay here a few more days."

Grandma protested. "I don't understand why I'm here?" She fumbled over the words and turned away.

David leaned over her with a slow soft voice, hoping to draw her back. "Fred found you outside in the rain. He was concerned about you. Your mind is confused at times. It's called Alzheimer's. That is why you can't remember what's happened." David wished he could assure her everything would be fine, but Dr. Smith's words resounded in his head. *"Your grandmother's Alzheimer's is only going to get worse."* It had taken ninety-four years, but the disease had robbed his grandmother of her identity and left only a frail shell of the once outgoing and intelligent woman.

"I don't understand what's happening. I want to go home. How come I can't go home?" Grandma struggled against the tightly tucked sheet and blanket and attempted to climb from the bed.

"You're in the hospital. We've been through this already." David winced at the sharpness in his voice and took a few deep breaths, counting to ten slowly. He wasn't sure how much more help he could offer without additional support from other family members. He wished Nathan's transfer was sooner rather than later. His head pounded and his neck and back tensed.

"No. I was sitting in my chair for a while to rest, but now I'm in a meadow."

Grandma's voice changed, it took on softness and innocence. Her panicked look had disappeared. She lay calm and relaxed. He rolled his shoulders and rubbed the back of his neck, trying to relieve the tightness, wishing the whole situation would merely disappear. He didn't know who was more helpless in their present situation, he or his grandmother.

Intrigued by the story, David tossed the blue hospital robe onto the neighboring empty bed, pulled up the orange molded chair and sat down.

"What are you doing in the meadow Grandma?" He patted the back of her hand.

"Mother and I went to visit Pearl for a picnic. Now we're gathering wildflowers, which I so much like to do. Can you smell them?"

Her delusion fascinated David. He spied the bouquet of lilacs, lilies, and daisies. Did their scent trigger her memories? "Yes, I smell the wildflowers. How did you get to the meadow?" Her trips of fantasy were becoming more and more vivid to her, but this was simply too weird for him.

"We took the train to Pearl and Stanley's like we always do. Then we took their car through Monahan and Issaquah down to the Raging River. We could see the snowcapped mountains in the distance."

David recalled the stories she'd told about her sister, Pearl, and how fond she was of her older sibling. He remembered Dr. Smith saying often Alzheimer's patients' minds go back to the point in their lives when they were happiest. It was bittersweet that in her mind she was in a far better place than the reality in which she was living. David patted his grandmother's arm which lay limp by her side. Her eyes sparkled, and her face flushed with more color than he had seen for some time. The deterioration of her mind saddened him, but she was at peace, wherever she was. He stroked her thinning hair, worried her fantasies would take over to the point where reality would cease to exist. It was a sobering possibility. It was possible she would be happier that way. Chilled by the frightening thought, he pushed it aside. Emotionally drained, David's head hurt like it did when the pressures of difficult problems at work bore down on him. He knew the next phase in his grandmother's life would be difficult for everyone. He mentally prepared himself for the possibility she might even fail to recognize him as time went on. He shuddered at the notion his grandmother could lose her identity that much. Her eyes fluttered shut. Engulfed in uncertainty and indecision, he hesitated to leave her side, but he needed to get away from the desperate, yet inevitable, situation that ate away at Grandma's life and controlled his. He whispered. "Come back safely, Grandma." He then turned and walked out.

Taking the elevator to the ground floor lobby, David fished the cell phone from his coat pocket as he strode toward his car. Dialing Dr.

Smith's office, he paced until the receptionist connected him to the doctor, who made time for him immediately.

"Thanks for seeing me so fast." David extended his hand as he approached Dr. Smith, seated at his desk.

"Thanks for coming. I hate to be abrupt, but I only have a few minutes. Your grandmother's health is only going to get worse. She's going to need an increasing level of assistance; more than she can get from the CNA's she's currently using. I'm willing to discharge her, but I recommend you begin immediately searching for an adult care

facility, unless you think you want to try to find twenty-four-hour care for her."

David stared at the doctor unable to stifle a brief laugh. Grandma's grudging acceptance of her nurse assistants during the day was stressful enough. Considering full-time live-in care was simply not an option. Assisting Edna had turned into an uphill battle. His fatigue and constant worry made him feel battered like a salmon fighting the fish ladder at spawning time. The inevitable, which hung over him since he first took over his grandmother's care, had arrived. It was something he managed to push aside until this moment. "I don't think that's an option, she's like a five-year-old pushing everyone's limits already."

Dr. Smith's broad grin relayed his understanding. "You are fortunate. There are a number of very good retirement homes that offer the extra nursing services your grandmother requires. You might want to look at some facilities specifically for Alzheimer's patients. If she gets worse it will be to your advantage, and hers, to place her somewhere with a more controlled environment to prevent her from wandering off."

"Great." David shook his head. He hadn't considered the possibility of her wandering off. He didn't need anything else to worry about.

"Let me know if you have any questions. If you plan on staying a few days to be with her and make permanent arrangements, I'll sign her discharge papers."

"Actually, doctor, if my grandmother requires assisted living arrangements, I think for my sake, in particular, I am going to suggest to her moving closer to me."

"I see." Dr. Smith rested his chin in his hand focusing on David's comment. "I think that's a smart move."

"The problem right now is, I'm going to need more than a few days. Is there somewhere she can go for a few weeks until I find permanent arrangements and can make the move?"

"There are quite a few facilities in the area that offer respite care for up to a month. You might want to check them out." The doctor scribbled some names on a slip of paper before handing it to David.

Reaching for the paper, David thanked the doctor, turned and somberly returned to his car. He sat for a few minutes with his hands on the steering wheel, allowing the news to bounce around in his head. "So much to do, so little time." Jean used the line often. He now knew how she felt. He started the car and headed to the golden arches for a quick burger, and then he'd go to his grandmother's house and make some phone calls. Tomorrow he would head home and begin his search for permanent arrangements on the eastside of Seattle. He cringed, thinking about the outburst he would face when he broke the news to Grandma. And then, there was informing Alicia.

With new significant decisions looming, David called Nathan from the now-familiar table at the fast-food joint to discuss their grandmother's options.

"I know you can be involved only from a distance, but it's good to have another sounding board. Quite frankly she's driving me a bit crazy. I'm beginning to understand how Alicia and her family felt."

"I'm trying to work a transfer. I know you've spent a lot of time helping Grandma Edna. When I get home, I'll see what I can do to lend a hand."

"Thanks, that means a lot. I only want to do what's best for her, but I have to keep my sanity too. Right now, I'm not sure how best to do that."

"What type of accommodations are you looking at?"

"An adult care facility is the only way to go. It's obvious she can't live on her own and she is fighting everyone who comes into her home."

"Ouch, that's not going to go over well. Is it?"

"No." David paused, "But there are no other options. I'm also going to suggest she move closer to me so I can stop making myself crazy with all the driving."

"Makes sense. How is the money situation? Do you need any financial help? It's got to be expensive. I can start sending a few hundred a month."

Nathan's offer caught David off guard. It took a moment to digest his brother's words. "No, thanks. Her financial situation is much stronger than I initially thought. Her income is currently covering her expenses, she has some savings and she has dividend checks coming in which helps cover her medical costs. I think her finances are okay for now." David experienced a tiny sense of relief. Maybe when Nathan moved back to Washington, he would get a break in spite of Nathan's career.

"So you still haven't heard from Lorraine or Alicia, huh?"

"I haven't heard from Alicia in a while, but Alicia and Lacey apparently stopped by and visited her in the hospital. They brought Grandma flowers and a card Lacey made. I need to call Alicia. I owe it to her to let her know I want to move Edna to the Seattle area. It would be so much simpler if they stepped up to offer more support, even if they aren't willing to take on the role of primary caregiver. I think Alicia initially called me to get me involved so I would take over. I always thought she had a hidden agenda." David bit his lip, feeling guilty over his resentment toward his stepsisters, yet still unable to completely bury the fact Grandma's silverware had never been located.

"Could be. I hate to say it, but maybe getting involved with Kora-Lee and her family was a dumb thing to do."

"Maybe, but where would she be right now with Larry gone? Frankly, I'm glad I can help in some small way and repay her for how much she and Granddad did for us when Mom wasn't around. I just wish she wouldn't fight me every step of the way."

Saying goodbye to his brother, David gathered his tray. He noticed the over fifty-year-old logo of the McDonald's chain printed on the paper tray liner. He chuckled as the slogan and song from the restaurant chain during his teenage years popped into his mind. *"You deserve a break today."* He laughed out loud, drawing a few odd looks. He definitely deserved a break today, but he also knew he wasn't likely to get it. He had practiced over and over in his head alternate scenarios on how he would inform his grandmother about his intention. He sighed in surrender. It didn't matter how he worded it, there was no way to put a positive spin on this news.

The familiar antiseptic scent assaulted David when he arrived back at the hospital a few hours later. He found his way to his grandmother's room, hesitantly stepping inside the gloomy room, feeling a bit like Judas, about to betray her trust. "Hello, Grandma. How are you doing?"

Her moist eyes immediately made his task more difficult. "Oh, David, I'm so glad you're here. Nobody will tell me when I can go home."

David took a deep breath and swallowed. Sitting next to his grandmother, he took her hand. "The doctor says you can be discharged as soon as we find a new place for you to live."

The panic rose in her voice. "I don't want to move." Her eyes narrowed and filled with anger. "You're sending me to a home, aren't you?"

David knew trying to convince her modern retirement homes offered beautiful decor and plenty of activities would not help calm the situation. To her, any place that wasn't her house was a nursing home. "I'm not going to put you in a place you don't like."

"You don't know what it's like to be old. It's not fair."

David shut his eyes momentarily. She was right. He didn't know what it was like to be old and helpless and dependent on others, to have others talk down to you, and tell you how you were expected to live your life. She was also right; life wasn't always fair. He sighed before he took her hand and spoke softly. "You're right, I don't. But I do know I want what's best for you, and I want you to be safe." David nearly pulled away, feeling the tension from his grandmother's trembling hand. "Grandma, what would you think about moving closer to me?" He recoiled slightly, remembering earlier attempts in approaching the subject always resulted in brutal defeat.

She looked at him while she considered his question. Her anger faded. "Closer to you? That would be okay."

"Are you sure? You won't be able to see your friends nearly as often." David knew she had many good friends from living more than half her life in eastern Washington. The move would be difficult for her.

"That's alright, as long as I have you and Nathan. You're my family. If it's easier for you, I can come live near you. I don't want to be in your way though. I don't think I should move in with you. You'll have to find me my own place, maybe next door to you."

David grimaced at the thought. He found it humorous she had interpreted the suggestion as an invitation to move in. It was best to let the details go for now and be thankful Grandma would be moving hundreds of miles closer, and he would be able to reclaim some leisure time again.

"Do you think I can take Missy when I move?"

"It's hard to find a place that will allow dogs, but I'll try."

"When will that be? I want to get out of here now."

"I'm going to need some time to find a nice place for you near my house. In the meantime, ..." David paused before proceeding. "I'm going to find a temporary place for you where there are full-time nurses and doctors. Until I have done that, the doctor won't sign your release papers."

Edna narrowed her eyes again and frowned, glaring at David. "I don't want to go to a place like that. You think I'm losing my mind, don't you?"

"No, Grandma, I don't think you're losing your mind. Some people's minds start to fail when they get older and things can get confusing. You can't live by yourself any longer. Something could happen to you."

Edna looked down and wrung her hands. "I want to live in my own home until I move closer to you. You can't take me to a nursing home." Edna's voice rose, she took a breath to calm herself. "It's not fair getting old and not being able to care for yourself. I've never been one to depend on others. I just want to be left alone, why can't anyone understand?"

"I understand that's what you want, but it's not safe anymore. You need to be where someone can watch you around the clock."

"Why can't I stay at my house with the girls?" Edna glared at David.

David sighed, "Since your last fall, Dr. Smith has been concerned for your well-being. For your sake, you need full-time care. I've called a few places that will allow you to stay for a short period. I thought we could look at one of them together. Do you know about Riverside Lodge?"

"I think a lady who was in the Master Gardeners with me may have gone there. Though I always wondered who would put someone they loved in a place like that."

"I hear it's a nice place. It's a retirement community, not a nursing home.

"I don't care what you call it. They're all the same."

"Well, you can stay here in the hospital if you want for a few weeks until I can move you closer to me."

Edna puckered her lips before she responded. "At least it's here in town, so my friends can visit easily."

"Okay, then, tomorrow we'll go look at the Riverside Lodge."

Edna's eyes glared hawk-like at him. Her command was straightforward. "You're not selling my house."

"No Grandma, I'm not going to sell your house."

Chapter 31

"I'll discharge you on the condition your grandson finds respite care before he returns home."

Edna fumed at Dr. Smith 's command the following morning. She'd been independent her whole life. The thought of depending on others infuriated her. She glared at David, knowing he was behind this.

David watched her from his chair next to her bed. "You know what that means, Grandma? We need to find a place today so we can get you moved in by tomorrow."

Everyone was plotting for her to move. She eyed David with resentment at his interference in her life. "Why do I have to move? I want to stay at my house with my girls."

"We've already talked about this. You heard the doctor; you need full-time care. Part-time caregivers aren't enough anymore."

Resentment roiled even as she recognized no one else cared enough to assure she had someone looking after her. She calmed, if she had to depend on someone, she was happy it was her grandson, her own flesh and blood, not Alicia or that family. No, Edna could never stand for that. Too tired to argue any more, Edna grudgingly allowed the staff to dress her while David signed her release papers. She sat on the bed with her coat by her side, dutifully awaiting their visit to some old person facility where she didn't belong.

They drove in silence the short drive to the Riverside Lodge. She made up her mind, no matter what, she was going to convince David she didn't need to stay there. Walking toward the entrance, Edna refused to let David help her. "I'm perfectly capable of walking on my own."

David walked next to her, running ahead only to open the heavy glass door.

A middle-aged woman dressed in blue slacks and a blazer approached and extended her hand. "Good afternoon. I'm Nanette, the social director." The woman thrust out her hand like an over-eager salesclerk. "Would you like to see our facility? I'm sure you'll be very pleased."

Edna frowned as the woman took her hand. "We'll see about that."

David made the introductions then added, "Thank you for taking the time. We do need a room immediately, but only temporarily until I can make long term arrangements on the other side of the state."

"I understand. We do have availability right now. Please feel free to join us for lunch after the tour. It will give you a chance to see what you can expect before you make a decision."

Nanette led the way through the facility and made a few introductions to the activity's director and some housekeeping staff. They were friendly enough, but Edna knew it was all an act to impress the families of the elderly residents. She couldn't help but notice the place was tastefully decorated in inviting shades of peach and sage green. The numerous silk and dried flower arrangements placed on tables and in large vases in the halls also made it quite pleasant. Still, she shrugged, it wasn't as nice as her home, and she'd be forced to live with someone else's schedule.

Nanette stopped near the end of a hallway. "Here is a typical one-bedroom unit, and it's available for immediate occupancy." She turned the key in the door and pushed it open, allowing Edna and David to enter.

David stepped in and looked around. "It looks nice, doesn't it, Grandma?"

Not willing to be coerced into something she didn't care for, Edna made a face. "I don't particularly like the light-colored beige carpet. How will it stay clean? I prefer a darker color that doesn't show the dirt." From the living room, she could see into the bathroom and the bedroom, but they were the only other rooms. She furrowed her brow and stared at Nanette. "There's no kitchen. How can I cook?"

"This is a facility for people who are unable to care completely for themselves. Our residents all eat in the dining room."

"Well, I don't like this place anyway, it's much too small. I presently have three bedrooms. Besides, this is furnished. Where will I put my furniture?"

David brought his hands to his temples. "This will be only for a short while. We can't move all your furniture twice. You will have a furnished room only until we can move you closer to my house. Then you can move some of your furniture."

Ignoring her grandson, Edna shot a look at Nanette. "This carpet isn't going to work too well for Missy."

"Missy?" The director looked puzzled.

Edna stood, hands on her hips, as David explained about the dog.

"I'm sorry, I thought you knew. We don't allow pets."

Panic seized Edna. Her voice wavered. "I need Missy's companionship. What's going to happen to her?"

"Don't worry about that now, we can talk to some of your friends. I'm sure someone would love to take her for you."

"I want to find another place."

Nanette attempted to take Edna's hand. "I'm sorry, but you aren't going to find a respite care facility that allows pets."

Edna pulled her hand away. Her eyes burned. Everything was getting increasingly unfair. She had lost control of life. Her life.

"How about we check out our dining room? It's nearly time for lunch." The director put her arm around Edna's shoulder and attempted to guide her from the room.

Edna planted herself firmly. She hadn't even moved in, and she was already being told what to do. She scowled at the director's too forward manner but accepted David's help to a round table at the edge of the dining room. The room's formal decor reminded her of a fancy overpriced restaurant with its white table cloths and fresh roses in crystal vases on the tables. Though she couldn't see the kitchen, the smell of meat and spices flowed into the dining room. A flicker from her past crossed her mind, long ago fancy luncheons with the military wives. Soothed by the happy memory, Edna took a seat. She looked around the room. A jet-black piano gleamed majestically in the corner of the room. Hard-of-hearing residents spoke in loud voices above the otherwise tranquil elevator music from the piano.

A young worker, neatly dressed, approached. "Today, you may choose between a green salad and cottage cheese, and for the main dish, there is either an open-faced turkey sandwich with mashed potatoes or beef stroganoff. Dessert choices, as always, include sherbet or pudding, and today only, we have apple pie."

Edna grumbled to the worker, "I never eat stroganoff out. You never know what you'll get." She sullenly ordered the turkey. At least it came with mashed potatoes with gravy.

David pulled a menu from the napkin holder and glanced over it. "It looks quite nice and there are plenty of choices on entrees. And they have apple pie, your favorite."

Edna knew he was trying to make things sound good. She preferred not to think about it. She stewed watching the other residents with their painted smiles and school girl chatter, sitting at the tables surrounding her. Within a few minutes, the server returned with two white plates. Edna looked over her meal which, she had to admit, looked surprisingly appetizing and plentiful, but that wasn't the point. "I don't want to eat like this every night with this many people around. I much prefer to eat on my own terms and on my schedule." Edna cast a warning glare at David.

"You'll get used to it."

"Oh, you. I don't want to get used to it. I don't like to eat a big mid-day meal. I prefer a light meal, like soup. Why can't I eat in my room?" Edna put her fork down. Sometimes David made her so furious. He didn't even try to understand. She didn't want to get used to doing something differently than she had done her whole life.

David lifted a bite of stroganoff to his mouth. "The food is pretty good, don't you think?"

Edna knew he was over-acting to try to convince her this was where she wanted to move. "The food's okay, but it doesn't taste the same when they prepare food for such crowds. You can always tell."

"I think it's a fine place. And it's only for a few weeks. We don't have many options; I think you'll like it here."

Taking a deep breath of resignation, she sighed. She'd lost all control of her life. "So, I guess It's finally winter."

David turned and glanced out the large windows facing the courtyard. "Yes, but it's almost spring, you can see the buds beginning to form on the trees and the crocuses are popping up."

Edna shook her head. He didn't understand. How could he? He was still young. He hadn't yet seen autumn. "I'm not talking about the season." She hung her head and looked at her hands, wringing them as her voice quivered and her tears salted the leftovers on her plate. "I'm talking about life. It's the end for me. The winter of my life."

Chapter 32

Astonished by the ease of getting his grandmother moved into a vacant room right away, David's tension eased. His long drives were nearing an end. But as he had grown accustomed to, Grandma had to grumble. With little time to pack many personal effects, Grandma bemoaned the place didn't feel like home without her furniture.

"I promise, it's only for a short while. I can stay and help you move more things or I can go back home and begin searching for a place where you will be able to have some of your things permanently."

"I don't want to spend my birthday here alone." Grandma plopped down onto the soft gray sofa, so unlike the dated, worn sofa left behind. "I don't know how many more birthdays' I'll have, and I still haven't seen Nathan."

David thought about the timing. It didn't seem right for her to spend her birthday without family around. "I'll try to find a place and get you moved in before the middle of March so we can have a nice party for you, even if Nathan can't be here."

Edna looked around the room. "I don't like it here. It's not my home, and this sofa is too hard."

Exhausted from touring, signing papers and packing some clothes and grooming supplies, David didn't have the energy to fight her. He let his grandmother's comment go without a response. Already after the dinner hour, and still facing the long drive home, David hugged his grandmother goodbye in spite of her protests. "I promise I'll see you soon."

The following evening, with Grandma settled at the Riverside Lodge, his tension released like an unwound spring. For the first time in months, the ringing phone didn't spark a tremor of fear in him anticipating what might have happened with Edna. For the next week, he focused his evening hours on finding a permanent home for his grandmother and called her nearly every day. Fred and Barbara had visited her and eased her sadness at leaving her home. Finally, he found what he believed to be the perfect option for her long-term arrangements. Only fifteen minutes from his house he found a large residence owned by a geriatric doctor and his wife. They lived in the upper level, with the second level specifically designed with full handicapped access for up to six residents, and a basement apartment for two live-in CNA's. Even with one of the larger rooms in the home, many of Grandma's possessions would have to be left behind. David knew how much she valued her belongings. Leaving them behind would be difficult for her.

Calling to give her the happy news, David put together his news with a sentimental remembrance of her youth. "It is a very beautiful home with a lovely view of Lake Sammamish. It's not far from where you told me you taught when you first became a teacher."

"I remember the lake. How large is my new home?"

David bit his lip. Now for the hard part. "It is a large home, but six people share it. You will have your own bedroom and a private bath. The kitchen and dining and living rooms are shared by all the men and women who live there." David sensed her heart-ache through the silence before his grandmother's soft voice cracked across the line.

"How will I fit all my furniture into one room?"

"We talked about this. You will only be able to take what will fit. If there are pieces of furniture you want to leave to some of your friends, we can make those arrangements."

"I need to go to my home David and sort my things out. When can I do that?"

David's neck muscled tensed. He drew an extra-long breath, realizing she was right. It would be easier to allow her time to sort and reminisce in her home one final time. An extra trip east of the mountains before the move was out of the question. He cursed to himself, he hadn't thought about the time involved allowing his grandmother to sort through her lifetime possessions and whittle them down to what would fit in one room. He had no choice but to impose upon Barbara one last time.

Dialing Barbara's number, David anticipated a quick call. Surely, Barbara would be able to take Edna to select which items to bring to her new home. He was certain Edna had shared the news of her upcoming move during one of Barbara's visits. He was wrong.

After ensuring Barbara's husband, Robert, was doing well, David mentioned the reason for his current call. "I hate to ask, but I was hoping you might be able to make time during the week to take Grandma back to her place to go through her things."

"Sure, that's not a problem. Is there anything in particular, she wants to get?"

"I don't think so." David thought about possible necessities for a moment. "I think she just needs some time to walk through the house and see what she wants to take when she moves."

Barbara's tone notched up. "You're moving her again? Where? When?"

"I'm sorry, I thought you knew her stay at Riverside Lodge was only temporary until I found permanent arrangements."

"Well, yes, but I thought it would be longer than a few weeks, though. Where is she moving this time?"

Straightening and breathing deeply, David tipped his head back and blew out. "She didn't tell you?" He paused long enough to know the answer. He winced in advance of the onslaught he knew was coming. "I found a place near me, in Issaquah. It will be a lot easier to visit and look after her."

The harshness in Barbara's voice instantly relayed her disapproval. "You're moving her to Issaquah? How can you move her so far from the only place she's lived for the last half of her life? After all I've done for her, and for you? Don't you think I should have had some say?"

David imagined banging his head on the desk. He rolled his eyes and huffed in exasperation. Damn, he couldn't get the break that even that white-faced red-haired clown from the golden arches told him he deserved. "I'm sorry, Barbara. You've been great. I appreciate all you've done for Grandma, and you how much your friendship means to her. With her ongoing health issues and Alzheimer's, I need her geographically closer to me and my family."

Barbara interjected. "The only reason you're moving her is to make things easier on you. Who will she know there besides your family? Does she even understand she's leaving?"

David glanced at the clock. His heart pounded so hard and quick he thought it might burst from his chest. So much for the quick and painless phone call. "Of course, she understands. Since I'm the only family member right now who is looking after her, I have to do what I think is best. And honestly, other than you and occasionally Fred, she doesn't get many visitors. Alicia's only been by infrequently."

"Obviously you've thought this out. I don't see how I'll be able to visit her after she moves. It's not easy on me to make a long trip like that at my age and with my husband, Robert, ill."

David noticed the change in her voice, now more restrained. Of course, she was hurt, what did he expect? She had invested a great deal of her time and energy in helping Edna, especially since Larry died. She almost certainly valued Edna's friendship as much as Edna had valued hers. The move would leave a hole in Barbara's life too. "I'm sorry to upset you. You've been like family to her, even closer than many of her family members, but as family, I have to make tough decisions. I understand if you don't want to help me."

As the silence lingered, David began to think Barbara had disconnected.

Finally, she spoke, "I need time to reflect and pray about this. I'll call you tomorrow."

David wished her and Robert a good evening and said goodbye. Since he'd already been beaten up, it was a good time to call Alicia and get that conversation and those licks over at the same time. He pulled up her phone number on speed-dial and punched the button. While the phone rang, David practiced the deep breathing from his occasional yoga exercises. In and out through the nose for relaxation. After several rings, David heard Alicia's greeting.

"Hi, Alicia, it's David."

"This is a surprise. What's up?"

David continued his slow breathing. "I wasn't sure if you knew Grandma was released from the hospital to respite care at Riverside."

"No. I assumed she'd been discharged and gone home, but wasn't sure. I visited her there."

"I know. I saw the flowers and card. Grandma couldn't stop talking about them. I guess Barbara called you to give you the news?"

"No. Fred called and told me he had to call the EMT's again. He said her mind is failing pretty badly."

"Yeah. That's what I'm calling about. She has dementia, likely, Alzheimer's. It's only going to get worse. I have no choice but to move her permanently to an adult care facility, one that will be able to give her the attention she requires."

"Have you told her yet?"

One deep breath later, David continued. "Yes, she's not thrilled, and she won't be able to take Missy, so you can imagine how she feels about that."

"Did she throw anything at you? Because you haven't seen her truly mad unless she's thrown something at you."

David's laugh loosened the tightness in his chest. One last carefree moment before the moment of indifference or as they say, all hell would break loose. He decided on the diplomatic tactful approach. "I know you and Lacey love Edna, but you also recognize, I'm the one who's been caring for her the past two years." Not pausing long enough to hear any defensive attack, David pushed on. "I'm moving Edna across the state. Close to me." *Whew*. He'd gotten it out.

"Wow. Just like that?"

David ignored the syrupy sarcasm. He could pour it on too. "No, not just like that. After two years of back and forth driving once or twice a month." He shifted the phone to his other ear. "I have the address and phone number if you want. I'm sure she'd love to have you visit." David heard fumbling on the other end of the line. "Lacey means a lot to her and she'd love to see her again."

"I'm sure."

Not certain how to read Alicia's tone, David offered a half-hearted apology, but there was no regret. His decision had been made in Edna's best interest and neither Barbara nor Alicia would convince him otherwise. "I'm sorry if you're upset, but right now, whether you believe it or not, I'm only doing what is best for Grandma. If you want to take over and assure her bills are paid and she has visitors regularly, we can talk about her staying in Richland, otherwise…"

Alicia cut him off. "You certainly are something. Mom and I spent years doing things for her. We were never good enough for her. No, it's your turn now."

Alicia's words washed away any trace of reservation in his decision.

The next evening Barbara called. "I prayed about your request last night. You're right, she needs family in her last years, and though I'll miss her a great deal, I need to focus more on caring for my husband. I'll be happy to take Edna home and let her go through her things."

Relieved his grandmother would have time to sort through her belongings, reminisce, and say farewell to her home before her move across the state, David thanked Barbara for her willingness to help. He could see no downside.

Chapter 33

Three weeks after his grandmother's move to respite care, David and Jean hooked their small trailer to the car, hoping it would be one of their last trips to the Tri-Cities. Arriving at Riverside Lodge before noon on Saturday, they found Grandma sitting on her neatly made bed wearing the burgundy velour cardigan they'd given her for Christmas. Though the TV was on, Grandma didn't appear to notice its blaring noise as she stared out the window.

"Hi, Grandma, how are you doing? Are you all set for your moving day?"

His grandmother turned to look at him through frightened squinty eyes. "What? Why am I moving?"

Jean sat beside her. "David and I are moving you closer to us. Won't that be nice?"

Edna offered a sideways glance. "Do I know you?"

"I'm Jean, David's wife."

Edna tipped her head in thought then turned her attention to David. Her worried look disappeared. "Are you sure you have room for me?"

David raised his eyebrows and grinned. "We found a very nice place for you with your own room, and it's not too far from where we live. How about we start packing your clothes?" He went to her closet and grabbed a bunch of hangers.

Edna jumped to her feet. "Stop. What are you doing? Those are mine. Why are you taking my clothes?" She rushed to David and reached out to grasp her clothes.

"It's okay." Jean hurried after her and put her arm around her. "We're taking them to your new home." She led Edna back to her bed.

Edna's tone relaxed. "I have a new home? Where is it? How come no one told me?" Her eyes widened but remained distant, her mind elsewhere.

David continued to empty the closet, flinging clothes over the back of the stuffed chair.

Sitting on her bed, Edna rocked slowly, clutching her quilt and drawing it close, caressing it as a child might with a small kitten. "Did I ever show you my quilt?"

David smiled. Hearing the story again was well worth the comfort it would bring her.

"I made this in 1935 when the children were still young." Edna clutched a corner of the full-size quilt with its white background and large pastel tulips of blue, green, pink, and orange, bordered and backed with bleached muslin. "See."

Jean ran her hand across the testament of Edna's skill. Holding out the quilt, she showed David the lower right corner. He squinted at the small embroidered initials and the date commemorating her achievement. The quilt was in remarkable shape for something nearly seventy years old.

"Mother and I are going to start another one at the next quilting bee." With great ceremony, she awkwardly folded her prized possession. "Will I have a place to put this in my new home?"

David winced at her words. There was no point in reminding her that her new home was merely a bedroom in an adult home. He fought the pang of deceit knowing now was not the time to burden her with the hard emotional truth. "Yes, we can put it on your bed." He took the quilt from her, refolded it, marveling in how soft it still felt in contrast to the other linens in her house, and placed it in one of the boxes. Though the decision had been difficult, he knew he'd made the right choice in moving her closer to him. His grandmother's mind was fading, her reality shifting more and more to another time, another place.

Grandma demonstrated a sudden burst of excitement as they led her to the car to take her back to her home for one last time. After one more night at Riverside Lodge, tomorrow they would pack her remaining grooming and personal belongings and would head to her new residence, over two-hundred miles away.

Accustomed to the disorganized manner in which Grandma lived, David still didn't expect the total disarray that greeted him when he followed her into her house. He looked at Jean and rolled his eyes in the same manner which annoyed him when Rachel or Emily relayed the same response. He stood wide-eyed and stared at the dining room table. "Now what?".

Not a single square inch of the table surface showed though underneath the piled household goods. Chipped mismatched dishes, rusted and burned on aluminum baking pans marred with dents from a lifetime of baking, and grease-stained and blistered plastic ware covered the table. Assorted glassware and canning jars sat amidst two produce boxes piled with fabric remnants, orange knits, and scratchy brown upholstery fabric woven long ago. David eyed the dozens of clothing items sewn over the decades, both as a hobby and likely out of necessity, during the hard times.

The overly warm temperature in the house heightened the smell of the old fabrics and dusty old wares scattered about. He checked the thermostat in the hall, set at eighty, and turned it way back, making a mental note to call the utility companies the coming week to shut off services.

"Barbara helped me gather some things for a yard sale before I move." Grandma's eyes looked down. Her voice trailed off.

David detected her despair. She'd talked about a yard sale several times over the past year, but David dismissed the idea as a whim, hoping it would be forgotten.

Grandma sat at the table and ran her hand across a couple of vases and figurines. "I've always liked to collect things. When I was little, I lined Mother's kitchen windowsill with jars filled with caterpillars, spiders, grasshoppers. One time I even had tadpoles. I still remember Mother getting upset with me whenever any of the contents got out. She didn't like it, but she tolerated it." Grandma giggled like the little girl in her memories. "I guess it's about time to start getting rid of some of my things."

David never held a garage sale in his life and had no intention of having one now. "We aren't going to have time for a garage sale this weekend. I'm sorry, we have to get you moved by tomorrow."

Grandma held out a sheet of labels upon which she had written shaky illegible prices. "I've already started gathering things to sell."

Jean browsed through the once precious belongings, now reduced to worn and used junk. "Let's see what you have." She picked up the remains of an old flower arrangement. A few sad faded yellow flowers with broken petals stuck out from among dusty wheat stalks, small cattails, and ragged stems stuck in a brown ceramic vase, now cracked and chipped.

Grandma beamed. "I picked and dried those flowers myself. Aren't they beautiful? I hate to sell them, but I have to start getting rid of some of my things. I'm old. I've lived longer than any of my kin and I know I can't hang on to these things forever." Her voice faded like the once vibrant flowers as she turned to busy herself, peering inside the china cabinet searching for more treasures.

The irony pricked David like a bee sting. The once beautiful arrangement was now dried and withered like the woman who fashioned it, the flowers faded like her memories. The heaviness in his chest caused him to pause and ponder the eventual progress of his own aging. It depressed him. But he was comforted he had family who would assist him in his old age.

An assorted hodge-podge of dated magazines lay stacked on the table. David thumbed through several dog-eared pages, clipped of easy-fix recipes and elegant desserts, that most likely now bulged from inside cookbooks and overflowed files and drawers, meals intended to be prepared at a later time. Overwhelming sadness gripped him knowing the time she wished for, of baking and sewing, would never again come. Whole sections were ripped from the large-type edition of Reader's Digest. "Grandma, these magazines are no good. There are too many pages missing." He held a butchered magazine.

"I ripped out some stories. I want to read them when I have time. Maybe when I've moved."

David's heart sank. Someday he would find the stories of romance, perfect lives, and adversity, stuffed in some folder, stashed on a shelf, or under a table. Stories to be read when there was time. Time, he knew that would never again come. Her aging eyes had played a cruel trick, the macular degeneration had destroyed her ability to see clearly, and her weakened mind crushed any ability to derive joy or understanding from the stories. One of the cruel ironies of age struck him. When you're old you have free time, only, in many cases, the time is rendered useless by failing health and mental clarity.

His grandmother bustled about and gathered what appeared to David to be even more useless belongings, still, he guessed to her, they were valuable finds.

Holding a chipped urn, he considered the value of so many of her things. "Grandma, since we can't have a garage sale maybe we can donate some of your things to a charity."

"Oh no." Her resistance was strong. "We can't do that; I can't make any money that way."

Jean, remembering all of the donations they'd made over the years, proceeded with her case. "I'm sure Goodwill would love to have your donations and you could take their value as a tax deduction."

Suspicious, Grandma looked at Jean. "How much would that be?"

"As much as you'd make on a garage sale, possibly more." David held his breath and waited for her response. He knew eventually he would be forced to dispose of many of her treasures. Her worn clothing, greyed linens, and ratty furniture would be tossed. Goodwill would welcome dishes, trinkets and some of her furnishings, and David would hopefully find friends of hers who would value some of the souvenirs from her trips. Still, he wondered what he would do with her many crates of photos and mementos.

"Okay," Grandma finally nodded. "But only if you take them to the Goodwill in town. I don't want to donate them to any other group. We should keep track of what we giveaway so I have a record."

David groaned under his breath; he'd forgotten how she liked to make lists. His neck muscles tensed. How had his simple plan become so complicated? Making a list of the items before him was an impossibility. "We can do that later." He turned around to catch Grandma sneaking up the stairs. "Grandma, wait for me. You shouldn't be taking the stairs alone."

"I'm not." She pouted. "I was going to wait for you to help me when you were done. I need to find some things upstairs."

David fought back his exasperation and took her arm.

Jean followed. "Let me give you a hand."

Grandma led them to her craft room. "Can you pull out that old wooden army trunk?" She bent over to sort through the assorted envelopes and bulging files of papers.

A musty odor drifted through the room as she shuffled through the old keepsakes. The glare from the sun shining into the room highlighted the shower of dust particles dancing in the air. David coughed, turning away at his allergy to dust.

As Grandma straightened, with her hands filled with papers, a bundle of letters spilled out. David reached out, catching them. The brittle paper and faded pencil marks warned him to handle the relics like the gems they were to his grandmother. He glanced at the childish scrawl on one of the faded fragile sheets. "Dear Mrs. Pearson, thank you ..."

"What are these?" David held a letter out for his grandmother to see. She took the letter and stared hard. David reached across to the pole lamp laden with dust, flicked on the switch hidden underneath the yellowed shade, and tipped it so the bulb shone toward her.

With more light to aid her, she held the old paper, focusing intently on the keepsake from long ago, concentrating, evoking memories from the past, before a slow broad smile spread across her creased face. "It's a letter from one of my students. Where did you find it? I have a whole stack of them." Her voice newly animated and eager to get side-tracked deep into her new finds.

Resigned the exploring would take some time, David pulled the small chair out from behind the sewing table. He eased his grandmother into it and handed her the packet of letters and cards bound by brittle rubber bands that broke when he removed them. Sitting on the floor next to her, he and Jean were amazed she still had the vintage notes, the memories of her days as a teacher, memories of the lives she had touched. His interest piqued, he rummaged through the trunk and lifted out a black framed Certificate of Recognition, issued by Goodwill Industries. '*For twenty-five years of faithful service.*' David knew Grandma donated many hours and her talents to the organization, she'd talked about it many times. He had seen notes on her old calendars and photos of the dolls for which she had made dresses, but he had no idea her volunteer work spanned so many years. "You must be very proud of this." David handed her the certificate, interrupting her as she thumbed through the precious letters. She ignored it, laid it down, and moved on with her hunt for another treasure.

Grandma jutted her chin out. "I actually volunteered for twenty-eight years. I volunteered for three more years after I received that."

For all her difficult manners and stubborn ways, David couldn't help but be awed by her spunk, her energy, and her kind heart. He smiled at the old woman, proud to know someone who had touched many lives in a positive and inspiring way. Leaning in, David took a banded packet of papers. "Can I help you find something?"

"I can find it." She continued her search. "The newspaper wrote an article about me and even took my picture when they gave me this award." She beamed with pleasure before continuing, "I bet you can't guess how many dolls I dressed for Goodwill to sell." Not awaiting a response, she continued. "Several thousand. I also made hundreds of beaded Christmas tree ornaments for the store to sell. Did I ever show you my ornaments?"

"Yes, we've seen them, you gave some to Jean the last time we were here. Did you find what you came up here for?"

Lost in her thoughts, she shook her head. She reached deeper into the chest and pulled out a photo album. She ran her hand across the front of the old-fashioned album then opened it to reveal pages of black and white photos affixed to black pages with small red gummed corners, much like the old-fashioned photo books from the early 1960s.

David noticed the frustration in her befuddled expression. His grandmother's eyes focused with intensity on the images as she slowly flipped through the pages, gazing at the photos in wide-eyed amazement. "May I see?"

Grandma smiled weakly. "These were taken so long ago. But I remember so many of these like only yesterday." Edna ran her gnarled index finger across a photo. "See? This was Larry and Kora-Lee when he came back from Korea, married to her."

"And this must be Lorraine?" David pointed to a small child around five-years-old.

"Yes." Edna tapped on one of the figures. "And Kora-Lee is pregnant here with Alicia." Her eyes narrowed. "I could never understand why he married her like that, carrying another man's child."

David sighed and looked at his watch. It was apparent her happy memories were taking a turn for the worse. He pushed his chair back. "It's getting late. Are you ready to go back downstairs?"

She sighed, replacing the discoveries into the trunk, and closed the lid. David pushed it back into its place in the closet. At least for now.

With Grandma's arm linked in his, David led her back down the stairs to the dining room. Her eyes glistened and tears welled up as she gazed upon her life represented in broken trinkets. "Let me help you with these things, we can decide what to do with them later." David packed a few into a box. He knew he was stalling. He would eventually have to deal with what to do with these vestiges from her life, including tossing so many of her memories. A twinge of guilt about his deceit and easy way out crept over him. For now, it was important for her, or maybe for him, to let her hold on to her past for a little longer.

A knock at the door drew David's attention.

"Sorry to drop in like this, I noticed your car and trailer. I guess this is goodbye." Fred stood outside holding a wooden chest about a foot and a half across.

"That's okay, it's nice to see you again. Come in." David stepped aside motioning Fred in. He called out to Edna and Jean as Fred handed him the chest.

Questioning the contents, David hoisted the chest, analyzing the weight, onto the table, already guessing its contents. "What's this?" He forced a closed-lip smile, squelching any uncontrolled vocalization.

"I came by to say goodbye and to return the silverware set which Edna had asked me to keep when she had so many visitors in and out after Larry died. She didn't want the additional worry of it being stolen. I'd forgotten all about it."

Edna shuffled to the dining room and smiled at the chest on the table. "My silverware. You brought it back. I almost forgot about it." She opened the small chest and plucked out several pieces. "Now I have two sets."

David resisted the head thump. He held back the mix of frustration and absurdity churning inside and focused on Fred's weary appearance. "Thanks, Fred. I'm glad you brought it by. It gives me another opportunity to thank you for all you and Marge have done for Edna. I hope Marge is doing okay."

Fred's eyes welled up. He responded she was doing fine, but David suspected she wasn't doing as well as Fred was saying. David's decision to move his grandmother closer to him would no doubt also benefit Fred too. Without feeling obliged to check in on Edna, Fred could now focus all his time and energy on caring for his wife.

With hugs and handshakes exchanged and difficult goodbyes spoken, Fred walked out the door. David stared at the silverware chest. He didn't know whether to laugh or cry. After months of suspecting the worst in Alicia, he wondered now if he'd judged her too harshly. Recovering the silver after so many months, he now wondered if the questionable checks had another reasonable explanation. He looked at his watch. The weekend was getting away from them. He stood by the mahogany chest, shaking his head. He brought his hands to his temples and smiled at Jean. "Do you want to call the insurance company and explain this, or should I? I guess I have to take back some of my doubts about Alicia too." They laughed before heading back to the living room.

"Grandma, you need to decide what you want to move to your new home. We can take your bed and one of the dressers. Remember, you are only going to have one room." David looked around the room once more, its contents ran the gamut from the tackiest of dime-store trinkets to artistic porcelain hand-painted vases from Korea which were purchased on a trip almost twenty years earlier, with Alicia. Most of the living room furniture was beyond well-worn, almost shoddy. There wouldn't be room for much. Either her recliner or the rocker, and maybe the antique secretary. "You should have room for your secretary if you like. That way you'll have a place for some of your travel keepsakes."

Grandma scanned the room. She shook her head. "That's my favorite piece of furniture, but I want you to have it."

"It is a very beautiful antique, how about I take it after you're gone. For now, you should enjoy it while you can. I can make room for it and it will help your new place feel more like home."

Tapping the watch on her wrist, Jean moved down the hall. "Do you want to pick out a few wall hangings?" Jean removed a gold-framed needlepoint picture of bright red poppies.

"Oh, no. I want you to have that, too."

Jean turned over the needlepoint. "It has Lorraine's name on the back." She held it out to Edna.

She waved Jean's comment aside. "Oh, never mind that. I wrote that on the back years ago, Lorraine never particularly cared to have it anyway, and I want you and David to have it." Edna proceeded to remove a matching needlepoint set of a boy and girl, then handed the pictures to Jean before shuffling to the armoire. "I want these."

David watched her move through the condo. The realization stung it would most likely be her last stroll through the home of which she was so proud. David returned upstairs to the guest room where he had spent a few nights, certainly more than he had cared to. He still flinched at the sight of the crushed red velour bedspread that cloaked the bed like a draped casket. He shuddered every time he stepped into the room, even knowing the carpet was clean and he had washed the sheets. He yanked open drawers revealing fabric and yarn, patterns and magazines. Nearly ninety-five years of stuff. Only it wasn't stuff, it was her life. The uneasy feeling in his stomach returned. He looked at the vivid pastel drawing of a garden, bursting with vibrant colors and framed in gold. He marveled at her love of bright, vibrant, overbearing colors. It was a reflection of the personality he was certain Grandma once had. He turned off the light and looked over his shoulder, knowing someday he would be back in this room. He guessed the next visit would be to bury his grandmother and empty her home.

"Can I give you a hand?" Jean poked her head into the bedroom.

David turned around and shrugged. "Nah. There's nothing in this room we need to take right now." He looked at the clothes draping Jean's arm. "Are these the clothes we're taking?" David scooped them up, folded them in half, laid them on the top of the biggest box and carried the bundle downstairs.

Grandma stood surveying at the half-empty living room. "What about the rest of my things?"

"After you get settled, we can go through a few more things, but you're not going to have room for everything."

"First, I couldn't take Missy, now I have to leave so many belongings. Are you sure I have to leave Missy with Barbara?"

"I know it's hard, Grandma. But you can't take Missy. You have to be able to care for a dog on your own."

"I can take Missy out and feed her just fine. Why is everyone treating me like I'm incompetent?"

Noticing she was visibly shaken, David put his arm around her. "We know you're not incompetent. But you do need assistance."

"You don't understand. I want to stay at my house. How come no one understands." The tears flowed.

"It's going to be okay. I've given all your friends your new address and phone number. Barbara said she has a brother-in-law in the Seattle area. She might visit, and most importantly, Jean and I live only a few minutes away from your new home." David patted her shoulder and drew her close.

She sniffed into her hanky, refusing to look at him. "What about my violets?" Grandma's voice cracked. She hurried to the plant stand.

Overwhelmed by their ongoing prolific growth, in spite of recent neglect while at Riverside Lodge, David stared at her purple and pink African violets.

"Are we going to have room for these?" Edna reached down and lifted a pot displaying a single plant with a one-foot diameter.

"Of course, you will." His conscience jabbed at him knowing he would be keeping most of them, as Edna would not have the space, and in time they would go the way of neglect. Then again, knowing how Jean cared for plants, it was probably sentencing them to death either way. "We'll put them in the truck last."

With the pickup loaded with her personal effects and a few large items, it was time to return her to Riverside for the night. With a last look around, David regarded the house in a state of disarray. Grandma's eyes followed his gaze. His heart ached for her. "Are you ready?"

She turned away. "When will I be able to come back?"

David and Jean exchanged a sad look. This time he couldn't lie. There would be no coming back. Not for her. Her Alzheimer's had slowly but steadily stolen more and more reality. Age and disease were going to win. Grandma would never again know the freedom of living on her own in her own home. His heart felt an unfamiliar heaviness that he guessed echoed his grandmothers'. He took her hands and urged her to look at him. "I don't think you will, Grandma." David forced back his tears, turned the thermostat off, and flicked off the lights.

The next morning, David and Jean shut the door, for the last time, to what had become their regular hotel room. It didn't take long to gather the remaining belongings from Riverside Lodge and load them into the car. To their relief, Grandma appeared at ease, even happy. They said goodbye to the staff and headed home, this time, for good.

As always, Grandma chatted up a storm during most of the drive. Despite her confusion, she knew she was going back to a place where she had spent some of the happiest years of her life.

"My sister, Pearl, lived outside Issaquah, in Monohan. We had such lovely times on picnics and walking through the woods picking wildflowers."

Somehow, the trip back to the place of her young adult life seemed appropriate. Grandma rambled on about her first teaching job in a one-room schoolhouse on the eastern shores of Lake Sammamish. David smiled observing her enthusiasm as she shared the memories that danced through her mind. With only one brief stop, after four and a half hours, David pulled the car off the freeway onto the Lake Sammamish exit. "Here's Lake Sammamish, Grandma. Does it look familiar?"

"Where's the ferry? Will we be taking the ferry across?"

The unusual question caught David's attention. He raised his eyebrows and smiled into the rear-view mirror at Jean. "What ferry is that?"

"The ferry. We always take the ferry across the lake."

David glanced over at his grandmother. She sat as calm as the lake that lay before them. "There is no ferry on Lake Sammamish. You're remembering the ferry on Lake Washington or Puget Sound."

"Well. You'll see. There certainly is." Grandma clipped her words and threw back her shoulders in defiance.

David dropped the subject. Her new home was only a few minutes away, a block off the west side of the lake. "Did I tell you the man who owns the house is a geriatric doctor?"

Grandma's eyebrows rose in question. "I don't need a doctor."

Pulling the car up the steep drive, he looked across the seat. "He's a doctor for older people. He'll make sure everyone is well taken care of. You'll have several other residents to keep you company." Parking the car as close to the front door as possible, David looked over at his grandmother. "Here we are."

"Where are we?" Grandma turned; her eyes vacant as she gazed past David to the large white house which loomed before her. She brought her hand to her cheek. "This isn't my house."

David banged his head against the car seat. He sighed. Any optimism he had his life was going to be simplified by the move seemed short-lived.

Chapter 34

No longer facing the long frustrating drive to eastern Washington, it was easy for David to visit his grandmother several times a week on his way home from work. Without the worries about what surprises he would find when he arrived, his drive was tension-free. Instead of checking off mental lists of what needed to be done, he relaxed to the music from his latest CD. From the moment he pulled into the long drive, with the professionally maintained lawn and the pruned arborvitae lining the way, he relaxed knowing her home and surroundings were clean and comfortable. Rubbing his hands on his arms against the cool evening, David grabbed his jacket from the front seat and strode to the front door.

He greeted Joanne, the live-in CNA and entered to a pleasant scent of floral air-freshener, a warm welcome from her home that reeked of musty fabrics and pet odors, or the sterile antiseptic-smelling hospital environment from which she had recently come. David greeted the two residents watching television in the living room as he passed.

"Hello, Grandma." David stood by her bedside, where she sat solemn, dressed in a laundered and coordinated blue top and slacks, lost deep in her thoughts, her own world.

"Gracious, is it that time already? Is it dinner time?"

"No. I'm just here for a visit. How come you're not out in the living room with the others?"

"I prefer to be left alone. I don't like mixing with the old people who live here. They're simply not my type."

Convinced he'd made the right decision to move his grandmother closer, he wished she would find some enjoyment in her new home. Though his worries had eased and he now had more time with his family, now he and his family were the only people near enough to stop by to see her. Several of her friends had said they would make it over to visit in the future, but David's practical nature told him it wasn't something he could count on. He wondered if he called Alicia with an update if she would bring Lacey by. He wondered too if that would bring any joy to his grandmother's near joyless life.

After his visit, David pulled into his driveway, pushed the button on the garage door opener, and closed the door behind him, and shutting his mind off from his work.

He called out as he went to his bedroom to change clothes. "I'm home."

Jean met him in the bedroom. "Tough day?"

David shook his head. "What else is there?" He cocked his head, seeing his wife's serious expression. "What's up?"

"Alicia called. Says it's important. She wants you to call her right away."

David tossed his blue dress shirt in the hamper and grabbed a T-shirt. "Did she give you any clue what it's about?"

Jean shook her head. "She wouldn't say."

Grabbing a beer from the fridge, David walked over to the phone on the kitchen counter, sat on a stool, and sighed. "I was thinking of calling her anyway. Might as well get it over with." He scrolled down the list of stored contacts to Alicia's phone number and hit dial. The call was answered right away. "Hi Alicia, It's David."

"David. Thanks for calling me back."

Immediately, David sensed an urgency in her hoarse and panicky voice. "What's going on?"

"Lacey's sick. Her kidneys are failing."

David straightened on the kitchen stool and focused on the shocking seriousness of the conversation. "I'm sorry. That's got to be incredibly difficult for you and your family. Is she going to be okay?"

"We have no guarantees. She needs a kidney transplant within the next few days. I was tested for compatibility, along with Mom and Lorraine. My blood type is not compatible, but fortunately, Lorraine's is. Lorraine is donating one of her kidneys. Surgery is scheduled the day after tomorrow."

"That's good news. You know Jean and I wish her only the best." David's throat had gone dry, his words cracked as he spoke and his eyes welled. In spite of the tension between him and his stepsister, there could be no ill wishes for Lacey. "I'm sure Jean will be praying for her too." Slow measured breathing came across the line before Alicia continued.

"That's not the only reason I'm calling, though."

"What else is going on?" David glanced around, hoping to get Jean's attention.

"When I was screened and tested to see if I might be a potential match for Lacey, the blood and tissue typing discovered something odd. Further blood tests were ordered and confirm what the doctor suspected."

David shifted uncomfortably on the wooden stool. "Okay."

"I don't know a lot about what blood types can result from different combinations of blood. I do know Mom and Lorraine have type O, and I have type B negative."

"I'm sorry, Alicia. I don't have much understanding either about how all that works. What does that indicate?"

"The doctor concluded with my B negative blood type, it was highly unlikely that my biological father could be the same as Lorraine's, especially taking into account Peter, our supposed father, was Chinese."

David hit the speaker button on the phone, quickly motioning to Jean. He sucked in air. "So, what are you saying?"

"I confronted mom. She told me she and your dad had an affair while he was still married to your mother. You knew my mom was pregnant with me when she and Larry married, right? Everyone assumed Peter was both Lorraine's father and mine, but Mom always considered the possibility that Larry was my biological father." Alicia delayed before continuing. "Larry's blood type was AB negative, which is rare, but extremely unlikely in the Asian population, and can result in a B negative offspring."

David's hand hurt from clenching the phone tightly, stressed with all the earth rattling news being lobbed at him. "Wait, there's too much going on here. You're saying you're my half-sister, not my stepsister because Larry had type AB blood? Are you sure about his blood type?" David took a long swig of his beer, wishing it were something a little stiffer.

"That's what was on his organ donor card."

David's heartbeat accelerated like a race car speeding toward the checkered flag. His thoughts whizzed out of control. He had so many questions, but he breathed deeply, gripping his emotions to maintain focus on the innocent child facing a life-threatening illness. "Does Grandma know?" David hesitated. "About Lacey, I mean?"

"Not yet. I'm going to call her next and tell her. I'm still not sure how to break the other news to her."

"I'm sorry, it's a little hard for me to wrap my head around this. I have to admit, you look different enough from Lorraine, your mother must have suspected Larry was your father, not Peter?"

"I guess she did. At first, she didn't want Larry to feel compelled to marry her only because she was pregnant with his child, and since she was still married to Peter...." Her voice trailed. "Since she wasn't sure either way, it was best to assume I was Peter's child too. There was no reason for my mother to pursue it." Alicia chuckled. "I don't think Larry could face telling his mother about his affair. You know how she can be." Alicia's chuckle progressed into a laugh, slicing through some of the tension.

"You're laughing. What's so funny?"

"Don't you see? Mom wanted Larry to love her, and accept me as his daughter, even if I was not biologically his offspring. On the other hand, not being Larry's biological child is the reason Grandma Edna never accepted me or Lorraine completely as her family. I think it's ironic that as it turns out, I am her granddaughter. I wonder if that will change her opinion of me."

David mulled over Alicia's comment. He couldn't dispute it. Several times Edna told him Alicia and Lorraine weren't family because they weren't blood. He too, wondered how his grandmother's view might change with this new-found development. He wondered if Edna was simply too old to comprehend how much the family unit had changed since she was a child. Now, modern families were often blended families, inter-racial families, adopted from not only different parents but different countries, and of differing skin tones, even same-sex couples. Was it too much to hope that at this late stage in life, there was still time for Edna and her granddaughters to forge a familial relationship?

Chapter 35

Hearing Gloria calling out to her, Edna glanced up from watching television with some of the other residents. The cheeriness in Gloria's voice told Edna it was good news.

"There's someone on the phone for you, Dear."

Edna brightened as she pushed off the cushion, strutting toward the kitchen with her cane, proud to have a family that loved her and called her. "Gracious. David just left. Who is it? Did they say?"

"It's your granddaughter." Gloria smiled, handing Edna the receiver.

Rachel hadn't called her since she returned to school. Her hand trembled in excitement waiting to hear about school. Taking the phone, Edna greeted her caller. "Rachel?"

"No, Edna, it's not Rachel, it's Alicia."

"Alicia?" Edna's hand gripped the phone tighter hearing sadness in Alicia's voice. She moved to the small chair by the phone and settled into it. She hadn't heard from Alicia since David moved her to this place. She thought back to Alicia's phone call the day Larry died. Something must be up for Alicia to be calling her now, at this time. She wouldn't call if it weren't serious. Edna's chest tensed and her voice broke. "Are you okay?"

"I'm calling because Lacey's sick"

"What do you mean? What's wrong with her?"

"Her kidneys are failing quickly. Without a transplant, she will die."

Blood rushed from Edna's head and her hands shook. "Lacey? How can that be? She can't die." Edna felt her breath weaken while her heart raced. "She was fine when I saw her."

Gloria reached for Edna's hand, bending over her with concerned eyes. "Is everything okay, Edna?"

Edna shook her head "My-great-granddaughter could die." Edna returned her attention to Alicia. "I never knew young children could need a kidney transplant. Will she get one in time?"

194

"It turns out Lorraine is a perfect match and is donating one of hers to save Lacey's life."

Alicia's words soothed Edna's nervousness, but her muscles tightened with concern. "Oh, Lord. What about Lorraine? Will she be okay?"

"Without Lorraine's kidney, there may not be enough time to find another suitable donor. They should both be fine within a few weeks."

Edna's hand steadied, but her mouth was parched like desert sand. Edna took a few sips of the water Gloria had placed next to her. "I never imagined someone could donate a kidney while they were alive. That's very brave of Lorraine."

Alicia agreed. "It's pretty amazing. I think Dad inspired her by being an organ donor himself."

Edna stiffened as she recalled her resentment and anger when she was told Larry was donating his organs. Unable to hold back the tears, Edna's grief turned to pride. The bitterness of her son's death sweetened at the realization he possibly saved another life with his unselfish act.

"Grandma. There's something else we learned while I was being checked as a potential donor for Lacey. I need you to listen and to understand what I am going to tell you."

Edna's back ached from the wooden chair. She shifted to settle herself through Alicia's firm words, dabbing at her tears with a tissue. "What's that?"

Alicia's tone softened. "The doctors performed lots of blood and tissue tests for organ compatibility. I found out Peter, Mom's first husband, Lorraine's father, is not my biological father. It turns out Larry was my biological father."

"My word. That can't possibly be right. Your mother was extremely pregnant before Larry married her, and he had only been divorced for two months." Edna grabbed her water glass and took several gulps, helping still her woozy head. "Oh my, what are you saying? Are you sure?"

"Blood typing is very accurate, very scientific. Based on his blood type and mine, Larry was my father."

Edna's mind spun in dizzying confusion. She struggled for a clearer understanding. "Larry was your real father?"

Was it possible, after all these years of deception? Edna fought to remember the day Larry had said he was married again and his new wife had a child and was pregnant. Had he known all along that Alicia was his biological daughter? How could he not have known? Kora-Lee must have known and lied to Larry. Edna never trusted her. Nothing made any sense.

"Grandma, are you okay?"

Edna shook her head. "No. It doesn't make sense. Why didn't Larry tell me? How could your mother not have known?" Was Alicia really her granddaughter? Edna brought her hands to her eyes. If only she'd known. Perhaps things could have been different.

Chapter 36

David tried to dissuade his grandmother from going to the airport with him to pick up Nathan. "The walk from the parking garage to baggage claim is going to be too much for you."

"I haven't seen Nathan since he was a child. I want to go with you." Her firm teacher voice demanded his agreement.

After double-checking the flight arrival information, David calculated the drive time and tacked on an extra hour, knowing the walk would be slow and tiring for Grandma. He quickly realized he should have insisted she get reacquainted with Nathan at his home instead of the fast-paced, hectic airport.

The smile never left his grandmother's face for the entire hour-long drive to Sea-Tac International Airport. As David eased her from her car seat, her moist eyes and wide grin offered some reassurance Grandma was where she needed to be. He shrugged in defeat. Hoping to simplify the slow shuffle across the parking lot and down the long hallway leading to the baggage carousel, David pointed out the rack of wheelchairs available. "How about we get you a wheelchair? It will be a lot faster than walking with your cane." David held his breath hoping for an affirmative response. Even before he asked, he knew the answer. Grandma's eyes cut like a laser. He wouldn't push any further. Holding onto her frail arm he cautiously guided her through the packed crowd of travelers scurrying by. Spotting the overhead sign pointing the way, he led her toward the airline's baggage claim. "Nathan's been looking forward to finally seeing you again after all these years, Grandma."

"That's nice. I'm sure he's a wonderful young man, just like you." Grandma patted David's arm.

In spite of the years of competition between him and his brother, David missed him. With the distance separating them, and infrequent calls, the relationship had waned. He looked forward to getting reacquainted with his brother again, as well as getting some relief in decision- making and the future care for their grandmother.

Edna broke David's train of thought. "I've always thought the service was a pretty good life. I enjoyed the years Jacob was in the service. I wish he had stayed on. It's so nice Nathan followed in his father and his grandfather's footsteps, isn't it?"

David reflected on his past, twenty-five years earlier, to when Nathan graduated from high school and was uncertain about the direction of his life. Now here he was a First Sergeant and career soldier. David paced, checking in all directions in between glances at his watch hoping there wasn't a last-minute delay.

"Hey, David."

David turned toward the husky voice he detected across the congested airport. He recognized Nathan approaching with a brisk walk. David unconsciously grinned. He had to admit Nathan looked good in his uniform. Nathan also carried about twenty fewer pounds around the middle than he did. For a moment, David's mind flashed to the photos Grandma had shown him of his grandfather, Jacob. David hadn't previously thought his brother looked that much like his father or grandfather, but seeing him now compared to the family photos, the resemblance was striking. During the past two years, Nathan's hair had grayed significantly. His deep-set eyes and the prominent nose so characteristic of the Pearson family emphasized his likeness to Larry and Jacob. David wondered if his grandmother noticed the same resemblance.

"How are you doing?" David extended his right hand to his brother and slapped him on the back in greeting. He looked at his grandmother. "Well, Grandma? Are you glad to finally see Nathan again after all these years?"

"Well, you're quite a handsome young soldier, aren't you?" Edna tipped her chin with a shy and nervous voice. "I have to admit."

David started to laugh but hesitated upon seeing his grandmother's flushed complexion.

"I've always been smitten by men in uniforms." Edna brought her hand to her lips, seemingly embarrassed by her words.

Nathan exchanged looks with his brother, his raised brows questioning. "I'm happy to finally see you again after so long." Nathan reached out to hug her.

"Not so fast young man, we just met." Grandma pulled away, instead, extending her right hand in a handshake.

David placed his hand on Nathan's shoulder. "Grandma, this is Nathan, your grandson." He noticed his grandmother's expression. No sparkle in her eyes or wide grin, like she wore the entire trip to the airport, and like he expected after finally being reunited. Instead, she looked at Nathan with suspicion. She was lost in another place, another time. Once more, David knew Grandma was in a separate reality.

David sighed as the announcement blared confirming the carousel numbers of the incoming luggage. Travelers scurried past to be first at their carousel as the baggage rolled down the belts. He tilted his head in the direction of the baggage carousels and whispered. "Remember, Grandma's not always in the same world as the rest of us."

"Can I give you a hand, Grandma?" Nathan extended his arm to link hers.

"Do you come to Dehoney's often?"

Nathan's eyes widened in confusion, struggling to understand. "Dehoney's? We're not at Dehoney's, we're at the airport."

She ignored his response and continued. "There's always plenty of action here. Look at the crowd. It's the best dance hall in the whole city of Seattle. Come on, soldier, let's dance." Grandma's flushed cheeks revealed a self-conscious grin and she giggled like an awkward teenager.

David smiled, shrugged, and looked at his brother. "I warned you about her delusions. You do look a lot like Jacob, I'm sure she thinks you're him."

Nathan hesitated for only a moment, then shrugged too, and played along with a smile. "Okay, let's dance." He handed David the duffel bag from his shoulder and took his grandmother's arms and swung her around.

She beamed. "I love coming to Dehoney's." Edna swayed back and forth. "Come on," she tugged on Nathan's arm. "Let's see how you dance."

Nathan awkwardly danced her around, side-stepping toward the baggage carousel.

David noticed the smiles and nudges as passers-by watched the six-foot soldier sway back and forth with a fragile old woman. The tension of the afternoon escaped through his laughter. "Welcome home, Nathan."

Chapter 37

Edna took a deep breath, taken by the scent of his cologne. She looked around the big hall with crystal chandeliers. The large wooden planked floor once perfect for dancing had been replaced with buffed tile. Edna loved to kick and sway to "Sneak" and "Cat Whiskers." She knew all the latest tunes. Music spilled into the hall, but she didn't see the stage or the jazz band that normally performed. The blaring sounds from the crowd hurt her ears and she turned to look for the wooden stage in the front of the massive hall. Confused it no longer existed, Edna laughed as she watched her date awkwardly step and tap in time to the foxtrot and the two-step waltz. His lanky arms swinging out of tune to the music.

"You're out of practice, Mr. Pearson," Edna batted her eyes coyly at her date.

Jacob wasn't much of a dancer; he was clumsy on his feet. Edna, however, moved with the smoothness of fine scotch. She was quick and athletic as she jitterbugged across the floor to the sax of Duke Ellington. She looked over at the young soldier's flushed face, seemingly embarrassed as he looked around the crowded floor. She knew they turned heads when they were in the room. Jacob, so dapper in his army uniform, and her, quite in fashion in her red satin dress, swaying as she danced. "Do you know the Charleston, soldier?"

Her beau shook his head.

"I don't much like dancing with only one partner. But it's different when it's a man you admire and like the best."

"I like you, too, Grandma." The soldier slowed his step and escorted her off the dance floor.

She gazed into the dark eyes of her handsome beau, beaming with pride, knowing someone cared about her.

Chapter 38

Nathan shook his head, he'd experienced many frightening and life-threatening circumstances in the past twenty years, but none had prepared him for the discomfort he felt with his grandmother's erratic behavior. He cast a sideways glance to his brother, his eyes pleading for help.

"Sorry, perhaps I should have given you a better idea of what you might expect."

"What do I do?" Nathan tensed with the awkward situation, aware of the flush on his burning cheeks as passersby looked at them with amusement.

David shrugged and tried to take his grandmother's arm. "It's easiest to just go along." "Come on, Grandma. Nathan needs to get his bag. It's been a long evening and we can catch up on everything on the way home."

Ignoring David, Edna continued her hold on Nathan's arm. "You know, soldier, before you take me home don't you think you should offer to buy me a drink?"

Nathan steered her to the conveyor belt spewing luggage out for the eager recipients. "How about when we get back to David's, we all get something to drink?"

Grandma narrowed her gaze at him. "You know I'm not much for alcohol, but I wouldn't mind a little something with someone as handsome as you."

Spying his army green duffle bag, Nathan freed himself long enough to snatch the bag. As he approached his brother and grandmother, with the large bag strapped to his shoulder, Grandma winked at him before turning to David. He heard her whisper to David. "Just you wait, you'll see. He's the one I'm going to marry someday." She giggled again as she took her soldier by the arm and proudly strutted down the corridor.

"Grandma, I think you're a bit confused right now." Nathan led her through the crowd.

"Never you mind now." She grinned as they walked through the crowd.

David stepped to his grandmother's other side and attempted to steer the conversation. "Grandma, Nathan sure looks a lot like his great-granddad, Jacob, doesn't he?"

She stopped walking and huffed at David in protest. "You don't know anything about Jacob."

Nathan patted her arm. "You'll have to tell me all about my great-granddad sometime, especially since I remind you of him." Arm and arm, they headed for the parking garage.

Chapter 39

Her room was nice enough, but Edna was homesick. The more time she spent in the confines of someone else's home, the more she missed the freedom to wander around her house and stroll through her yard. The grounds around her new home were beautiful, but the steeply sloped terrain made it almost impossible for her to maneuver around, so she settled for soaking in the color and scents from the cushioned and wicker seats and wicker table positioned around the small patio area. A gardener came by weekly and weeded and mowed. Edna valued the few minutes here and there the middle-aged man spent chatting with her about the shrubs and various trees planted in the backyard. His knowledge of horticulture brought back many happy memories of her years as a master gardener.

The new electric bed David bought allowed her to sleep with the bed at a slight angle and helped ease some of the pain that accompanied aging. And on top of the bed, was her most revered display of talent, her most precious keepsake from the past, her quilt. A pencil drawing depicting a lake surrounded by tall pyramid-shaped trees, from Emily, hung in a wood frame on her wall along with the needlepoint tapestries of a young boy and girl which she made for Bernice's college dorm, shortly before she died. Occasionally Edna received updates from Barbara on how Missy had adjusted to her new living arrangements, and how much consolation Missy brought to her ailing husband, Robert. Her heart ached when she thought about Missy, but she was happy Missy brought joy to her new owner. Twice, Alicia sent updates on Lacey, and Lacey sent drawings that Edna cherished, tucking them inside the frame of the mirror over her dresser along with Lacey's school photo.

Gloria poked her head inside. "David will be here soon. Are you ready to go?"

"Of course, I'm ready." Edna gathered her coat and purse and shuffled to the living room to wait for David. The hardwood floor made it easy to maneuver especially with her cane and occasional walker. Though a three-story home, all Edna ever saw was the floor she lived on, which consisted of six bedrooms, all with a toilet and sink, one main bathroom with a large shower stall, as well as the common living space with a kitchen and dining area. For the most part, the residents spent their days in this area, staring at the nonsense that flashed across the television screen or babbling about their families and how they were going to visit someday. Today the living room was calm and quiet without the noise from the television.

Simon's son was visiting, and as usual, Henrietta and Gladys sat alone. Gladys looked at Edna with longing in her eyes. "Are you going to your grandson's for dinner again?"

Edna beamed. In addition to David's weekly visits, Nathan came by once a month or so and even joined her for dinner at David's. It was nice living closer to both of her grandsons. "Yes, I'm lucky to have him. Maybe someday I'll see my granddaughter and great-granddaughter again too."

The white walls and large picture windows, framed in heavy champagne color brocade drapes, and held back by a thick gold cord, always left her chilled, despite the sunlight spilling in. Plopping her things onto the plush rose-colored sofa, with overstuffed sage and deep purple pillows, she hobbled over to the window and gazed far off into the distance. The glare from the sun burned her eyes as she strained to see the lake she knew lay before her, somewhere. But it lay beyond the scope of her failing eyes' ability to see. Even though she couldn't see it too well, David had told her the view of the lake was spectacular. Staring off in the direction of the lake, she reminisced about her teens and young adult life where she spent so many days on the shores picnicking with Pearl and her husband, Stanley. The cold seeped through the large plate-glass windows. Her eyes scanned the blazing palette of early fall colors that streaked across the horizon. She squinted against the light and longed for her ability to see with more clarity again.

Edna turned as a sudden gust blew into the room. She crossed her arms tightly across her chest, shivering against the cold as David stepped inside.

"I didn't see your car coming?" Edna shuffled past the others. Gloria retrieved the coat and scarf from the sofa.

"Is it cold outside?" Edna grabbed her red wool scarf from Gloria and wrapped it snugly around her neck.

David held her coat out and eased her arms into it. "It's a bit nippy."

Edna grinned as Gloria put her arm around Edna's shoulder, patting it with a caring touch. "Have a nice evening, I'll see you later."

Edna shivered against the crisp fall air as David helped her into the warm car. She snuggled into the seat. Heading down the tree-lined two-lane road toward David's house, Edna looked out the window to the expanse of water almost hidden by houses. "It's a shame they've built so many homes. It's not at all the way things used to be." She sighed at the memories of her childhood years on the shores of the lake. Edna stared across the water to the vastness which lay beyond and diverged into a blur. "It's not right. We used to have such lovely picnics here."

David reached across and took his grandmother's hand. "I bet it was a lot different back then."

"It was a more relaxed life." Edna settled back in her seat. "Are we taking the ferry today?" Edna's eyes squinted from the sun's glare reflecting off the water as they came around the end of the lake, with a more open view.

"Grandma, we've been through this. There's no ferry on Lake Sammamish, we have to drive around the lake."

Edna pouted, squirming against the tight seat belt. "We always take the ferry across the lake to visit father." She opened the purse on her lap and fumbled around searching for change. "That's okay, I have money."

"You took the ferry on Puget Sound to Vashon Island, that was a long time ago."

Edna wrinkled her brow. "Oh, you." Frustrated by his response, Edna gripped her coins in her fist and watched out the window. The car moved away from the water and the scenery shifted. Edna noticed all the small businesses and houses along the way. Finally, the car turned down the gravel road lined with near-naked maple trees with a few stubborn golden leaves holding on for another day. The serenity of the country returned. She couldn't wait to get home. She had missed her family while she was away.

When the car pulled to a stop after her ride, Edna hungered for the cozy feeling inside where her mother always had a fire in the stove. Struggling to climb out, David took her arm and helped her to the door. The odor from sharp onions assaulted her, signaling meatloaf, which Mother often served on Sunday before Daddy had to leave for work again at the logging camp on Vashon Island. She looked around the surroundings, confused she didn't see her mother. "Where's Mother? Is she out in the garden?" Edna called to the emptiness of the house as she walked over to the wood-burning stove in the living room to take the chill from her hands. Edna rubbed them vigorously.

David came in. "Your mother's not here, but we can see if Jean is outside?"

Edna dutifully followed him outside as she tried to remember who Jean was. "Where's Mother? I don't see her old burlap harvest bag hanging by the door. She must be gathering produce for dinner." Edna looked around the yard and brightened when she saw a familiar figure picking lettuce leaves for tonight's salad.

Mother smiled and handed Edna the salad greens. "Are you hungry? Dinner's about ready. I only have to make the biscuits."

Edna cocked her head, her mother looked younger than she remembered, but she was put to ease as mother took her hand as they strolled inside. "May I help?" Edna loved the baking powder biscuits they had most evenings. She opened the cabinet door under Mama's cupboard and rummaged around. Out of the corner of her eye, she spotted her mother shaking her head, but always patient, Mother said nothing, she simply smiled at her daughter. Edna opened and closed the drawers. Finally, in the third drawer, she pulled out a yellow and orange apron. Someone had moved it. Her fingers fumbled as she struggled to tie the strings behind her back.

"Here, let me help you."

Edna welcomed the help, tying the apron around her waist.

The flour slopped out as she dug deep into the canister with the white plastic measuring cup, and with slow careful moves, she scooped out two cups. She laughed as flour drifted down and settled on the countertop. Knowing the recipe by heart, Edna measured out two teaspoons from the red can of baking powder while watching her mother reach to the top shelf for the shortening.

"Let me help." Kind gentle hands guided Edna's hand helping dice the shortening into a coarse mixture.

With the warm milk poured in, Edna stirred gently with the wooden spoon until Mother stepped in and removed the spoon from her hand.

"That looks perfect. I'll take over now."

"I can do the kneading. I'm old enough." Edna pouted, feeling pushed away.

Her mother smiled, gathered the dough, and slapped it on the board. Edna reached for the baking pan to help place the cut biscuits on the pan for baking.

"How's it going in here?" David appeared in the doorway.

The oven door closed on the biscuits. "Dinner in ten minutes. Can you show Grandma where to wash up?"

Edna gripped David's arm and shuffled to the bathroom. She could hardly wait for her father to return from the town. He should have been home by now. She couldn't understand what had happened to him and why the family was gathering to eat without him.

David led her to her place at the table. The aroma of warm bread wafted into the dining room. Edna beamed with pride, knowing she helped with the family dinner. "Where's Daddy? Shouldn't he be home by now? We can't eat without him." Edna's chest tightened. She stared at the blank faces looking back at her.

A strong hand reached out and grasped hers with a firm but kind voice. "Grandma, you're confused again. Your mother and father are gone. I'm your grandson, David. You're having dinner with my family, remember?"

"Oh, you." Edna shot an indignant glance across the table, shocked by the woman who sat in the chair where Mother always sat. It wasn't her mother sitting there. She didn't understand. Jean looked nothing like her mother, whose eyes were green and her hair much darker. Edna blinked back the tears, silently cursing her confusion. Her cheeks burned. "I know that. I remember your family. I'm not senile you know."

Edna ate in silence while David, Emily, and Jean chatted about work and school. Her eyes burned, but she couldn't let on how everything seemed so jumbled to her lately. After dinner, David led her to the living room. She sat by the stove and soaked in the warmth, reminding her once more of the old stove in her house when she was a young girl. Edna smiled, wishing they could stay together always, but she knew soon David would take her back to that other place. "I wish I could see Alicia and Lacey again. But they're so far away. I hope they come to visit me soon."

David leaned forward in his recliner. "Have you talked to Alicia recently?"

"Oh, yes. She calls me nearly every week. Her last call was comforting. Lacey's getting stronger every day"

"That's good news. Alicia sent me an email keeping me up to date too. I guess Lacey's doing well enough to resume a full schedule, including playing volleyball."

"I should get a computer so I can learn how to do that email thing too. I was always very adept at typing you know. Did Alicia tell you that she's your half-sister? Larry was her father too."

"Yes, Grandma. She called and told me. Isn't it nice for you to have more grandchildren, like Alicia and Lacey?"

"Don't forget Lorraine; after all, she saved Lacey's life."

"You're right. David kicked the footrest of his recliner down. "It's getting late. We'd better get you back."

She cast a downward look. It couldn't be time to leave already. A knot seized in her throat as David held out her blue quilted coat. Edna hated saying goodbye and going back to that other place. Hugging Emily at the door, loneliness took hold and gripped her once more.

David opened the door and led Edna down the walkway, helping her into the front seat.

"How long until we get to the ferry?" She fought to control the cracking in her voice and hummed to distract herself from the wave of sadness that swept over her. She had always been fascinated by the large white sleek vessel Daddy got to ride on. She loved to watch the boat bellow smoke from the towering stack, and listen to the horn blast its alert as the last-minute riders dashed for the boarding plank.

She must have dozed off because she didn't remember the ferry ride, and before she knew it, the car stopped in front of the large white house. "We're home. I'll see you next week."

The front door opened and Gloria met her at the car, helping her out. Edna stood cold, alone, saddened as her father waved goodbye and drove away. When Daddy could no longer see her, Edna stiffened her resolve and wiped the small drop from her cheek. But she was brave, as he had asked, and next week he would be back to visit her again.

Chapter 40

The ring of the phone interrupted the family's Saturday evening cribbage game. Emily dashed to answer it. Handing the phone to her father, David noticed her usual smile had disappeared. When David heard Gloria's voice, his breath caught for a moment. She called only when there was news concerning Edna. The calls were coming with increasing frequency. His throat tightened and he swallowed to relieve the dryness.

"David, I'm afraid your grandmother has wandered away. This time, beyond the neighboring houses. Carl called, he found her down by the lake."

David took a deep breath and counted slowly in his head. How could his grandmother, who required a cane or walker to get around, walk the four blocks to the lake without somebody stopping and realizing she was a confused, lost woman? "Where is she now?"

"They're still at Vasa Park. Your grandmother's fine, but I thought it might be less traumatic for her if you came and calmed her a bit. She's pretty mixed-up about things again."

"I'm on my way. Thanks for calling." Still clutching the phone, he clicked it off and stared at it for a while.

Noticing his concern, Jean put her arm around his shoulder. "What's going on this time?"

"Grandma wandered off again. Do you want to go with me to pick her up?"

"Of course, you know I do." She headed for the coat closet.

David grabbed his keys and a coat and within moments they were on their way to the west side of Lake Sammamish for Vasa Park. "Don't you think people who are trained to take care of the elderly should be more aware of where their clients are?" David heard the irritation in his voice, knowing it was misplaced, but needing to vent, he continued. "Maybe we should consider moving her to an Alzheimer's facility where they can lock the patients in. I won't have to worry about her so much."

"Take it easy. You know they can't watch everyone every second. You can't get all upset over it. You're not doing your blood pressure any good."

"Well, what do you propose I do?" David glanced over at Jean to see if she had a better plan.

"Remember what we read about people with Alzheimer's? They are easily confused, and any change in routine can be upsetting, maybe, even set them back. I think keeping her where she is, as long as she is safe, is her best option." Jean paused, reached for his arm and patted it. "You know it's only going to get worse. That's the way the disease works."

"You're right, but she can't keep wandering away like this." David's neck muscles tightened as the tension crept in. He sensed a headache coming on. "You can bet my blood pressure's going to be high when I take it tonight." David mulled over his current situation. His children were nearly grown, the oldest now in college. It should be a time for more freedom to enjoy leisure activities. But even with Grandma's move nearer to him, the time commitment of caring for her, which began as a slight imposition on his life, had grown like a sinkhole, engulfing his whole life in some form or another.

The sun was starting to descend as they pulled the car into the near-empty lot at the park. The sky wore a cloud tinged in gold and pink. David spotted Carl and Grandma sitting side-by-side on a bench, looking east, across the lake. The cool late fall evening hadn't deterred the small crowd of parents who brought their children to the park to burn off some energy, before settling into bed for the night. David hurried to the beach with Jean alongside. Across from a small wood picnic shelter, they joined Carl and his grandmother.

"Hi, Grandma." David squatted and patted her hand. She continued to look out into the distance. Her eyes lacked their normal feisty sparkle. David leaned in. She turned, cocked her head, and regarded him without acknowledging his presence.

Jean sat next to Carl. "How is she doing?"

"She's been better. She's been staring out at the lake for the past ten minutes, talking about Pearl and her mother again."

Jean tapped him on the shoulder. "Thanks, Carl. Gloria said you walked here. Why don't I drive you home and they can visit a bit."

The cold night air made the blue veins bulge against Edna's translucent skin and her hands shivered. Jean took her coat off. "Here you go, Grandma. This will help keep you warm." Jean draped the coat across Edna's shoulders covering her red sweatshirt. "I'll be back in a few minutes to get you."

As Carl and Jean returned to the car, David took Carl's place on the bench. He put his arm around his Grandma's delicate frame and followed her gaze. Her vacant eyes stared far off into the distance, across the vast lake to the glow of lights dotting the other side. Sorrow overshadowed his anger, recognizing his grandmother's complete helplessness in the grip of Alzheimer's. "What are you looking at?" He took her gnarled boney hand, cold from the chill of the evening, placing it between his hands on his lap. David watched a young couple walking by the water enjoying a late evening stroll. Then he looked out across the dark calm lake, a peaceful sight under normal circumstances. Tonight, he couldn't help but feel like a monster lay in wait under the smooth surface, ready to pounce. Peace for him and his grandmother seemed elusive right now.

"I can't see the school. I thought I would be able to see it from here." His grandmother spoke with a wistful longing tone.

Turning to her, David's eyes and nose burned as he fought the despair that swallowed him up like a buffeting bitter wind. He filled his lungs with fresh air and continued to pat her hand, wanting to help ease his grandmother's troubled mind. "What school is that, Grandma?"

"You know the one. I told you about my first teaching job in Monohan. It should be right over there. It's not far from Pearl's house. Can you take me to Pearl's house now?" Grandma struggled to stand and shuffled closer to the water's edge toward the shelter. She pointed across the lake toward the flickering lights on the other side.

She was right. There once was a small lumber town called Monohan on the east side of the lake. The area still survived, though not recognized by many these days. Over the years it had given way to the rapidly growing sprawl of houses for the upper-income folks and commercial space for eastside startups. "There was a school there once, but it's not there anymore." David's throat tightened with sadness at his grandmother's present situation, living more and more in the past.

"What are you saying? Of course, it's there. I just got a job there last week when my teaching certificate came."

"You're right, Grandma, I forgot." Over the past two years, David learned not to fight the situation. It was much easier on everyone and even encouraged, to go with the flow and the time she was in. "I don't know if I can take you to Pearl's now." David hoped Grandma would forget about her sister soon so he wouldn't have to remind her Pearl had died over twenty years earlier.

Grandma's eyes widened and David saw a slight glint reflecting in her wet eyes. A slow smile turned up the corners of her mouth. "I can see the school and my students. Do you see it?" She grabbed David's arm for support, gripped her cane, and shuffled toward the small park facility building at the water's edge. Upon reaching it, she gazed at the building and ran her hand over the white painted surface.

Chapter 41

Edna guessed the old country school was from the era of the children's grandparents, built around eighteen-seventy, or so. She smiled at the man next to her. She guessed he had been assigned by the district to escort her to her new school. "I can't imagine this one small room holding all grades from one through eight. Attending high school in Seattle, she never imagined her first teaching job would be at such a rural school. "You know I always imagined a larger school. Though I do like the opportunity to stay close to where my sister, Pearl and her family live."

"Yes, it is important to be near family."

Her opinion reinforced; Edna looked over at the cistern at the corner of the building. "Is this the drinking water?" The stink around the area smelled like a ripe outhouse and drew flying insects. Edna bent over to inspect it. It was flavored with dead bugs and the like, obviously unfit to drink. "How can the school district allow children to drink this water? I know I certainly won't?" Edna looked down at the cistern and cleared her throat. "I suspect one of the reasons students in small rural schools have a lot of sickness, is from the water supply."

Her escort looked surprised at her direct manner. He shrugged and stuttered, "This faucet isn't drinking water. The park has a drinking fountain." He looked at her confused, but Edna was not about to let him get away without inspecting the water. She demanded the district analyze the water and make it fit for drinking. "I expect it analyzed immediately." She stood firm until she heard the schoolmaster concede, then went to the front door and ran her hand across the siding, where the white paint peeled away like birch bark on the weathered wood. "There are some other changes that will need to be made. Perhaps a fresh coat of paint for this tired building." The man's eyes widened. Edna suspected he wasn't used to such an outspoken, young, beginning teacher.

He paused then muttered something. Edna knew about the district's limited resources, but she didn't want to hear excuses. Nonetheless, he surprised her and quietly agreed.

"Of course, whatever you want."

The sounds and sight of children playing outside reminded Edna to prepare the classroom for the students' arrival. She pushed on the door. It groaned as it opened into the small room. The sun fought its way through dirt-encrusted windows, casting a dim light on the dirty, planked, wooden floor. A large, black, three-foot iron stove stood in the back of the room on a brick hearth. "I imagine in addition to my teaching responsibilities; I'll have to keep the stove going?" Edna looked over at her companion.

He smiled but didn't answer.

She bent over the dirty black steel and struggled to stoke the stove with the coal that she knew would be delivered in loads of large pieces. She poked and prodded with an iron rod as the embers struggled to life like fireflies. She coughed. Her eyes burned as the gritty dust settled on the wooden plank floor and furniture, coating everything like a black snowfall. She inspected the benches and found they were etched with many years of students' names and initials, including the parents or other relatives, who also attended the school during its fifty years of existence.

The children's voices got louder. She barely had time to compose herself before several children, from six to fourteen years old, dashed into the cold sparse room and stared at her. "Settle down now children and be seated." She motioned for the children to sit on the old plank picnic benches. Edna brushed the soot from her hands, her heart raced as she greeted the children. It was important to present an air of authority for her first impression, but her faltering voice threatened her position. "Hello children, I am your new teacher for this school year." Edna stood with confidence in her decision to teach. She smiled at their polite smiling faces, eager to tackle her first year as a teacher.

Waiting for the warmth of the stove to heat the small room, she noticed the children were still in their coats. The commotion started early; Edna stood helpless as the children ran about without paying her any mind. She wasn't prepared for how the children might react to her. She had to devise a quick threat of consequence for any misbehavior. The stove came to life with small cinders burning with an orange glow. It would provide a sure chore for her students. "If there is any misbehavior children, you know what you'll spend your recess doing. There is always coal that needs breaking up." Edna smiled smugly at her wit, confused the children had failed to acknowledge her threat.

"Grandma. You're going to get burned if you stand too near the BBQ pit."

Edna looked startled. She couldn't understand who was interrupting her instruction. She backed away from the hot surface. The children were gone. They must have all gone out to recess. She found a bench at a picnic table. She needed to rest.

Chapter 42

David struggled with the role-playing his grandmother had taken on. He was relieved for the reprieve when the sound of crunching gravel announced Jean's arrival. He urged his grandmother back outside to the now darkened sky with the sun almost completely descended from view and the diminished crowd of park visitors. Her eyes twinkled with mischief and her smile flickered like the distant stars dotting the sky.

"Are you ready to go home? Jean's here to take you back."

Grandma tipped her head and seemed puzzled by his words. She snickered. "Dear, it's right across the street. Don't you think I can walk that far?' Her tone mocked David's apparent ignorance regarding the matter.

"What's right across the street?" David raised his brows and studied his grandmother.

"My house. The house the district has provided for me as the teacher."

David took her by the arm. "At least let us walk with you. Will that be okay?"

Edna didn't acknowledge him but trudged along slowly with her cane and Jean on her other arm. At the car, Jean opened the door. David helped Edna in. She didn't comment or resist as they made the two-minute drive back to her home.

Gloria met them at the door with a blanket. "Let's get you warmed up." She draped the plaid wool wrap around Edna's shivering body.

Grandma swung around. "There is still a lot of work to be done at the school. I expect it in top shape before the school year begins."

217

Chapter 43

Gloria walked into Edna's room with Edna's coat draped over her arm.

"Ready, Edna? David will be here soon."

Bewildered, Edna looked at Gloria. "Is it Sunday already?"

"No, it's not Sunday. David's picking you up to take you to his home for Christmas Eve, remember?"

Edna glanced around her room. A big red bow hung on her door and a fresh wreath graced the wall behind her bed. "Of course, I didn't realize it was that time already. I haven't done my shopping yet." Edna shuffled to the nightstand and snatched her purse. "Christmas was always my favorite holiday, with all the gaily colored decorations and the sweet aromas of mulled cider and gingerbread houses." She recalled memories from long ago when her children were small. Their first clue she was starting preparations for Christmas was the whiff of cinnamon from the freshly baked snickerdoodles. Bernice always loved pulling out the stool and rolling out the dough for the cut-out cookies and together they frosted the cookies and decorated them with silver candy beads and sprinkles. Even Larry helped stir the walnut fudge and divinity. Edna yearned for those days when she'd strung the cranberries for the tree and hand-painted the greeting cards as she did in college for extra spending money.

"Even when I was older and alone, I spent many weeks making ornaments to donate to Goodwill for them to sell during the holiday season. These days. . ." She looked down at her now gnarled knuckles, "My fingers lack the dexterity for such crafts and things." Gloria grabbed Edna's stability cane and positioned it in front of her. "Let's get you ready. It's almost three-o-clock. David will be here any minute."

Edna frowned at the awkward aluminum cane, a constant reminder of her increasing limitations, and shuffled to the living room. "I need my

218

hat. Somebody get my hat." She gazed out at the cloudy gray day which endeavored to dampen her bright mood.

Bundled in her winter coat and hat, Gloria pinned a poinsettia-shaped broach on her coat. "Merry Christmas, Edna."

The doorbell chimed bringing a surge of excitement as she followed Gloria to the door. Edna shivered from the draft that swept in when the door swung open.

"It looks like you're ready." David tugged at her hat, pulling it further over her ears.

"I haven't had a chance to do any Christmas shopping. Nobody reminded me."

"Don't worry Grandma. You don't need gifts. We're just happy to spend Christmas with you." David helped Edna out the door and into the car. With her cane stowed in the backseat, David clicked on the radio, filling the car with holiday music and joyous voices.

Edna smiled. "Where's Nathan? Will he be there?"

"Yes, he'll be there. Jean's whole family will be there too. There'll be a lot of people to share Christmas with this year."

The front door to David's house opened to a warmth that instantly shook the chill off. Surprised by Jean's green shimmery dress, Edna puzzled over what it meant, Jean had never made such a fuss about their Sunday dinners like this before, she must be holding a formal event.

"What kind of affair is this? Is it a summer affair or a winter affair?" Edna furrowed her brow and scrutinized Jean who appeared dressed for church or such. She looked down at her navy-blue knit slacks.

"It's Christmas Eve."

"Oh, my." She blushed. "Christmas already. Someone should have told me. I don't have gifts for anyone."

"Having you here is our gift from you." Jean took Edna's purse and set it on a small table opposite the entry door.

"Gracious." Edna smiled as she stepped to the table with the mirror hanging above it. "You found the perfect place for this table." She ran her hand over the glossy finish of the mahogany.

"It does look nice, doesn't it?" Jean nodded as she led Edna to the living room sofa facing the fresh pine tree which graced the corner of the high-ceiling room.

A sharp cold breeze sent a chill across Edna's neck. She strained to turn around to see David opening the door. A crowd of noisy people rushed in with their arms filled with bags and packages, along with plates and bowls of food. Never before had she seen such a commotion for a dinner. Confused by all the strangers, Edna's voice broke above the ruckus. "Who are all these people, David?"

"They're Jean's family, Grandma. We always spend Christmas Eve with them. This year you get to join us."

"Oh, I wondered about that." Relaxed, she watched the twinkling lights of red, blue, green, and gold dance along the branches of the tree.

Sitting next to Edna, Jean looked over her shoulder at the door and called out to the crowd still arriving. "Just put the gifts under the tree. Rachel and Emily are upstairs playing pool if the boys want to join them." Footsteps trampled up the steps.

Edna stared at the tree dominating the living room. "It's quite a big tree isn't it?" Edna strained her neck to look at the star adorning the top of the evergreen. She loved the pine scent reminiscent of her walks with her sister and mother along the Raging River.

"Come on, let's go look at it." Jean took Edna's arm and led her to the tree.

"Oh my, I've never seen anything like it at all. It's lovely, Dear." Edna fingered the many different ornaments. Jean removed several and told her where she got each of them. A gold angel came from the German village of Oberammergau, and an artisan's hand-painted silver ball was brought from Leavenworth, a Bavarian village in eastern Washington. There was a small stuffed walrus from Alaska, and a silver heart from Florida, which Jean told her was one of the last items Jean's mother had bought for her.

"You have quite a collection, don't you? I need to give you some ornaments I made."

Jean searched the tree and retrieved two ornaments, a pearl beaded angel and a crocheted and beaded snowflake, and handed them to Edna.

Edna's eyes widened and a broad smile appeared. "Gracious, I made these many years ago." She blushed. "I forgot I gave you these," Jean explained to Edna she had well over one- hundred ornaments and she remembered where most of them had come from. Edna stood and absorbed the sights and sounds of the holiday. Evergreen boughs draped over the upstairs balcony rail overlooking the living room. Small white lights snaked through the greenery with red silk poinsettias poking through here and there. Jean led Edna back to the sofa so she could greet the guests. Edna didn't know this family. There were so many unfamiliar faces. She wondered when she was going to see Nathan.

As the crowd disbursed to other parts of the house, the room quieted except for the commotion from the kitchen. The robust smell of roast beef and garlic floated into the room.

The sharp knocking at the door made Edna flinch and a moment later, her heart fluttered at the touch of a hand on her shoulder. Startled, she turned to see someone standing beside her. Her heart leaped as she reached out to take Nathan's hand. "I'm so glad you made it." This was the first Christmas she had spent with both of her grandsons in over thirty years and her emotions overflowed.

"Merry Christmas, Grandma. It's nice to see you again."

Edna felt as warm as the glowing lights on the tree. She covered her eyes with her hand to control the waterworks that were coming. Nathan bent down and kissed her cheek.

"You're the last one to arrive again, I see." David laughed as he greeted his brother. "But not too late for dinner."

"I have a knack for timing that right. It's good to be back home again to spend the holidays with family. It sure beats being with a bunch of soldiers." Nathan went to the tree and placed a small red foil-wrapped box underneath.

Jean called out to the children gathered in the upstairs loft, "Dinner's ready." Moments later a stampede of ten kids moved down the stairs. "You guys fill your plates and head down to the basement. The table is set and sparkling cider's in the fridge."

David reached out to assist his grandmother. "I guess dinner's ready, let's get you seated." David helped Edna to a chair at a gloriously set table with a lace tablecloth and beautiful china and silver, enough places for ten. Her mouth watered seeing the platter of roast beef in the middle of the table.

"Do you recognize your silver, Grandma?" David handed her a fork from a place setting.

"What is this?" She turned it over in her fingers.

"We thought it would be nice to have your beautiful silver out when you shared Christmas with us."

She gazed upon the silver for a long time. Her face lit up. "Is this my old silver or the new set I bought?"

"I have both sets."

"I guess I don't have any use for it." Seated, Edna watched all the unfamiliar children and adults pile food on their plates, some scattering to find places to sit away from the table which couldn't hold the large crowd.

"Can I get you some roast, Grandma?" David picked up a plate and began to fill it.

Edna sat on the end of the table and took in the assorted plates and bowls brimming with all the makings of a real holiday feast. When her plate was set before her, she beamed at the piled-high plate, noticing all her favorites, including mashed potatoes almost swimming in gravy. Salad and vegetables sat on the other side. Her stomach gurgled and she giggled with embarrassment. Everyone gathered around the table eager to hear her stories. Edna found an unexpected audience in one of David's sisters-in-law, whom she learned was a second-grade teacher. "I used to be an elementary teacher, too. I can still remember when I made the decision to teach. I taught for twenty-eight years, though I did take some time off when my children were young."

"I've been teaching elementary school for nearly twenty years myself. I imagine children and teaching are a lot different these days."

Edna nodded. "I remember when I was a young teacher, I earned $1500 for a nine-month contract. Married women weren't allowed to teach, only to substitute. But during the war, there was a shortage of teachers, with all the men off fighting. I paid one dollar for an emergency permit that allowed me to teach until the war was over."

David's sister-in-law was so polite and inquired further about Edna's past. "I guess you liked it though. You taught for your whole career."

Edna allowed her mind to wander for a few moments. "I did. I always loved teaching. From the very beginning." She looked around the table at so many people gathered. "I also always loved Christmas, especially as a young girl. Mother always made so many Christmas treats." She squeezed her eyes shut and thought about earlier Christmases. "I always felt like Christmas was an obligation with Larry and his daughters, but they were the only family I had. From my youngest days, I was taught Christmas is a time for family." Edna paused as the events of the past month tumbled through her mind. "What a surprising Christmas revelation, learning Alicia was family all along." Her smile dazzled like the polished silver fork she held.

David reached over and took Edna's hand. "Alicia and Lacey are your blood relations. But family can be anyone in your life who wants you in theirs, the ones who make you smile and love you no matter what. We hope you will think of Jean's family as your family too. How does that sound?"

Edna smiled. "Barbara always told me; families are created in the heart."

After everyone was finished eating, they spilled into the living room. Adults sat on all the living room furniture and carried in chairs from the dining room. After searching under the tree for presents bearing their names, all the children gathered around on the floor, with a pile of gifts to open. Edna sat on the sofa, a sparkling apple cider in hand. She delighted in watching the children rip open their brightly wrapped presents. Several of the children smiled at her. She smiled coyly back as she turned and whispered to David. "They act like they don't know me, but I recognize some of them, especially those two boys. They were in my third-grade class when I taught in Monahan. I still have all the cards all the children made me that year for Christmas."

David smiled, walked over to the tree, and returned with his arms full.

"Oh, my." Edna was overcome with gratitude at the sight of the gifts in front of her. "How thoughtful you and Nathan are." Edna placed her glass on the end table and took the first present, ripping open the paper, revealing a lovely bottle of pink body lotion. Aware the room was quiet, Edna looked around. Everyone stopped opening their presents and sat waiting and watching her. Thrilled by the attention, Edna tore open a square box wrapped in green foil with red poinsettias. She clapped her hands at the unexpected treat. "A plate of peanut butter cookies."

"I made those for you. Chewy, not crunchy, just like you prefer." Emily grinned from across the room.

Next, Edna unwrapped a box wrapped in blue and white with snowflakes. She fingered the delicate white yarn scarf from Rachel and ran it across her cheek before she held it out for all to see. "This is like the scarves I used to knit. I also crocheted lots of yokes for corset slips, doilies, and edges for handkerchiefs which I always made for Christmas gifts."

"I'm glad you like it. I learned to knit from the internet after you told me how your mother taught you to knit."

Ripping open her last package, Edna gazed upon the framed photo of Lacey, clutching it to her chest. "To think, my great-granddaughter might have died without me knowing she was family. It's a miracle she's still here, and in my life." She looked around the room at the large group of strangers all still watching her. "These are such wonderful gifts. Thank you so much."

"Just a minute, Grandma. There's still one gift left under the tree for you." Nathan picked up the red foil box from under the tree. "This one is from all your grandchildren."

Still fingering the scarf around her neck, Edna tipped her head and stared at the small red box he'd placed in her hand. "All my grandchildren?"

"Open it." Even the youngsters fixed their gaze on the small box.

Edna carefully removed the adhesive bow from the top and placed it next to her on the sofa. Lifting off the top of the box, she gushed over the lovely ring with a blue center stone, and six other sparkling gemstones in a knot design wrapping around the band.

Nathan squatted next to her and lifted the sterling silver ring from the box. He held it out for everyone to see while he explained what the stones represented. "This is a family tree ring."

"Look at all those precious stones. I am sure this cost way too much for you." Edna looked at Nathan.

"They aren't real gems, only crystals. Each crystal represents someone's birthstone. The center stone is an aquamarine, your birthstone."

"Gracious." Edna brought her hands to her cheeks. "There's a ruby for Bernice's birthday in July, the garnet, for Larry's birthday in January, and two diamonds for David and Nathan, both born in April. I don't know these other stones." She brought the ring close and bent over it, turning it over in her fingers. "Thank you so much, Nathan."

Nathan smiled as he took her hand and slid the ring onto the finger of her right hand, explaining the other crystals were Alicia's and Lorraine's birthstones. "I thought you would like to have them remembered too, on your grandmother's ring. We can add your great-grandchildren if you like."

Edna knit her brow as she pondered all the stones in the ring. "Alicia is family, Lorraine isn't really my family, but she saved Lacey's life."

"That's right, Grandma. That makes her family too, don't you think?"

Edna sat erect. "I should think so." She held her hand out and beamed at the stones. "This is so beautiful. I don't recall getting jewelry with precious stones since Jacob presented me with my engagement ring." Edna's eyes moistened as she stared at the beautiful symbol of love on her finger.

An unexpected whiff of cologne took Edna by surprise. Jacob had not worn cologne for her previously. It was a nice change of pace from smelling like a pub, which usually accompanied Jacob, or worse, the faded scent of another woman's perfume. She noticed the glass filled with sparkling champagne, next to her on the table, and frowned. She knew his game well. He was intending to get her to drink too much so he could have his way with her. This time, she wouldn't fall for it. He liked to put her on the spot in front of any group they were with. In order not to cause a scene, she smiled sweetly and decided to play along with him, although she fumed inside. "It's warm in here." She wiped her hand across her sweaty forehead, wet from the hours of dancing. Her dance card had been quite full. She looked around the room. Dehoney's was a very busy place tonight. "I need to freshen up." She noticed all eyes in the dance hall were studying her. They could see she was angry and she didn't want to make a scene, so she calmed herself and excused herself to the restroom, to pin back her braids.

Returning a few minutes later, Edna couldn't believe her eyes. "What's going on here?" Another woman was sitting in her spot talking with Jacob. Her shoulders tensed as she strutted toward the table. Edna knew the game. She wasn't proud of it, but she'd enjoyed playing the game herself. She caught the eye of the offender with her gaze as she sauntered back to reclaim her seat. Standing over the woman, Edna stared at the floozy. "Excuse me, this is my seat." She couldn't understand how Jacob could be attracted to that other woman. She was much too old for him, nearly middle-aged.

"Is she another one of your many flirtations?" Edna stood hands on hips.

Jacob said nothing. He looked shocked by her outburst and offered no excuse.

Edna could tell his mind was involved with something. She feared what it might be. She glanced down at her ring finger. Her face warmed. She looked at the patrons and forced a smile to the large group of people who looked at her with confusion in their eyes. She turned to her handsome beau who had proposed with this symbolic ring. She heard herself mutter. "Yes, my darling, I forgive you, and I will marry you."

He squatted next to her and held her hand. "Merry Christmas, Grandma."

Chapter 44

Gloria led Nathan down the hall to his grandmother's room. The smell of age and its related problems assaulted him. Fighting the impulse to turn and walk out, Nathan choked back his stomach's urge to revolt. At her bedside he gazed upon her, pale and expressionless. If it weren't for the short shallow breaths that strained and snorted with each exhale, he would have thought he was too late.

Gloria stood next to him, a reassuring arm on his shoulder. "She's been sleeping a lot these past few days."

Unable to take his eyes from his grandmother, Nathan almost spoke softly to Gloria. "Is that a good thing?"

"At her age, it's pretty typical, but she's not eating either. Based on how she's been doing the past few weeks, I'm glad you're here and able to visit with her before it's too late. She'll be happy to see you." Gloria patted his shoulder. "This is all pretty new to you, isn't it?"

He shuddered, still struggling with the rising uneasiness in his stomach. "I've never dealt with anything like this before." He wondered how David had managed to stay sane for the past few years, juggling work and family, along with their grandmother's affairs. He finally fully understood the commitment which had been made and the patience and time his brother had dedicated to helping make Grandma's last years as pleasant as possible. He stepped closer. Reaching out impulsively, he took her skeletal hand, startled by the chill of it. She stirred in bed, her eyelids fluttering.

Gloria reached across and stroked Edna's forehead and thin straggly hair. "Look who's here."

Her eyes opened, only a sliver, not relaying any hint of recognition.

Overwhelmed with feeling helpless, Nathan looked to Gloria for direction. "Are you sure she's awake?"

"Give her a few minutes, she'll recognize you." Gloria turned to leave. "Let me know if you need anything. I'll be here."

Unsure what he should do, Nathan let her hand drop to her side. He exhaled with a loud whoosh as he released his jumbled thoughts.

Edna turned her head at the sound. Her blank eyes stared in his direction. "David?" Her voice came in a strained murmur.

Nathan bent over her and stroked her hair as Gloria had done. "No, Grandma, it's Nathan." Reluctantly, he again took her hand in his. "How are you doing today?" He forced a smile hoping she would read that instead of the nervousness of his shaky hand. It was an uncomfortable situation and he was unprepared to make idle chatter.

A tired smile crossed Grandma's face. "Nathan, is that you?" Her grip tightened. She clutched at the sleeve of his gray sweatshirt. "I didn't recognize you without your uniform." Her hoarse chuckle caught Nathan off guard. She was barely alive but her wit was still sharp.

Nathan allowed the muscles in his neck to relax. Perhaps the visit wouldn't be too bad after all. He was glad he came. Though well-intentioned, he hadn't visited as often as he should have since he moved back.

"I must be dying."

Her comment raised his eyebrows and he leaned in. "Why would you say that?"

"You never come to see me. They must have told you I was dying."

Nathan studied her face for an indication his grandmother was being facetious, but her expression was as serious as her words.

"No, Grandma. You're not dying." He awkwardly chuckled, attempting to make his words upbeat and convincing. "It's not easy for me to get away from the base, that's all." He reached for a water pitcher and glass on the bedside table and poured a little of the thickened water. He grimaced at the appearance of the clear gelatin consistency before realizing it was probably the only type of fluid she could swallow without difficulty. "Would you like some water?" Adjusting the pillows behind her, and supporting the weight of her shoulders, he assisted her to a seated position. Then, as he held the plastic glass, Grandma sipped slowly from the straw. He smiled at his small success until she began to gag. She coughed fitfully. Alarmed, Nathan pulled the glass away and yelled for Gloria.

Gloria came running. "It's okay, Edna." She rubbed Edna's back between the shoulder blades until the coughing slowed to a minor clearing of her throat.

Nathan's heartbeat slowed to normal. "Sorry. I guess I'm not too good at this."

"Don't worry, you'll feel more comfortable in time." Gloria reassurance comforted him.

With her breathing labored and the sound of gurgling still in her chest, Edna flopped back on the bed. Nathan reshuffled the position of the pillows behind his grandmother's head and shoulders. "How's that?"

She lay expressionless. Ill at ease, Nathan shifted his weight nervously, uncertain what to do next. Looking around the room, he noticed her cheery pictures and vases of silk flower arrangements sitting on her dresser and a small table. Framed photos clustered atop the four-drawer mahogany chest across the room. Nathan admired the photo of the young woman he guessed was Bernice. A black and white picture of his father, Larry, stood next to it. Nathan examined them. His Aunt Bernice had been a beautiful young woman, most likely favoring Edna when she was young. Nathan glimpsed at a dated photo of another soldier from long ago. He grinned. There was no doubt Larry took after his own father, Jacob. One more photo sat on the dresser, the color photo of him he had given her for her birthday. Seeing the resemblance to his father and granddad, he chuckled as he thought about his first meeting with his grandmother at the airport. He understood how the confused mind of an aging woman could deceive her. Though brothers, with similar characteristics, there was no doubt Nathan favored his grandfather's side. A heaviness thumped in his heart as he realized how much he had missed and how little time remained to learn about her.

"Nathan?"

Edna's weak voice startled him.

"Are you still here?"

He approached her bedside. "I'm here, Grandma. I was just looking at your room. David did a nice job decorating it."

"Yes, David is such a dear. He's done so much for me. Did you see my violets? I don't know where David put my violets."

Nathan glanced around and spied several large African violets in plastic trays on the window sill. "They're on the window sill. Do you want me to water them?"

"Are they dry?" Grandma strained to look over her shoulder.

Nathan picked up a pot and fingered the dirt. "They seem like they need watering." He carried the plant into the bathroom.

"Don't get it wet."

Nathan stopped in his tracks. "They're dry. I thought you wanted me to water them." Confused, he returned with the two plants in his hand. Edna's hand quivered as she reached for them. Nathan lowered the pots so she could reach them.

She fingered the dirt. "They need to be watered from the roots. Fill the trays with water and set the plant back inside. How do you think I've kept them alive for so many years?"

Nathan shook his head. Here she was on her death bed, and still concerned about her plants. David had said she loved plants and gardening. He found the whole experience ironic. He could see how David still considered her a sharp woman, even as her mind deteriorated. He did as he was told, and returned the plants to the window sill. Nathan looked at his grandmother's pale gaunt figure still struggling to find a rhythm with her breaths. "You look tired Grandma."

Her chest rose and fell in short rapid bursts, but for the first time since he had arrived, he noticed a sparkle in her eyes. He stroked her forehead once more. She beamed. He took another look around. Somehow in spite of what should have been a pleasant room, a gloom hung over it. It was only a matter of time, possibly a very short time, and the shadow of death would move in. With a knot in his stomach, Nathan bent over and kissed his grandmother's forehead as her eyelids drooped. "I'll be back again soon."

Her breathing slowed and quieted.

His jittery hands calmed and he breathed easier. Nathan hung his head as he walked away and departed for the base.

Chapter 45

"Your grandmother's health is deteriorating. She hasn't been drinking much and she's dehydrated."

Carl's words didn't surprise David. Nathan shared his concerns about her sunken eyes and physical deterioration during his recent visit and David suspected the news was coming. "Is there anything I need to do?"

"No, the ambulance is on the way. If you're able to stop by the hospital after work, I'll let her doctor know to expect you."

David hung up and dialed Nathan. He left a quick message for Nathan to meet at the hospital around five if he were able. He struggled with his tasks at hand, finding it difficult to concentrate on the graphs and data that lay before him. Focused on his grandmother, his brain refused to function as he reviewed the calculations. He glanced at his watch, wishing either the time would fly by or his brain would kick in so he could concentrate on his work. An hour later, Nathan's call relieved some of the stress, and David managed to push his worries aside and complete his report. The urgency of his task completed; David phoned Jean to let her know he was heading for the hospital.

Pulling into the hospital parking garage, David grabbed his portfolio of legal documents. The lobby was relatively quiet during the dinner hour and David settled into a sofa that faced the main entrance. His stomach growled. He hadn't eaten anything except a small pre-made sandwich and box drink on the plane, during the flight test. He reread the brochure he had acquired earlier, regarding living wills and durable power of attorney, until he heard Nathan call out. "Let's grab a quick bite in the cafeteria before we go to see Grandma. I need to get some food in me while you look at something." David handed a folder to Nathan.

"What's this?"

"Grandma's directives to her physician. It certainly isn't the most clearly understood form I've ever seen." David grabbed a ham sandwich and coffee and they took a seat. He watched Nathan review the legal documents thrust on him. "Well?" David put his elbows on the table, rubbing his temples with his palms. "I wish these darn things were more clearly stated than a standard box simply being checked. I don't know what Grandma intended. This whole thing is taking a toll on me." David regarded Nathan. "What do you think now that you've read it?"

"I can't make any sense out of all this legalese." Nathan scratched his chin. "The directives indicate if she is diagnosed with a terminal condition, she does not wish to be kept alive with life-sustaining procedures which would offer no hope of recovery."

The wording almost seemed bizarre to David under the present circumstances. "If old age isn't terminal with no hope of recovery, I don't know what is. Is a feeding tube life-sustaining? Carl hinted it might be the only means of keeping her alive at this point. Her life would be prolonged, and she would recover, but to what degree?" David struggled to interpret his grandmother's intent. "Grandma's not eating enough to stay alive. I'm going to talk to her doctor about a feeding tube." David looked at Nathan for confirmation.

"What's involved in putting in a tube? I don't think I would want one. Will it be painful to put it in?"

David shook his head. "I don't know. Her doctor mentioned it the last time we spoke and he recommended the Thick-It to help her swallow fluids." He rubbed the back of his neck and took a few bites of his sandwich before continuing. "I do know she can't keep going like she's been. You've seen her recently. Don't you agree? We have only two choices. Either force-feed her or let her drift away naturally."

Nathan stood up, paced in front of the table a bit, then looked at his watch. "It's almost time for our appointment. Let's go talk to her doctor. I'll support whatever you think she would want."

David narrowed his eyes, resisting the urge to shout he didn't want to be the sole decision-maker or play God. Instead, he took a deep breath. "It's time to make some tough decisions, and I don't want to make them alone. I want your input." His ability to handle this responsibility was being tested. They took the elevator to the third floor. The disinfectant smell of the hospital by now all too familiar, still made him flinch when he exited the elevator. They walked down the hall to Dr. Bonner's office and knocked on the open door. Dr. Bonner waved them inside.

Dr. Bonner put his pen on the desk and leaned back in his chair. "I'm glad you came." He extended his hand to Nathan and introduced himself before greeting David. "I'll get right to the point. If your grandmother doesn't receive a feeding tube or start eating on her own, she'll most likely die within the week."

Feeling as if he'd been punched in the gut, David's words popped out without hesitation. "We have to do something." He paused. "Don't we?" David looked at Dr. Bonner. "What if she were your mother?"

"The feeding tube can be uncomfortable. There's always the possibility it will be pulled out. Knowing how stubborn your grandmother is, that is a distinct possibility. The alternative is letting her pass on naturally."

David rubbed his forehead feeling a headache coming on. "You're saying let her starve to death. I don't think I could do that."

"It truthfully is a very humane and natural way to allow someone to pass on. After the first two or three days, especially in her already deteriorated condition, her body will stop craving nourishment. We will continue to administer fluids. But as her system shuts down, the rest of the body begins to shut down, including the kidneys. The need for fluids decreases dramatically. There's no pain or suffering. She won't even be aware of her weakening state." The doctor rose and went around to the side of his desk to stand closer to Nathan and David. "Take a little while and think about it. Let me know what you decide. Soon."

They thanked the doctor and turned to leave. At the door, David turned back to the doctor. "What about discharging her? She's been staying at an adult home, owned by a retired geriatric doctor, Carl Hoffmann. Do you think her need for fluids could be met in a home environment?"

"Of course. I know Dr. Hoffmann's reputation; hospice providers are as capable as we are of administering fluids as desired. During the last few days, fluids may actually increase nausea, vomiting, and diarrhea. Dr. Hoffmann may prefer swabbing her mouth with a damp sponge. This will help keep Edna comfortable at the very end of life. Dry mouth is what causes most people to feel uncomfortable and IV fluids don't relieve the dry mouth as well as moist swabbing does."

David's mind raced as he mentally tossed dice in his head, attempting to achieve the right roll for his grandmother's fate, yet still uncertain what that roll might be.

Grandma was in the bed farthest from the door. David pulled open the tan curtain separating the beds. As before, she lay propped up in bed staring wide-eyed into space.

"Hi, Grandma, how are you doing today?" David and Nathan exchanged glances upon seeing how pathetic she looked. David drew the window blinds partially, allowing some sunlight to find its way into the depressing room.

Edna turned her head toward the light. "I saw Mother again today."

"What did she want?" Surprised by her response, David swung around and looked into his grandmother's eyes.

"She took me to visit Larry and Bernice, only it was hard to understand."

"What's that? What was hard to understand?"

"Well, it's just that I thought Larry and Bernice were dead."

David struggled to comprehend how his grandmother's mind was functioning. Her dreams or hallucinations, whatever they were, were becoming more frequent. Some of her statements made David think she was rational, though confused, caught between two worlds. But most of the time she seemed to be in her own place and time.

"We went to the 4-H fair where Larry showed the pig he got from the Future Farmers of America. Bernice won a blue ribbon for the bread she entered into the baking contest."

"That's great, I bet you're proud of your children." David scooted a chair over and joined Nathan by their grandmother's bedside. Nathan was stroking her forehead and watching her labored breathing. Her wrinkled skin was almost translucent and her veins and bones showed through the ghostlike tissue. David took her frail hand and spoke softly. "Grandma, since you haven't been eating enough to stay alive, we may need to put in a feeding tube."

"What's that? I don't want any tubes in me. I've had enough tubes in me." Her words were clear and abrupt. "What will happen if I don't get it?"

David's eyes widened. He hadn't heard her speak this coherently in many weeks. Feeling some relief, he swallowed hard and took in a deep calming breath before continuing. "If you don't get one, you'll die."

Her eyes focused intently on him. She didn't hesitate. "Well now, that would be okay with me."

Edna's words and calm delivery shocked David. He cocked his head and studied his grandmother's aged face. There was only one way he could interpret her words. He believed, at that moment, she was in as competent a state of mind as she had been in months. Her statement could not be taken lightly. Grandma was ready to join the rest of her family who had preceded her. Her family, who, on some level, she had been visiting with for some time. He looked across the bed at Nathan for assurance.

"Grandma, do you understand what David said?" Nathan took her other hand and held it in his. She shifted her gaze to Nathan.

"It's okay, I'll be just fine." She closed her eyes. Within minutes she was snoring faintly, her mouth curled in a wry smile.

A weight lifted, David wondered if she was off with her mother again somewhere. He recalled reading about death with dignity, having the patient's wishes honored. David considered his grandmother's words and Dr. Bonner's reassurance there would be no pain or suffering. In the end, it was not his decision to make. It didn't matter if he agreed or not. Nathan and David walked quietly from the room, arranging to meet later in the evening to gather the family together, for possibly one last time. They stopped by the nurse station to relay a message for Dr. Bonner to make arrangements to have his grandmother discharged without a feeding tube.

Chapter 46

Edna lay in bed; the room void of any color or cheeriness. Boredom blanketed her like a heavy veil. She missed David and Nathan. She didn't want to die. She thought about it a lot. She didn't long for death but sighed with an acceptance and willingness to move on to the next world. Mother understood as she visited more frequently than she used to. Mother wanted Edna to go with her, but Edna puzzled over where exactly that was. Her mother kept insisting it was peaceful and there were meadows of flowers for her to stroll through.

"Come, my sweet girl, come with me. We'll visit Larry and Bernice and your father, too."

Edna looked up at her mother smiling. "Where are we going?" Edna wanted to know, but Mother wouldn't answer. Instead, Edna followed her to the old farm Jacob and she owned when her children were young. Edna watched as something was moving through the wheat field making the tall golden stalks part as it moved. She recognized the car, the jade green Ford Jacob sold when they moved to New Jersey. Larry sat behind the wheel with Bea next to him. When they emerged from the tall stalks, Larry's eyes grew wide. "Don't be upset, Mother" Larry met her gaze. "Bea wanted me to teach her how to drive."

Edna wanted to scold them but it was hard to stay mad. She found herself laughing instead. She stood and watched as Larry and Bernice wove the car back through the wheat fields for home.

Her mother's soft voice was insistent. "You can stay here and be happy with your children again.

A voice called from across the dusty air of the wheat fields. Edna closed her eyes and struggled to hear the voice more clearly. "I can't hear you, Mother." Her voice strained against her dry throat.

"Mrs. Pearson, are you okay?"

Edna opened her eyes. The golden stalks blowing in the wind had disappeared. She searched for her mother. "Where's Mother?" She was gone. In her place was a younger woman wearing blue scrubs.

"I'm sorry, Mrs. Pearson, I don't understand. There's no one here visiting you right now. Your grandsons were by earlier."

The voice from the wheat field was no longer her mother's. "Never mind." The pain deepened. Edna knew her mother had left her once again. Edna strained to lift her head and look around. Her mother had said she could stay with her and her children, but she was gone, and Edna was back in the dreary hospital room.

The young woman feigned a smile. "Someone will be in shortly to clean you." She turned and rushed out. Edna became aware of a wet, uncomfortable situation. Disgusted with herself and her lack of control, she burned with anger and shame. The door opened and Edna's anger and embarrassment rose. A male nurse was coming to clean her. How humiliating, to be like a newborn with no control, and no dignity.

"Where's David? Where's my grandson?" Edna brushed away the tears with her hand.

"Mrs. Pearson, stop moving. You're making it worse. You'll be cleaned up in no time."

Ninety-five years of independence, reduced to this stage. No human being should live this way. There was a knock at the door. The nurse called out to the visitor to wait a few minutes.

When the nurse departed, David poked his head in the door and greeted her.

Aware a mist of Lysol melded with the odor of her mishap, Edna reddened as she turned and reached out for David. "Thank God you're here."

"It's okay, Grandma. Don't cry. You're not having a good day are you?"

David's wrinkled nose and frown told Edna he was aware of the situation.

"I want to go home. I don't like it here. I've had enough." Edna struggled to free herself from the confines of the fresh bedding, now tightly tucked in, restricting her movement.

"I've spoken to your doctor. Do you think you can eat something?"

"Oh, you." Edna pouted. "You're just like Jacob, always telling me what I can or can't do." David didn't understand. She had no desire nor hunger for food or water. Besides, she was never one who liked being told what to do. Jacob had always tried to dominate her. "Fine, I'll have some water."

David handed her the glass by her bed. She tasted the syrupy fluid.

"This isn't water." She pursed her lips and handed the glass back.

"It *is* water, Grandma. You know you can't swallow liquids without almost choking. That's why the doctor says we have to add thickener to anything you drink."

"I don't like it. It tastes awful."

"There's no taste to it at all. It's just your imagination."

What did David know? Edna fumed. She didn't see him drinking it.

The door creaked open a little further and a small crowd piled into Edna's room which was already cramped with machines and tables. Nathan and the rest of her family were all there to see her.

"Hi, Grandma." The voices mingled in a warm greeting.

Edna looked around. "Where are Alicia and Lacey? How come they're not here?"

"Alicia lives too far away to make it right now. She wants you to know she's thinking of you."

Edna wished she could see her great-granddaughter again. One more chance to make peace in person for all the tension between her and Alicia, one more chance to hug Lacey, a great-granddaughter whom she'd almost lost. She looked at the ring finger on her left hand. "David, did you see my wedding ring?

"It's very nice."

"It's old. From 1922. I want Lacey to have it when I'm gone. It should go to her."

David held her finger for a few seconds. "I'll make sure she gets it. It's a wonderful gesture of peace."

With everyone at the hospital at the same time, Edna knew what it meant. They thought she was going to die. David must have told the family she wasn't eating and didn't want to prolong her life. She studied the forced smiles staring down at her, uneasy in what to say. Tears welled up. "I love all of you. You are my family."

The nurse poked her head in and smiled at the group, reminding them the evening was getting late, and to be aware of the time. The lateness didn't matter to Edna. The people who were gathered in her room were all that mattered. She wanted their visit to last as long as possible. She didn't want to face an empty quiet room again. But their visit couldn't last forever and her eyelids were getting heavy.

Edna woke as the sun played peek-a-boo through the window blinds. It had been a fitful night, but she smirked at the realization she had fooled everyone. She was still alive for another day. The doctor came in with the good news. She was strong enough to leave the hospital. David came later in the morning and drove her back to Carl and Gloria's. Edna ached for her old house, for the freedom to cook her own meals, and most of all, she ached to have Missy by her side to comfort her, but she'd accepted her small room in someone else's home was the last home she would see. Upon her return home, she immediately sank into the boredom of her standard routine. Too weak to walk much, she seldom left her room. Her Sunday visits to David's had ceased. Her bed and wheelchair were where she would be spending her remaining days. The small television, atop her dresser, was on all the time but was only a distraction. Edna saw only blurry images and heard only muddled sounds. She was unable to concentrate and held no interest in the news which once held her interest. A general weakness overcame her and she spent most of her days sleeping. Eating would likely give her strength, but her stomach and her mind had stopped craving food.

Chapter 47

David didn't expect Grandma would be strong enough to leave the hospital, but she didn't live to be almost ninety-six by being weak. She'd spent her entire life fighting for what she believed and spent the last few years, in particular, contradicting everything and everyone, especially him. Determined to fight the doctor's prognosis, she wasn't about to stop now.

After her release back to Carl and Gloria's, David received urgent calls twice from Gloria that Edna was dying. Both times David rushed to his grandmother's side. Still, she lingered, continuing to eat just enough to hang on as the days turned into a week and beyond. Every day after work, David stopped in to see her, each day uncertain what he would find. Sometimes he found her barely able to move, but her mind alert and sensible. Other times she was entirely lost, only babbling a string of guttural sounds with random words not tied to any coherent thought. His nerves were like exposed wires ready to ignite at the slightest provocation.

As the days went by, it was obvious they were only playing a game of Russian roulette against time. The only unknown was how long she could hang on. After almost a year of enjoying Edna's company and enchanting stories every Sunday afternoon, it was heartbreaking. Grandma had very little cognitive quality left and David sensed she knew her mind had surrendered to advancing age and dementia. The ultimate end, which every being on earth must ultimately meet, was near for his grandmother. David called Nathan to share his concern. The sudden emptiness he felt surprised him, as he faced the prospect of his grandmother no longer being an integral part of his life.

The eighth day after Edna returned home, Gloria called. "Edna is unusually disoriented and agitated. She hasn't taken any liquids for the past two days. We're trying to keep her comfortable with the moistened swabs. I think you should come soon. I'll call Nathan for you."

David and Jean rushed out the door. David focused on his breathing, fighting back the burning sensation behind his eyes. His brain clouded with a sense of foreboding as they drove. "Maybe I should have agreed to the feeding tube." David poured his guilt out to Jean.

Jean glanced across and rubbed his shoulder as he drove. "You made the right choice for her. But that doesn't make it any easier."

His heart pounded fast and frantic by the time he pulled into the driveway at Gloria and Carl's house. He took one last deep breath, and with resignation, climbed out and hurried to the front door. He knocked twice before opening the door and walking in. An unfamiliar faint odor greeted David. He gulped in fresh air and courage before heading to his grandmother's room. Gazing at her body, ravaged by time, something inside David's throat lurched. Unsure of the basis for the overpowering urge, David rushed to the window, pulled back the curtains, and flung the window open. The cool late afternoon air brought welcome relief. The light added a feeling of life to the aura of death in the room.

"Hi, Grandma, it's David." He inched closer, with Jean on his arm. He gazed upon his grandmother's pallid face, not sure if she were aware of his presence. Leaning in, he studied the dark sunken eyes that looked as if she were staring straight through him. He reached out for her bony arm and patted it. The chill of her flesh forced him to look one more time. He pressed his fingertips to her wrist. Cool relief washed over him at the realization her heart was still beating and she was still breathing. "It's okay, Grandma, I'm here. How are you doing?"

"Are you there? Is that you ...?" She quivered all over, her gaze fixed and emotionless.

David and Jean sat by her side stroking her arm and her hair and soothing her like a frightened child. Suddenly, she shifted and yanked at her clothes, struggling to throw the blankets off and tearing away at her bedclothes.

"Help me, Jean. Why is she acting this way?" Panicked, David tried his best to calm her, patting her shoulder. "Are you too hot? Do you want some water or anything?" David went cold. He shot a glance at Jean. He'd never experienced anything like this. His neck tingled from fear as if he had seen a ghost, not just the pale skeleton of the woman he had grown to love, so much.

"She doesn't know where she is. She's frightened. Keep talking to her to calm her down. Right now you are the only familiar thing she has." Jean helped restrain Grandma with a gentle pressure on her shoulder and gentle stroking of her hair.

David's heart regained its normal pattern, his neck muscles relaxed, thankful Jean understood his grandmother's bizarre behavior. Her reading about Alzheimer's patients and the elderly had prepared her for this. Gripped in helplessness, he wanted to flee, to be released of the inevitability of what he predicted would follow shortly. But he knew his place was by her side. David and Jean sat by her bedside for the next few hours, reluctant to leave as long as she was awake and responding on some level. Their vigil was interrupted by a soft knock on the open door. Nathan started to step inside. David motioned with his head toward the hallway before he could enter. He met Nathan outside the door with an update on their grandmother's state.

The increased activity in the room made Grandma stir and she became aware of their presence. She lay quiet, listening to her grandsons' recount stories of the times they shared with her.

As Edna faded off again, Nathan offered a reprieve. "You've probably been here quite a while. Why don't you take a break?"

Nathan's words were a welcome invitation. David needed to get out of the room, away from the smell of salty perspiration, away from the musty bedding and stagnant air, away from the ghostlike figure who was once his spunky grandmother. A quick break would be nice in spite of his churning stomach and lack of appetite. David and Jean bid Nathan goodbye and escaped outside to soak in the fresh air.

After a quick stop for a deli sandwich and a cold drink, they returned to Edna's bedside again. "How is she?"

Nathan stood as they entered. "In and out."

David stared at her unsure what he should do next. She turned, smiled, reached out for David's hand, and mumbled some faint words, then, dozed off. Nathan and David realized from past experience that as bleak as things looked, she could still linger for days. Satisfied, and relieved she was peacefully asleep, they said their goodbyes and departed for home.

Chapter 48

Lying in bed, a shroud of loneliness veiled Edna. Darkness cloaked her room except for the dim stream of light which spilled in from the hallway. She dreaded the darkness. The specter of solitude haunted her nights as dementia induced ghosts and shadows of reality drifted in and out of her weakened mind. But specific memories remained. David had told her she wasn't crazy, just confused. The doctor had warned her the Alzheimer's would only get worse. She sighed as she looked at the ceiling, half expecting to see her mother whom she'd seen with increasing frequency lately. Edna tried to reminisce on her life, but only fleeting thoughts danced across her mind. She hummed a melody from her long-ago past, attempting to stay in touch with reality. Salty tears tracked down her cheek. She blocked out the vague surroundings and allowed her mind to dwell on the happy memories of her loved ones. Familiar faces flashed like strobe lights through her mind which had long outlived its useful life. Now, at ninety-five, her body was catching up as memories from her past were eaten away like moths on the fabric of her life.

Her once acute vision that delighted in the beauty of nature and the intricacy of her needlepoint and crafts, now narrowed like a dark tunnel with only blurry images cavorting in and out of its constricted scope. She sensed the presence of people surrounding her. Her heart skipped knowing loved ones gathered for her. She shifted in bed, attempting to sit. Garbled tones spilled from moving lips, Edna struggled to decipher them. The caring tones were familiar, but their names had slipped from her mind like so many memories. A soft touch of lips brushed against her cheek. She reached out into the shadows and held a warm hand, her sole connection to reality. She knew the hand and she stroked it. She fixed her attention on the figure. "I'm so glad you came to see me." Her garbled words struggled to emerge past her droopy lips and thickened tongue. Her breath came in short shallow puffs. Her joy in her visitors sent a calm serene sensation over her. She was at peace.

All the prayers of her last years had been answered by the love she had shared with David and Nathan. She had made peace with Alicia and Lorraine and had come to know Rachel and Emily, as well as Lacey. She fumbled with the fingers on her right hand feeling the ring that all of her grandchildren had given her for Christmas. She had experienced the love of family, a love that she thought she would never truly know again after losing her children. She willed words to come. She needed to tell her visitors she knew they were there and she loved and appreciated them, but the coordination of her thoughts and words was not in sync. She reached out and grasped a warm hand, attempting to focus and manage one last smile toward those she loved. Surrendering, she closed her eyes in defeat. She wiped her damp cheek with her nightgown sleeve. She was tired. It was time. Contentment cocooned her as she lay still and listened to the slow faint pounding in her chest. Tiredness overtook her and she drifted off.

Chapter 49

Minutes after David and Jean arrived home, the phone rang. His pulse quickened with an uneasy feeling. A lump formed in his throat. He swallowed and noticed his hands shaking as he stared at the phone for a beat before picking it up.

"Edna passed away a few minutes ago." Gloria's compassion carried across the line.

The words stung. "Is there anything you need me to do?" David sat at the dining room table with a pen and a note pad in hand. His look and actions drew Jean to his side.

"No. I've already called the funeral home, they'll pick up her body tonight. You can call tomorrow to coordinate the rest of the arrangements. They'll be expecting your call. I told them she was going to be buried in eastern Washington, not locally."

David scribbled the name and phone number of the funeral home on the pad. He thanked Gloria, relieved that the immediate task was handled. A pang of guilt struck him as he returned the phone to the receiver and looked at Jean. Grandma had skirted death for weeks, possibly months. Everyone knew her time was looming. Nonetheless, the finality was difficult to confront. Only a half-hour had passed since David and Nathan left their grandmother's bedside. Her ramblings had been increasing over the past few days and her last words to them were incoherent. Still, David remembered her final action. When he bent down to kiss her goodbye on the cheek, she gripped his hand and looked intently into his eyes. He searched for an indication of recognition. She had smiled. The sparkle in her eyes made him believe for that brief moment, she knew him again. The thought comforted him. "We should have stayed 'til the end." David looked over at Jean, fighting an emotion that was new to him.

"It wouldn't have mattered." Jean's voice cracked. "We've visited every night since she left the hospital. You know how long she lingered. There's no way we could have known it would be tonight."

"You're right. Besides, knowing how stubborn she is, she hung on until she'd seen Nathan and me one last time, and she hung on until we left before she allowed herself to drift away." His grandmother planned the timing of her last breaths as much as she could manage. It was all according to her design and her being in control, as so much of her life had been. She had lived independently for so many years and liked things her way. It was fitting and proper her final moments were according to her wishes.

The small white tent did little to break the wind's icy chill as the brushed stainless-steel casket was lowered into the hard, still frozen, snow-dusted ground, alongside Jacob and Bernice. Edna's remaining family were there to pay their respects and say goodbye. Nathan joined David, Jean, and their daughters. Lorraine had gathered along with Alicia and Lacey. Only Kora-Lee was absent. Though chilled outside, a warmth cloaked him as he looked out at the bare trees and the sparse floral arrangements of the nearby plots, including her husband and daughters' gravesites. He sighed remembering how badly Grandma had wanted Larry's remains to be buried with the Pearson family and how his cremation almost severed all ties with Larry's daughters. Still, Larry's death and Lacey's illness, in the end, brought healing to the family. As the last of Edna's remaining friends and few neighbors departed from the site, David turned to his brother and sisters. "I'm sure Grandma is happy. She's finally with Larry, Bernice, and Jacob. She is at peace with her parents, and her sister, Pearl." David removed the funeral wreath from the large metal easel and placed the circle of vibrant flowers on the grave. He silently said one final goodbye to Edna Pearson, his grandmother, who left behind, as the obituary read, "four grandchildren and three great-grandchildren." As he looked up to the single ray of sunlight breaking through the gray clouds, he hoped, on this winter day, Grandma was in heaven with her sister and her mother, and once again, picking wildflowers in a meadow somewhere, smiling.

She had finally made it to her own family reunion for which she had waited so long.

About the Author

Naomi Wark lives with her husband on Camano Island. She loves the natural beauty of living near Puget Sound where she enjoys long strolls along the water and exploring the many beaches of the island. When not writing, she is active in several volunteer efforts including the Stanwood Camano Food Bank. She loves spending time with family, a theme in her novels. To quote Archbishop Desmond Tutu, "You don't choose your family. They are God's gift to you, as you are to them." It is up to each of us how we choose to view the gift of family which we have been given.

Wildflowers in Winter is her first novel. A prequel to Wildflowers in Winter, Songs of Spring, is planned for release in late 2020. Songs of Spring, is an historical novel which takes place in the Seattle and Puget Sound area between 1902 and the mid-1920s.

If you have enjoyed this book, please consider writing a review on Amazon or your favorite reader's platform.

Made in USA - North Chelmsford, MA
1178288_9781734432916
10.09.2020 1545